APOCALYPTIC

ALEXA O'BRIEN HUNTRESS BOOK 14

TRINA M. LEE

APOCALYPTIC
Copyright 2018 by Trina M. Lee

All rights reserved. No part of this publication may be reproduced, stored in a retrieval system, or transmitted in any form or by any means, electronic, mechanical, recording or otherwise, without the prior written permission of the author.
Published in Canada

Cover art by
Marvin Lee Cover Design

Edited by
B. Leigh Hogan

Published by
Trina M. Lee

This is a work of fiction. The characters, incidents and dialogues in this book are of the author's imagination and are not to be construed as real. Any resemblance to actual events or persons, living or dead, is completely coincidental.

CHAPTER ONE

"The trail just ends, Jez. I'm not sure what to make of it. The residual energy left behind feels strange. I wish I knew how to describe it. Sticky is all that comes to mind." I reconsidered my word choice but nothing else fit.

With my phone pressed to my ear, I studied the bloodstained sidewalk outside one of the most popular dance clubs in the city. A heavy bass beat pounded from inside, something the nearby residential neighborhood must have really appreciated at this time of night.

One of Smudge's sources at the police department had tipped her off to the body the second it was called in. Unfortunately, this one had happened on the doorstep of a heavily populated human establishment. It had been found moments after the kill, the vampire already long gone.

So we'd split up. Jez and Smudge were scouting a location where a body had been found a few days prior in an apartment. Both vampire kills. Related? Not always but most likely. Most vampires had been on their best behavior since shit had gone down with the FPA. I was seeing more of them at The Wicked Kiss than prior as well.

Still, not everyone was content to play by the rules, especially when Arys and I so often blurred the lines ourselves. Yet something about this situation felt different. This had to be a new vampire. Although not stupid enough to have been caught already.

"Sticky?" she repeated, pausing to respond to something Smudge said in the background. "Sounds gross. So what now? Can you track it? We're not having much luck here. The place is clean."

With a little concentration I could feel the energy of every supernatural creature in the city. But it wasn't like a Google map in my head. I couldn't see the exact location of those outside my vicinity. A few city blocks or so.

"I'll see if I can hunt down the energy signature I'm picking up, but it's a shot in the dark really. This vampire could be anywhere by now." I scanned the group of people milling about outside the club, smoking and talking. All human.

After glancing up and down the street, I headed in the direction I'd have gone if I were taking off after a kill. Away from the lights and noise. Toward the park a few blocks down. Slip through the park to another neighborhood and be gone. It would be safer than running the busy streets right after a public kill.

"Keep me posted if anything turns up." Jez snapped her gum loudly in my ear. "Catch you later."

I stuffed my phone into my shoulder bag and kept moving. I suspected that, whomever this vampire was, they either didn't know who ran the city or they didn't care. It didn't matter much now anyway. Public kills didn't fly in any city. There was too much at stake. Too much to protect.

After a recent incident involving trophy hunters coming to the city because of a video leaked by a newbie werewolf, I wasn't going easy on anyone breaking the rules. A cunning, clever vampire could hunt and kill without drawing attention. Anyone taking reckless risks either didn't know any better or wanted to get caught.

Strange.

I pondered this, happy to have something to keep my mind occupied. Keeping busy, mind and body, kept me from falling apart.

It had been three weeks and four days since Kale died. Correction. Since I had killed him.

It did not get easier. Every night it got a little harder. But properly grieving Kale's loss, healing, was next to impossible when I could barely keep my shit together.

It had been the hardest three fucking weeks and four days of my life.

The darkness loomed larger in me these days than it ever had. I too had slaked my dark hunger tonight. I'd chosen a local gang leader who'd just murdered the wife and child of a rival. Their shady business was none of mine, but that crap was an open invitation.

The effort it took to maintain a semblance of rational and sane required frequent feasts of blood and power. Because the balance between Arys and me had been tipped well past the safe point. Each night the rift grew. Each night we became more unbalanced. More mentally unhinged.

Apocalyptic

Uneasy, I paused outside a small, quaint house with a family of decorative deer in the front yard. Winter was coming to a close. Soon such items would be stashed away for the spring.

Still there was a chill to the night air. I raised my nose to the breeze. Car exhaust and general city pollution. No telltale scents to explain my disquiet. Because the danger that had triggered my wariness came from within.

Panic gripped me. He was out there. He shouldn't be out there. But he was.

Seconds after my intuition spoke, that cool wind blew inside me. I both dreaded and loved it.

Arys Knight. My dark half. Hunting me.

Moving faster, I hurried toward the park ahead. Maybe if I could stay ahead of him I could lose him.

We had good nights and bad nights. Tonight felt like a bad night, although it was too soon to tell. Thankfully we still had more good nights than bad. But when we had a bad night, it was off the charts horrible.

I could feel him getting closer. Unable to detect the exact direction he advanced from, I broke into a run. With inhuman speed, I darted down the street and into the park.

Then I froze. The park was heavily treed in parts. Then it gave way to a large grassy area with picnic tables. A building housing guest services and washrooms formed the center point. Sticking close to the trees, I made my way toward it. From there I'd figure out which neighborhoods were in which direction and get gone fast.

Heading west would take me back toward The Wicked Kiss. I had to get there before Arys though, and he'd anticipate such a move. On the other hand, I could go in the opposite direction and have Jez pick me up somewhere.

Arys drew closer. I felt it. But I was pretty sure he hadn't gotten a visual on me yet. Hoping to keep it that way, I reached the pavilion and pasted my back up against the side of the building.

A sudden swell of cool power flared up in my core. Fuck me.

I might have liked to think I was a badass, but Arys had been doing this for three centuries. I was but an amateur next to him. Hunting me was in his blood. He existed for it.

Holding my breath, I listened hard. Not so much as a crunch of dead grass from where the snow had melted. Closer he came. From which direction though? He was toying with me, keeping me on my toes.

"Goddamn you, Arys," I muttered.

Step by slow, careful step, I eased toward the corner of the building. I glanced behind me before daring a peek around the pavilion's edge. Clear. I stepped forward, readying myself to break into a run.

Strong arms grabbed me from behind, jerking me against a firm chest. In my ear, a sexy snarl. "Trying to escape me, my love?"

I froze in Arys's embrace, the rabbit caught by the wolf. Struggling would only encourage him. With his lips on my ear and his hard on nestled against the top of my ass, I mustered a half-hearted, breathy, "Always."

The seductive pull of his low chuckle weakened me. It was dangerous for us to be alone together. For obvious reasons. For both our sakes, I needed to break free of him. The touch of his mouth on my neck beneath my ear made that especially hard.

"I need to feel you, Alexa. Not touching you is making me crazy." The urgency of Arys's desire racked me. His palms were hot through the fabric of the long sweater I wore over black leggings. Grabbing the hem, he slowly peeled it up.

I waited for the touch of his fingers on my skin. Then I sighed, melting into him as his lips found a ticklish spot on my neck. His hands slid over my midriff, up to caress my breasts through my bra.

"Arys, we can't do this. It's not safe." My protest sounded less than convincing. Telling myself to make him stop was easier than actually doing it. Because I did not want him to stop.

"It isn't safe not to." He kissed the vein in my neck before tearing himself away with a growl.

He shoved me against the wall of the pavilion and turned me to face him. His actions were rough but not aggressive. The truth was, he wasn't wrong. We did need to connect as badly as we needed to disconnect. A constant push and pull comprised the battle we waged every moment.

"Not like this." A feeble attempt to shove him away went ignored. It wasn't like I'd tried very hard. "We need Shaz."

Holding my face gently, he kissed me with a demanding passion. Nothing else existed but Arys. Dragging his lips lazily over my jawline, he whispered, "We need to be alone sometimes too."

Apocalyptic

As much as I enjoyed having Arys and Shaz together, he was right. Because he always friggin' is. To truly reconnect and recharge, we needed to be alone. Together. Just us and the night.

And a fuck ton of power.

That little voice of reason inside my head shouted, *He'll kill you, you dumb bitch!* As much as I feared that very thing, I didn't completely believe it. I wasn't so easy to kill now. If anything, we'd kill each other. In a blaze of glory.

If there'd been any hope of me resisting him, it had been tiny. Once his hands were on my hips, pulling me tight against him, I didn't stand a chance.

Just the sensation of his erection against me brought forth a swell of arousal. We moved together in the dark, hurriedly disrobing as much as possible, needing to feel each other. When I wore nothing but my bra and my boots, Arys took me. There against the rough wooden siding.

I sighed as he thrust inside me. It was a waterfall after the desert. Sunshine after the storm. Being with him after being so horribly forced apart felt like coming home after a long journey.

Overhead the sky rumbled. Our union had become a volatile thing, affecting the energies around us stronger than ever before. A streak of lightning followed, yellow with a splash of blue. A small storm broke out above us. But only above us.

Arys filled me with frenzied thrusts, like it had been months since we'd been intimate rather than days. Although it had been quite some time now since we'd been intimate alone.

Resting his forehead against mine, he kissed me, messy and hard and desperate. "I can't lose you."

Fear. The driving force of the dark flame's insecurity and all-around bad behavior.

Not knowing how to comfort him, because there was no comfort for us, I did my best. I kissed him back, a hand on his jaw, the other in his mess of black hair. "I'm right here."

"But for how long?"

"Forever."

A pause. A soft groan. Then Arys's quiet declaration. "I don't know if I believe in that anymore."

His fear echoed inside me, and I forced him to meet my eyes. "You waited so long for me. Don't you dare give up now."

We moved together in perfect rhythm. Every slip of him inside of me, every slide out. It felt like finding myself. For a brief time. If only we could live in this moment of powerful peace always.

I didn't know how to make it happen. I just knew I had to.

Arys thrust deep and I gasped. His pupils dilated in response. But I knew the glint that followed. Not mere desire anymore but hunger as well.

"If it comes down to you or me, choose you. Kill me. You might survive it." His words came out in a rush, like they'd burst free of his restraint.

Horrified that this was even a discussion and especially now, I gaped at him. "No, it's not happening that way."

To shut Arys up before he could say anything else I didn't want to hear, I kissed him again. My tongue delved into his mouth. The steel of his lip ring was warm and smooth. I tightened my legs around his waist and gripped his hair a little harder.

With a groan he broke off the kiss and buried his face in my neck. His pants and moans so close to my ear made me come undone. I couldn't think of a better sound. His firm body against mine, the scent of cologne and laundry soap, the sound of his pleasure as he took me. It overwhelmed my senses. I was drowning in all that was Arys.

The touch of his mouth on my neck was hungry. Insistent.

I tensed.

Arys jerked his head back and stared at me with wide, scared eyes. "Don't let me do it. I won't be able to stop myself."

I watched it take him. The darkness. It stole over him like a cloud over the sun. Blocking out his light. His true self. Reducing him to a mere monster.

From Jekyll to Hyde. I knew the feeling. Once the darkness overcame you, there was no fighting it.

Slamming a fist against the building beside my head, Arys demanded, "Fight me off. Do it now."

He had me pinned against the building. His body was inside mine. There was only one way to make him back off.

Just blast him.

But I couldn't do it. Not now, not like this. It felt wrong.

Then he went for my throat.

Both hands came up, instinctive defense. Blue and golden-yellow light burst from my fingertips. The sky lit up with the same.

Apocalyptic

Thunder rolled. The blast hit Arys at point blank range, throwing him ass over teakettle onto the grassy sprawl in the picnic table area.

There was no time to struggle back into my pants. I slid the sweater on over my head and snatched up my pants and underwear, gripping them with my bag as I ran. Being nailed with his pants down bought me enough precious seconds that I was able to propel myself through the park and out the other side.

Only when I emerged onto a busy downtown street did I pause. I didn't see or feel him approaching. Quickly I slipped my pants on, flipping off the SUV full of guys who shouted out the windows at me.

Clinging to the shadows against the myriad office buildings and bite-sized skyscrapers, I headed for The Wicked Kiss. With shaky hands I tried to smooth down my hair.

"So fucking stupid," I cussed to myself as I hurried down the city street.

We'd played with fire and almost been burned. Too close, that call had been.

Arys and I stood on the brink of our own destruction. I'd promised to save us. I might be the only one that could. Or that might be a pie-in-the-sky, bullshit theory.

Either way, I had to try something. The darkness had escaped its barrier. The yin yang-like structure of our relationship teetered askew, the lines no longer perfectly drawn. Now it seeped through us, consuming us. The very thing Willow had fought so hard to prevent.

The real joke on all of us was that he'd taken my darkness the night I turned. To keep the balance from tipping with my death and rebirth as a vampire. But because fate could not be escaped, only postponed, Willow's actions, caused by the darkness he'd taken for me, had led us right back to this moment.

After everything he'd done. It was so *Final Destination*. But worse, because Arys and I would cause our own end. We were dangerously close to stepping off the ledge and plummeting headlong into the abyss.

My guardian angel had sacrificed himself for nothing. The darkness was coming for me anyway.

CHAPTER TWO

Only when I'd slipped into The Wicked Kiss through the back entry did I let myself stop moving. Partway down the hall I stopped and slumped against the wall. Letting my head fall back, I sucked in a deep breath and held it.

I would not cry.

The time for tears had passed. Now was the time for ideas and execution.

A door cracked open down the hall. Willow's hybrid energy preceded him, a mix of Arys and me and something else. Something all Willow, a spark of who he'd started this journey as.

I felt it when I took his blood, and I felt it now as he walked toward me. And I'd never speak a word of it to anyone who couldn't pick up on that ethereal hum. Everything about Willow was fascinating. Unfortunately, others would think so too. Starting with Briggs. So far nobody had come sniffing around Willow, but I was braced for it.

I knew I reeked of sex and death, but Willow didn't get weird about it. He played it so cool, like he didn't even notice, though I knew it had to have been an immediate punch to his senses.

"What's the damage?" he asked, easing to a stop a safe few feet away.

"No damage this time." I squeezed out a tight smile for him. He didn't need to be worrying about me anymore. He'd done enough of that and look where it had gotten him. "Arys caught up to me while I was tracking a vampire. I left him in the park. It's fine. We're fine."

We were so not fine and Willow knew that. Still he nodded, not calling me on my bullshit. "This is probably a shitty time to tell you that Salem is MIA."

The shitstorm just kept brewing tonight, didn't it? Absently I rubbed at the raw spot left on my back from the rough, wooden siding of the pavilion. "Of course he is. Because why wouldn't that happen now of all times? Do you think Lilah did something to him?"

Willow glanced up and down the hallway. Nobody cloistered away within these walls gave a shit about our conversation. Angels and demons were an especially secretive bunch though. And no matter what form Willow wore, to me he'd always be an angel.

"It's the most likely possibility. I can pretty much guarantee it has something to do with your visit there." His green eyes sparkled with tiny gold flecks. They caught me each time I looked at him, because I'd thought they would be red for all eternity. I continued to marvel at the wonder that was Willow.

"I knew I screwed things up the moment I got back." Cursing, I shoved away from the wall and paced the hallway. "I shouldn't have mentioned Shya."

Willow stepped back as I paced by him. Aware of the sensitive nature of our bond, I tried to clamp down on my power so it didn't flow freely around me. Like Arys, I tended to seep a little all the time. For people like Willow, who were bound to me on a deeper level, that could get painful.

In the weeks since he'd turned, Willow and I had established a routine: every few nights I gave him a little blood and he was good. For another few nights. We didn't go long enough to find out what would happen. I knew. I saw it with Jenner and Kale. But truthfully, I didn't want Willow to want me like that. He did. He couldn't help it. But we kept the desire controlled. It had to stay that way.

"It doesn't matter now. We'll have to go on without him. It can't wait much longer." Willow studied my face, and something he saw made him break his self-imposed distance requirement. He stopped me mid-pace, stepping in front of me. Pulling me into a hug, he smoothed back my hair with such gentle care. He still had a guardian's touch. "Let's go sit down and talk about it. We'll figure this out."

Because I knew it wouldn't last nearly long enough, I soaked up all I could in that hug. Within seconds he stiffened and pulled away, unable to touch me too long without wanting to ravish my body and take my blood.

"Let's go sit out there." I nodded toward the heart of the club, where barely muffled electric guitars screamed. "It's too quiet back here. I don't want to hear myself think right now."

With a sympathetic wince and nod, Willow followed me into the main room. Stepping from the back hall and its high-strung vibe rife with blood, sex, and excitement into the drunken shenanigans of the main room was like striding between two worlds. Both party zones but different kinds of party.

Right now, I'd pass on the one with humans and vampires meeting in a place where everyone could get what they wanted without leaving bodies in the streets. I needed the party with a dance floor and people cheering every time the band's singer called to them. The one with Falon swigging tequila by the bar.

Wait, Falon?

The silver-haired angel stood at the bar shooting the shit with Josh the bartender. In one hand he held a bottle of the best tequila we had.

A tall, leggy blonde vampire sidled up to him, flirtatious smile in place. They didn't always know what he was, especially the newer vamps. Falon could keep his power under wraps, so it went undetected by most unless he used it. They knew he wasn't human though, and he was stupidly good looking. Seemed to be an angel thing. I had yet to meet an ugly one.

Falon turned to engage her with a raised brow. He leaned in to listen to whatever come on she had prepared. I couldn't tear my gaze away as I led Willow to my favorite table near the door.

Whatever she said to Falon made him shake his head and laugh. His lips moved as he responded. What the hell was this cold, hard dagger-like stabbing in my chest? Jealousy? Fuck me.

They both glanced in my direction.

She nodded and held up a hand in a 'say no more' gesture. She slipped away as fast as she'd come.

He turned her down. Because of me? Or because she wasn't his type?

With a parting remark to Josh, Falon circled around the bar to meet us at the table as we reached it. I tossed my bag into the booth and plopped down beside it. Willow sat across from me. He scowled at the fallen angel who carefully ignored him.

"Shove over, wolf." Falon didn't wait for me to move. He looked me over with eyes as silver as his hair. "You're in one piece. That's reassuring. Wasn't sure what I'd find after the little storm you two started in the park."

I winced and settled in against the butt-hugging booth seat. "You felt that huh? All of you?"

Willow nodded his confirmation, but his gaze locked on the bottle of tequila. Poor bastard. Probably missed it like crazy. It had been his vice. Now his vice was blood and women, but Willow kept a tight rein on his hungers.

As virginal as an incubus could get, he enjoyed time with willing ladies, but he didn't sleep with them, much to their dismay. I didn't know how he did it. I suspected his control was off the charts. He knew how to handle power far greater than ours. Still, I wondered how long he could keep that up.

"You reek of sexual frustration and disappointment," Falon observed before taking a swig from the liquor bottle. I suspected he chose tequila just to taunt Willow. "He didn't even make you come before he tried to kill you, did he?"

Willow's eyes widened, and he sat back with a head shake. He and Falon had never been anything close to friends. I got the feeling Willow was recalling the time he'd beat the ever-loving crap out of Falon in the FPA building. Good times.

With an exaggerated sigh, I turned a scowl on Falon. "Must you be so obscene?"

"Spare us the good girl act. I'm sure Willow's not that naïve. You love it and you know it. The dirtier the better with you." He nudged my thigh and snickered.

After his next swig he dragged his tongue over his bottom lip, capturing a stray drop. A simple motion. Something we all did without thinking. Falon made the small act sensual. A flick of his tongue and my orgasm-denied succubus self demanded that I climb into his lap.

Not happening.

"Falon, did you just come here to see if I survived Arys? Sorry to disappoint you but, yeah, I'm still here. Now if you're satisfied, you can be on your way." The several inches between us was not nearly enough space. I was tempted to take him back to my office and do him until sunrise.

"Cut the dramatics. If I wanted you dead, I'd kill you myself. I just turned down a gorgeous woman because of you. Stop trying to run me off every time we're not fucking." Another long drink drained the bottle dry. He shoved it to the edge of the table for the servers picking up empties.

A drunken eyeroll followed, making me wonder how much he'd had to drink so far tonight. Angels were no lightweights, but I'd still seen one plastered. Many times.

I smiled apologetically at Willow who half shrugged. His gaze strayed to a woman with pink hair who sat near a pool table in the far corner, watching her friends play.

Despite not wanting to press the matter in front of others, I turned in the booth to face Falon. "Why? Why did you turn her down? If you want to take her in the back, be my guest. Who am I to stop you?"

It was a dangerous game I played. I both did and did not want him to answer. It shouldn't have mattered. There were far bigger bads to slay than the details of my relationship with Falon.

He twisted slightly, propping an elbow on the table. In a long jacket that screamed magazine trendy, his all-black attire made his hair and eyes astoundingly brilliant. From his dark t-shirt to socks that I knew without looking were argyle, Falon dressed to make a statement. Usually that statement was 'supreme asshole' but more often than not it was also 'do me any way you want me.'

"You, Alexa, are the bane of my existence." The sexy smirk he flashed me was one of my favorite things about him. Little did he know. "And you're toxic as hell. But you fuck like it's an Olympic event. There's not one woman I know who can do what you do."

I laughed, both insulted and amused. "Am I supposed to take that as a compliment? You turned down someone else because it won't be as good as it is with me? Touching."

"It's not a compliment. It's..." His gaze on my lips, Falon trailed off. A frown stole his smirk away. "Inconvenient."

Willow made a big show of clearing his throat. "We should discuss what we'll do now that Salem's out of the picture. I don't suppose you've seen him, Falon?"

The angel tore his gaze away. Turning to Willow, he repeated, "Out of the picture? What are you talking about?"

"Nobody has seen him in weeks," Willow discussed the matter in a respectful manner despite his hatred for the fallen angel. Just another trait I loved about him. "I suspect he's holed up in that room with Lilah. He's done this before. According to a friend, the last time he stayed in there with her for an entire year before resurfacing."

Falon rubbed a hand over his jaw. "Shit. That evil bitch has got to be keeping him there to screw Alexa over. Which means they must know something."

"She's screwing herself over too. She should want this to work." I'd like to throttle Lilah for being such a giant pain in the ass. "If I see that woman again, I'm going to kick her ass all over the place."

"Now that I'd like to see." One hand drifted over the seat between us until Falon's fingers lazily drew circles on my thigh. "So what do we do? Waiting on Salem probably won't be an option for much longer."

Although I didn't visibly react, I enjoyed his light, playful touch. It had become familiar, and right now I needed that. I looked to Willow as well, trusting his opinion over any other.

Willow frowned in the tequila bottle's direction as a server with a tray of empties smoothly breezed by and collected it. He watched it go, his expression wistful. "I'll reach out to a few other sources. I think we need to prepare to go it without Salem and Lilah. We shouldn't rush anything, of course, but we don't want you and Arys to reach the point of no return."

Nodding, I tried to stay on focus. Falon's finger danced along my thigh in sweeping motions that tickled. "I don't think we're there yet, but it's not the kind of thing I can really put a time frame on."

"The way I see it, the best option is for you to try to create your own keystone. One less fragile than a werewolf." Falon glanced from me to Willow. The two of them shared a look. "Reforming the keystone is the less dangerous option."

"Yeah, it is," Willow agreed. "Without Salem's help, it's pretty much the only option."

Falon's finger drifted to my inner thigh. What he'd said held my attention, but his touch dipping closer to my bikini line, fought a good battle for it. "Less dangerous than what?" I asked.

"A keystone is a solid way to tie both sides together, but to truly mend the rift, one would have to access the twin flame core, where your power resides. Fix the rift at the source." Willow didn't appear convinced it was possible. "Few have survived the effort, and none have succeeded."

Willow's explanation sounded far too simple. I glanced at Falon to see if he had anything to add. This had been his idea in the first place. He believed I could mend the rift. Either his confidence in my abilities exceeded my own, or he wanted to get me killed.

"If it goes wrong," Falon added, "the tie that binds you could be severed completely. Darkness would consume you both."

That was always a risk for the twin flames. I eyed him with a raised brow, trying to figure out if he had an angle in all this. "And you still think I can do it, even with the odds stacked against me?"

"I do," he didn't hesitate to say, "but it's going to take more power than even you have."

Salem and Lilah held vast, immortal power. Power like mine, but stronger and older. If they would help, we stood a greater chance of success. If we pulled it off, we could set us all free.

Lilah didn't want that. She feared what becoming truly whole with Salem would mean for her. So lost in her dark ways, she feared the light. A true balance for twins wouldn't eliminate the dark, but it would rein it in. To her current mindset that was a trap worse than the cage she dwelled in now.

My gaze went to Willow, and I searched him for some sign that he thought I could do it. He didn't look as confident as Falon. Still, he offered me hope. "I'll keep looking for Salem. No matter what happens, Alexa, you're not alone. We'll get you through this."

I wanted to believe him. But everything kept imploding around me lately. It definitely made for shaky faith. I wanted to fix the unbalance between Arys and me. Yet I couldn't help the stone of uncertainty that settled in my stomach, leaving me heavy with worry.

Suddenly the booth wasn't so comfortable anymore. I sat stiff, unable to relax. Without thinking I reached down to capture Falon's hand. Only after I'd slipped my fingers through his did I realize what I'd done. The action had come so easily. Natural, even. Panic-gripped I wondered if it would be too awkward if I yanked my hand away.

Apocalyptic

Then Falon settled his fingers in against mine and squeezed gently.

"It's cool, wolf. Willow will be the guardian and find the solution. And until you can find a way to pull it off, we'll keep you and your dark half from doing something stupid." Falon chuckled snidely. "Correction. You're both idiots outperforming each other on the stupid scale on a nightly basis. We'll keep you alive."

Sure, Falon and Willow were willing to do what they could. They each had their reasons. Willow, the guardian who couldn't stop protecting. Falon, the shady Circle member who knew more than he shared.

But they couldn't be everywhere. They hadn't been there tonight in the park.

If Arys and I were meant to destroy one another, no force in this world could do a damn thing to stop it.

CHAPTER THREE

ARYS

I raged through the night, trying to run from the urge to go after Alexa. With panic in her wide eyes, she'd thrown me on my ass with my dick out. No less than I deserved.

Then she ran.

Watching her go, I warred with myself. In the end it had taken putting a fist through the guest services' lodge window to keep me from giving chase. Blood dripped from the deep gashes in my knuckles and forearm. The pain had done its job. I'd come back to myself enough to let her escape me.

Fists clenched, I cut back through the park the way I'd come. To the street where I'd left the Jaguar, currently Alexa's car, formerly her piece of shit Alpha's. I gripped the hood with both hands and sucked in cold gulps of air. Inside me dark waged war with light.

Go after her.

Don't be an idiot. Go to him. Calm down.

The monster inside me wanted to hunt Alexa down, to the very ends of the earth if necessary. I'd become so fucking obsessed with her, it was killing me.

Because she was our light, our soul, I counted on her to keep us adrift on this raging sea of shit. She would save us. I just had to manage to somehow not kill her first.

It shouldn't have been so hard. Over three centuries, I'd mastered my hunger, learned to use it as a weapon. Now it was using me. Making me its bitch in the worst of ways.

I slammed my bloody fist on the hood, leaving scarlet smears. Dropping into the driver's seat, I started the engine and let my head fall back against the headrest.

Apocalyptic

In the quiet with just the purr of the engine to offer comfort, I heard the distinct voice of the light say, *Stand firm in the face of temptation.*

"Yeah, it's just that fucking easy."

The voice had begun to speak to me with growing frequency since Alexa's death and rebirth as vampire. I despised it. Promises of better things to come. Whispers of encouragement and assurance that there was more to me than I'd ever let myself dream back in Vegas, in Harley's harem of blood and sex. As meaningless as it gets, I'd been a whore for power, rolling around in filth to get it.

The whole time dreaming of her.

Then she came true. She brought me back to life. Filled me with it. And I killed her.

Woe is fucking me. Right? I know. Get over it already. Well it's not for lack of trying. Killing the one you love most kind of fucks you up.

Especially when you ache to kill her again.

In an attempt to drown out the angel and demon on each shoulder, I cranked up the stereo and put the car in gear. In record time, I made the drive. The parking lot was almost empty. But the black Jeep I hoped to see was there.

My hands shook when I got out of the Jag and clenched them into fists. I thrummed with pent up hunger. I'd fucked myself into a nice state of blue balls. So close I'd been to filling her, and bleeding her. Now I hungered on both counts. I knew better than to trust myself like this.

So I'd come here, Doghead. To the one person I trusted to keep me from doing something I'd regret tonight.

I burst through the door with more force than intended. It slammed open, drawing the attention of everyone inside. Owen, Shaz's beta wolf, leapt to his feet ready to defend. He relaxed slightly when he saw me but not completely. Smart wolf.

A handful of werewolves were scattered about. Other than Owen the only one I knew personally was Izzy. She eyed me warily before turning her attention back to the tattered paperback she held. Or pretending to. Her eyes may have been on the page, but she was keenly aware of any move I might make. Well of course she was hyper-aware; I knew what she tasted like.

Every wolf in the place was justified in treating me like an interloper. A danger walking among them. A few Doghead wolves had died by my hand. As much as I loved how hard I got at the very scent of wolf blood, not to mention the fantastic high, there were only two wolves I wanted to sink fangs into on a nightly basis.

One had just fled from me. The other was here.

Shaz stood at the pool table, a cue in hand. He and a few others were clustered around the table, drinking and shooting the shit. Like everyone else, his gaze found me. But his was the only one I'd been searching for.

Piercing green eyes scanned me as Shaz did a quick analysis, gauging my mental state before I got too close. Whatever he saw made him hand off the cue to another guy and excuse himself from the game.

With a slight head tilt, he directed me to the office at the back. Knowing better than to turn his back to me, Shaz waited for me to get a few steps ahead of him. He kept his distance, ready to defend himself until I gave him a reason to relax. He'd made handling the twin flame insanity into an art. Shaz learned how to read us, as a duo and individuals. He knew us, likely better than we knew ourselves.

The office was small. Painfully small. A narrow sofa had been crammed against one wall and a desk against the other. Not much else. The window had those annoying metal blinds that clattered together as I jerked them open. I needed to feel less trapped in this tiny room with him.

When he started to close the door, I raised a hand. "Might want to leave it open a bit."

Pausing, Shaz searched my eyes. I let him see it all. "Where is she?" he asked, knowing without me having to say a word.

"I don't know. I told her to stop me and she did. Then she ran. Somewhere safe by now. Her blood den, I assume." I didn't sit. I couldn't. So I stood stiff near the window, as far as I could get from him.

"Did you hurt her?" His tone was guarded, his expression expectant.

I sighed and rubbed my forehead, squeezing my eyes shut. "Didn't sink a fang. I would have though. I followed her. I shouldn't have. Cornered her in the park and… It doesn't matter. She's safe."

Apocalyptic

Eyes closed, his wolfish scent became my focus. I knew Shaz's scent well. Like forest, animal, and man all mingled into one intoxicating cocktail that reached down and grabbed me by the balls.

I felt him move. My eyes snapped open and he was there. Too close. Too confident.

"Do you want to hurt me?" A loaded question if there ever was one. He knew how this would play out.

"You know what you're asking for, don't you, pup? You won't get a chance to change your mind." I advanced on him, driving him back toward the door. Giving him one chance to leave before I took what he was offering.

We hadn't been alone together in weeks. It wasn't something we engaged in frequently, although I wouldn't mind changing that.

Without breaking eye contact, Shaz retreated, walking backward in slow steps. Upon reaching the door, he closed it and turned the lock. "You need it. I want it. And we both know I'm not the one you really want to kill. It's safer this way."

Shaz's willingness was an aphrodisiac all its own. It stirred my desire to life. The anticipation of tasting his flesh and coating my tongue with his blood had me rock hard.

I'd wanted him from the start, despite our rocky beginning. Because Alexa wanted him. I never expected it to evolve into something genuine. It had taken some time for me to come to recognize it for what it was, but I'd fallen for Shaz.

And only Alexa knew.

For a moment I simply held his gaze. I had yet to reach for my power. His attraction, his craving for my touch and my bite, it was all him. Shaz wasn't under my influence. His hunger for this moment was as real as mine.

Then I let my hold slip. A slow trickle at first. The erotic vibe grew steady and strong as I fed it. Catching Shaz up in my thrall took little effort. He all but threw himself headlong into it.

With a hand on his shoulder, I backed him up against the closed door. I filled my senses with him, seeking to escape the obsession for her with the infatuation with him. A hand in his platinum hair, I held his head tight enough to imply control. A silent challenge. Shaz wasn't the type to play submissive. Despite welcoming my bite, he was no victim. He was my lover. In almost every sense of the word.

I had no interest in forcing Shaz further than he wanted to take it. He could set the boundaries of our relationship, and I'd happily play within them.

Relaxing against the door, he affected a casual stance. Unafraid and eager. A hint of defiance glinted in his eyes. I searched for it every time, needing to see that he was ready to defy me.

I wondered if I would ever tell him that I loved him.

Sure Shaz had come a long way since we'd first met. But I doubted he'd come quite that far. Certainly not as far as I had.

With my free hand I traced a finger along his jawline, down the side of his neck, and over his jugular. Outwardly he appeared unmoved, but I felt the tremor that ran through him on the inside.

"You should have called me," Shaz said, voice husky with want. "I would have stopped you from going after her."

He had a way of saying so much with such a simple statement. Hands flat against the door on either side of him, we only touched where I touched him. My hand in his hair, finger on his vein. A breath of space kept our bodies apart. Just barely.

"I know." I wanted to close the distance, to feel his hard lines and soft flesh. To feel him shudder beneath my touch. "You're helping now."

When Shaz's gaze dropped to the silver ring in my bottom lip, I leaned in to kiss the edge of his mouth. He allowed it but evaded my attempt to kiss him more deeply. What a damn tease, and I knew that he knew it too.

I had to taste him. The faint stubble covering his chin and jaw was rough against the tip of my tongue. His skin was hot, his blood pumping faster in my ears. Despite the careful space I left between our lower halves, I knew he was rock hard.

And I knew I could bring him to orgasm without ever laying a hand on him.

The push and pull of sex-charged energy cycled between us, growing with each cycle. My mouth found his jugular. His pulse raced beneath the skin, faster with each second. Slowly I released a warm breath, an exhalation of abso-fucking-lution.

The white wolf set me free. His willingness and, most importantly, his trust helped me remember how it used to be with

Alexa. Before her death and my obsession. It gave me hope that we'd all have that again. Together.

His excitement grew into a force all its own. It sucker punched me, testing my control. My cock throbbed, and I groaned softly as I scraped fangs over his flesh. Shaz gasped, the sound shocking my system into overdrive.

My hunger for my wolves wouldn't be teased any longer. With Alexa lurking in the back of my thoughts, I sank fangs into Shaz. Then I held them there, buried deep, knowing it was both pain and pleasure. More intimate in some ways than even fucking.

The trust he gave me in that moment was priceless. I didn't know how bad I'd needed it, to be trusted again. Because Alexa didn't trust me anymore, and it killed me.

A sexy growl-like moan from Shaz made my balls tighten. I withdrew my fangs, letting the blood flow free. Swirling my tongue over the punctures, I sucked hard on the bite. I couldn't help but wonder, did he ever think about how my mouth would feel anywhere else?

With a snarl he grabbed hold of my hair and roughly pulled my head from his neck. Our faces were mere inches apart. Shaz's green eyes were wild and all wolf. He searched me for a moment before dragging my mouth to his.

Shaz dominated the kiss. It was aggressive and dirty, blowing my mind. He continued to surprise me. His tongue clashed with mine as he tasted his blood on my lips. Using both hands I braced myself against the door, able to shove away if things went too far. Although I'd started to question what his idea of too far was these days.

He caught my lip ring between his teeth and gently tugged. If he kept this shit up I was going to lose it.

"Shaz," I murmured, a soft warning.

He blinked at me with lust-filled eyes, like he was drugged. Which he very much was. Slowly he came back to himself.

His gaze lingered on my mouth when he said, "I should probably get back out there. Are you good?"

I backed off, freeing him from his place against the door. "Yeah, I'm good. Thanks. If you don't mind, I'm going to hang around here for a while. Play some pool. Cool?"

"Yeah, of course." He nodded his platinum head, scrubbing a hand through it so his slightly shaggy hair was tousled. "Stay as long as you want."

I didn't trust myself to stay away from Alexa if I left right now. And perhaps I wasn't quite ready to leave Shaz just yet.

CHAPTER FOUR

Across the room Jenner lounged on a bright-red sofa. An exuberant blonde sat splayed in his lap, bouncing and squirming. Feeling my gaze upon him, he slid me a mischievous grin and a wink.

With a roll of my eyes I looked away. Jenner had enough attention in this place. He didn't need mine.

He'd made himself quite at home here. On somewhat of an extended vacation away from his home in Las Vegas, he'd admitted he'd come here because he'd been run out of his city. His nightclub had been taken over by a vampire named Loric. The closest thing to a brother Harley Kayson had had. As the person who'd killed Harley, this was not great news for me.

Jenner had begged Arys to come back to Vegas with him. To take their city back from the vampire who sought to revive the blood ring we'd begun to dismantle, among other things. Arys and I had agreed that we'd go. After we dealt with our more pressing matter of not killing each other.

That was a trip I sure did not look forward to. I had a love/hate relationship with Las Vegas. I wasn't a big fan of Jenner either. He wasn't all bad. Sure, he'd been there for Arys and me, and he fucked like a champ, but he and Arys had history that they just couldn't let go of. And I didn't trust it not to cause problems.

I sat alone in the booth. Falon left after saying something about needing to see a demon about a horse. I'd flipped him off, and he'd chuckled. Over by the pool table Willow chatted up the girl with pink hair.

My phone buzzed in my bag, and I dug around to grab it before it went to voicemail. Shaz's name on the screen gave me the warm and fuzzies.

"Hey, babe," I answered with a smile on my face. Suddenly I very much needed to hear his voice. "What's up?"

I got up and ambled away from the booth, toward the corner by the pool table. The furthest I could get from the band. Pressing the phone tight to my ear, I tried not to worry. A call at random from Shaz after running from Arys didn't automatically mean something bad.

"Arys is here, Lex. I just wanted you to know. Is everything ok with you?" Heavy concern laced Shaz's voice. Arys must have told him what went down.

"Yeah, I'm fine. How's Arys?" I'd once felt left out from what had developed between Shaz and Arys. Now that I understood their bond, I just felt relieved that Arys had gone to him.

"Hanging in there. Better now. Calm." A pause. "He's going to hang out here for a while. But I'm going to swing by your place at sunrise. I want to see you."

The warm and fuzzy feeling grew, spreading through my chest. "Looking forward to it. Keep our vampire out of trouble."

Shaz's laugh released some of my tension. "Will do. Love you."

"Love you." I hung up with the sudden realization that I'd referred to Arys as our vampire, and Shaz had rolled with it. Arys and I referred to Shaz as ours all the time, but it didn't go the other way. Until just now.

Gabriel's dark energy announced his arrival. I turned in time to watch the black-magic vampire step through the entryway. His long raven hair was tied back. In a long black gothic-style trench coat and black jeans, he wore power like a fragrance.

People noticed him. Tall, a little lanky but firm. Not willowy or gaunt by any means. Every time I saw him there was less of the awkward teen I'd first met and so much more of the confident vampire. Young, twenty now, but all man nonetheless.

Immediately he took command of the room. They responded. Some were quick to get out of his way. Others gravitated closer. He'd grown into himself and everyone sensed it. How had I not noticed until now?

His dark gaze found mine across the distance. So he was looking for me. Crap. I'd been hoping he was here to play, like the others. If he was here for me, it couldn't be good.

I tucked my phone in my bag and met him in the middle of the club. "What's up, kid?"

It just slipped out. I pretended not to notice the flicker of irritation that passed over his face. I didn't blame him for being annoyed. I'd have been too. It sucked when people saw you one way but you knew they weren't getting the whole picture. That presence couldn't be forced. They either saw you or they didn't.

"I need to tell you something." He killed me with that statement. How many horrific confessions had started with those words?

His dark-brown eyes revealed nothing. I didn't have the luxury of telling him to get lost. That I had my own problems to deal with. Whatever he had to say, I had to hear it out. Because he belonged to Arys and me. Our responsibility.

"How bad is it?" Not the question I should have first asked but the one that spilled out. I grimaced. "Sorry. Do you want to sit?"

He glanced around before shaking his head. He eased out of the flow of traffic, and I joined him. Leaning in close enough to speak without shouting, Gabriel said, "The vampire you're hunting, I know who it is."

A prick on the back of my neck set off a chain reaction as a chill stole over me. *He'd turned someone?* No, I couldn't jump the gun just yet. I needed to be able to trust him. "Tell me what you know."

I didn't want to believe Gabriel was as bad as Hurst had predicted. He'd warned us not to turn him. And Gabriel had done some shady shit. All was forgiven, though never forgotten, and we'd moved on.

Still, I did worry that he'd become a liability. He knew it too. So it took guts for him to walk in here.

"Her name is Lizzy. I turned her." Gabriel looked me right in the eye, owning his confession. "But I didn't plan to. It just… Things got out of control and, shit, I didn't know this would happen." Gabriel had said he wanted me to trust him, to consider him part of my inner circle. I suspected he feared blowing any shot he may have had at that.

Decision time. Lose it and snap the kid like a twig or try to extend some understanding. I mean, who was I to act like I'd never fucked up?

"Tell me everything."

Gabriel nodded and paused to gather his thoughts. His gaze strayed past me. I felt someone draw close. He grabbed the wrist of the man who'd been about to make a grab for my ass.

The drunken idiot slurred something about having a good time. This shit happened. Most people knew better than to make uninvited grabs in my nightclub, but those who didn't, well, they learned. The hard way.

"Hands off," Gabriel hissed, twisting the man's wrist so he shrieked. Then he gave the guy a shove in the opposite direction.

Obviously I didn't need him to fend off drunken grope attempts. I could take care of that myself. Still, his courtesy didn't go unnoticed.

He asked, "Can we talk about this outside?"

The pressure inside my head had grown substantially at his arrival. The constant static from Willow and Jenner had already been loud enough. Four of us inside one building pushed my tolerance.

"Yeah, go." I waved a hand for him to head out, glancing back at the injured man holding his wrist. Gabriel's chivalrous act had been a plea. What he told me outside would affect how I chose to respond.

In the parking lot Gabriel lit up a cigarette. Taking huge drags, he strode to the far end of the lot, near the back of the building, where the streetlight didn't fall and most people didn't park.

Crossing my arms, I waited for him to start talking.

He paced back and forth a few times, puffing on the smoke. His energy was frazzled. Scattered. Like he was all over the place inside his head.

"I didn't mean to do it, Alexa. I swear." He jerked to a stop and sucked in another lungful of smoke. As he spoke, it spewed from between his lips. "I knew Lizzy from before. When I was just dabbling in witchcraft. Since high school. We were part of the same coven. I lost touch with her, and everyone else, when I got caught up with Shya. I ran into her at a concert a couple months ago. I knew I shouldn't take her home but I did. I screwed up."

"Looks to be that way. How did the whole turning her thing come about?" Try as I might to resist, the urge to feel him out won me over. Just a subtle poke at his aura.

So dark. Heavy with the succulent incubus vibes bestowed on him by Arys. If I studied him closely enough, I saw a faint ripple in the air around him. Like when hot meets cold. There were vampires pushing a thousand years old who'd never know half the power Gabriel had now as a relative newbie.

I had to admit, it was enticing. Running high and hot, and he didn't even have to try. I wanted to sample it for myself. To taste that certain something I could feel in his power, the part that made it all his own.

Gabriel had to have felt my intrusion, but he gave no indication. "We slept together a few times. She's a witch. She knew I'd changed and she wanted in. I refused though, Alexa, I promise."

Shifting my weight from foot to foot, I nodded, agreeing to withhold judgment a little longer. He tossed the cigarette butt to the ground and immediately pulled another from a pack in his jacket pocket.

"Lizzy got kind of obsessive. She came to the house one night, right before sunrise. I wasn't expecting her. She came to seduce me into turning her, used a spell to trigger the bloodlust." Puffing on the smoke, Gabriel stared at his boots. Remembering. "She didn't know what she was doing, messing with a vampire's hunger like that. It backfired. I lost it. I'm still not sure how I managed to keep from killing her before it was too late."

I stifled a groan as I put the pieces together. "You turned her to save her. Risky decision to make in the moment. But I get it. You thought you were doing the right thing."

"I only cared because we have history. She was a friend. You know?" More pacing, more smoking. "My first mistake was reconnecting with her in the first place. But I know I shouldn't have turned her. I'll find her. I'll fix this."

"*We* will find her," I corrected. "I was tracking her earlier. She was on the move. You can help. You know her energy signature. Help me pick it out from the rest."

Gabriel looked up in surprise. He must have expected me to tear him a new one. "Yeah, of course. I'll do anything to make this right."

"I'm sure I don't have to tell you why none of us should be too quick to turn anyone," I said with an annoyed sigh. Annoyed because all of us had turned someone at some point that we shouldn't have. "The power in our bloodline, it needs to be kept exclusive."

He grimaced around the cigarette. "No argument here. This never should've happened. I panicked."

In his dark gaze I saw wariness. Readiness. He really thought I might do him in for this. Was that the reputation I had with everyone? Or just Gabriel?

"I turned Briggs out of anger." I shrugged. "I've fucked up too. When the right time comes, I'll fix that mistake. Tonight, let's fix yours."

I turned back toward the streetlight that bathed the rest of the parking lot in an artificial glow. Gabriel hesitated before falling into step with me. There was something he had yet to say.

The hard set to his broad shoulders softened. He released a plume of smoke. "There's one more thing. Lizzy stole my grimoire."

CHAPTER FIVE

A witch turned vampire with an obsession had her hands on a grimoire filled with demon spells and rituals. What could possibly be alarming about that?

Everything. The answer was everything.

Together Gabriel and I returned to the dance club where we'd last tracked Lizzy. While he inspected the bloodstained concrete, I fired off a text to Jez to let her know we had an identity and a vampire who could sniff her out. So to speak.

The night had grown late. Last call had come and gone. The remaining stragglers leaving the dance club loudly piled into cabs and Ubers. Then the street was quiet.

"I can feel that she was here, but her energy signature crosses with so many others, it's hard to pick out." Gabriel extended a hand and lifted a dark brow. "Do you mind?"

Did I mind allowing the precognitive, black-magic vampire to touch me and access my power? Just a little. Did I show it? I hoped not.

I started to reach for his hand, then stopped midway. "Just a thought, did you see anything I should know about when you touched Lizzy? Like what she's going to do with that grimoire."

His gaze fell, and for a second that awkward kid showed through. Gnawing his lower lip, Gabriel ran a hand along the back of his neck. I caught myself staring at his mouth, watching the tip of a fang peek out.

"Nothing. That's not to say I haven't tried." Looking ashamed, like he thought it was his fault, Gabriel slanted a glance at the stain on the sidewalk. "I don't control the precog visions. They come when they come." His hand started to drop.

Hating that Gabriel's touch gave me anxiety, I caught it in mine. "Do what you need to do. Let's find her."

Gabriel's news definitely added a steaming heap to the already massive pile of crap tonight. But what could I do but roll with it? Obviously the girl needed to be caught. I was expecting the worst, that we'd have to destroy her. But hopefully not the absolute worst. I didn't want to have to destroy him.

Gabriel slipped his soft fingers between mine. Even though I expected the moment when our power merged, I wasn't prepared for the shock to my system when it happened. A shock of ardor. Straight to the groin.

Did he do that on purpose? He was an incubus, made by Arys. It came with the territory. Still, it seemed strong and sharp. Demanding my attention. Or had I just started to take notice?

With a gentle, smooth pull Gabriel drew on my power to heighten his own abilities. Eyes closed, he concentrated, searching the night for the vampire he'd made.

On top of everything else Gabriel had done since turning, this perhaps more than anything proved Hurst right. He shouldn't have been given our power. But old vampires with their wise old owl words of wisdom and foreboding didn't have to deal with it here and now. I did, and I was over premonitions and warnings.

This whole ordeal did force me to make the decision I'd been putting off. Trust Gabriel? Or kill him? Because there were no other options.

He'd asked for a chance to prove himself. I'd give him that. Killing off every threat or liability wasn't how I'd prefer to do things. Arys had turned Gabriel. That made him ours. We owed him a chance to act like it.

Another tug on my energy. The circuit running between us twisted and writhed. My power rolled over and through Gabriel, seducing him from the inside out. Lust spilled from him to test me.

I clenched my teeth, telling myself I didn't want to taste him. It was just the power talking. And I most definitely didn't want to throw him on the ground and straddle him.

Ok, so he wasn't really a kid. And in that moment I was forced to feel it. I glanced up to see that his dark eyes had opened. He watched me with the tortured wonder I'd seen in the eyes of several vampires before him.

Gabriel pulled his hand from mine, severing the connection so suddenly it felt like being doused in the face with a bucket of cold water. "I think I can find her."

We traveled in the opposite direction from the park where I'd encountered Arys. So I'd been going the wrong way. I followed Gabriel's lead, letting him guide the way as we left the streets and ventured closer to the river.

Neither of us were the type to force small talk, so we moved in silence. Until he randomly said, "I want to help you and Arys fix things. I know I'm not exactly skilled in light magic, but I want to help in any way I can."

We drifted farther from the street lights, into a treed area with a bench and trashcan. Nice for sitting and gazing out on the river. In the dark, the surface partially frozen, the water appeared black.

"Thanks, kid. I appreciate that. Sorry. Gabriel. I've gotta work on that. I know you're not a kid."

I wasn't stupid. Keeping Arys and I from blowing apart was in Gabriel's best interest. He wasn't the only one. Self-preservation drove all of us. There was safety in numbers, and vampires like us, we didn't lack enemies. Power had a way of creating them. Gabriel had more to gain from us alive than he did if we were dead.

He stopped, scanning the scanty trees. Leafless and bare. Skeletal against the night.

"Do you?" Calm despite the erratic way his energy caused the atmosphere to surge at random. "I meant what I said, Alexa. About wanting into your inner circle. I'm worth having around, and I'll prove it."

I had not forgotten our brief conversation. Naturally it had to come up again. I had yet to respond directly.

So I did now. There had always been this level of awkwardness between Gabriel and me. It had changed but it was still there. So I bulldozed right through it. Cut to the chase. "Tell me what you really want from me, Gabriel. A chance? Fine, you've got it." I took a careful step back, then another. Slow. Just to keep a safe distance between us. "But if it's blood and sex you want, then I don't think you've thought that through well enough."

A slip of a grin changed his usually solemn expression into something unexpectedly brilliant. Gabriel was quite handsome when his eyes lit up. "I'm trying to pledge my loyalty to you, Alexa. I'm at your disposal, and you can have me any way you want me." His sullen manner had dissipated, replaced with the growing confidence I'd been seeing in him a lot lately.

I laughed, mostly because I didn't know what to say to such a bold statement from someone I still didn't know all that well. It was ballsy for sure. Had to admire that. "Sounds like you're spending too much time alone in a demon's house," I half joked. "You need to get out more."

Without taking a step, Gabriel angled himself toward me. He held my gaze, arching a brow in silent invitation. "Look, if Shya taught me anything about surviving in this world, it's to choose your queen wisely. Because he sure as hell didn't. And to do whatever it takes to prove loyalty. Because the only thing really worth anything anymore is trust."

He turned away, following the trail he'd picked up. Keeping my distance, I followed. "Ok, I get that. Strategic alliance. Makes sense. But there's no need to make rash decisions that you can't take back. In case you haven't noticed, my lovers tend to form an addiction to me. And between you and me, it looks painful."

Casting a glance back over his shoulder, Gabriel ambled along, pausing here and there to reassess. "It's a small price to pay for power and protection. I've seen the evil that's out there, and I know who I want to be aligned with when shit inevitably goes down."

"Thanks for the vote of confidence but you might be overshooting the mark a little." Of all the motivations men had had to sleep with me, self-preservation had never been one of them. I chuckled a little to myself, finding it amusing. I had to. It was so hard to genuinely laugh these days.

Gabriel jerked to a sudden halt. Then he turned and came at me, stopping just close enough to make my breath catch but not so close as to raise my defenses. "I don't want to feel like I'm always on the outside looking in. I know where my loyalty lies, and I want you to know it too."

I swallowed hard and licked my lips. "Um, alright. Thank you, I think. I appreciate that."

Frustration seeped from him, raw and sharp. He didn't think I was taking him seriously. In all honesty, I didn't know what the hell to say.

Letting out a breath on a huff, Gabriel continued to surprise me by sinking to his knees before me. "You are my queen, Alexa. I know what that means even if you don't yet." Pausing, his hungry gaze slid down my body, slowly over my hips and thighs and back up again. "And I am willing to serve you, in any way you like. I want you to make me yours."

His declaration hung between us. He waited, allowing it to sink in. Holding my gaze, letting me see the vampire where the boy had been. On his knees, pledging himself like a warrior to his queen, Gabriel emanated an otherworldly awareness.

What did he know that I didn't?

Having him on his knees before me with darkness in his eyes and wisdom far beyond his years, it caused my stomach to tighten. A tremor shook me as the hunger encouraged me to take what he was giving.

His offer of service hung heavy on the air with its many intentions. My encounter with Arys had left me hungry and frustrated. Sure Gabriel was young at twenty, but already he'd gained a reputation among the women of The Wicked Kiss. So, so fucking enticing.

Part of me remained wary. Cautious. He saw things and that worried me. The rest of me was a little turned on. Our eyes locked and he saw it. My temptation. Darkness drove my hunger. I couldn't fathom a single reason why I shouldn't ravish him right there.

"I'll most definitely consider it," I managed to say. It came out smooth and seductive, a tease. "Let's see how you handle Lizzy."

I clenched my fists to keep from touching him. Arys's darkness streaked through me, determined not to make it easy for me to resist.

Having nothing more to add and likely sensing my internal struggle, Gabriel rose with a nod, and we continued on. My phone buzzed in my bag, and I busied myself with texting Jez. Anything to distract from the tension in my loins.

Gabriel wanted me to claim him. To give him my body and blood. To enslave him through blood and power as I had Kale, Jenner, and unfortunately, Willow. He wanted it. Requested it. And it blew my mind.

What would Arys think about this? He'd made Gabriel, and he didn't regret it. Would he want to immerse him that deep into the fold? Because what this was really about for Gabriel was belonging. To us. So that he could never be forced to belong to someone else. Like Shya. Or worse.

Jerking to a stop, Gabriel kicked at something etched into the dirt. A symbol? It looked like a series of intersecting lines. He bent to inspect it before hissing, "Fuck."

"Not loving the sound of that," I muttered, turning to scan our surroundings. We were alone. I couldn't feel anyone else. "Ok, how bad is it? What is that thing?"

He studied the mark, shoulders slumped. "It's a spell from my grimoire. A cloaking spell that Shya showed me. Lizzy's hidden her energy signature. The trail ends here."

"Well this is an unfortunate yet not entirely surprising turn of events. Want to tell me why the hell that spell book was accessible?" I pinned Gabriel with a stare that I hoped he felt to the soles of his feet. "Briggs used that book to make a goddamn zombie."

Brow furrowed in anguish, he clenched both fists and uttered something Latin that sounded like a curse. Fire erupted from his hands. It scorched a path straight to the symbol, destroying it.

"I spelled the book after that. The pages look blank, but anyone with enough magical ability and knowhow could crack it." Scuffing a boot through the small pile of soot, he grew sullen, Gabriel's customary expression. "Lizzy does have the knowhow, and I gave her enough power to crack the spell. Stupid. So much for earning your trust."

Yes… so much for that. Inwardly I sighed. Outwardly I remained calm and tried to shut out the dark voice shouting inside my head to destroy this waste of time and effort. This evil little part of me decided if it couldn't play with Gabriel, then it might as well kill him. That part of me was all dark, all Arys.

I was able to shut the voice out with focus and intent. It continued to beat at me though in the back of my mind. Did Arys feel this way all the time? The constant urge to fuck, feed, and kill.

Not anymore. Now he also felt the torment of humanity. After many years of living the most wicked of lives, I'd brought his heart back to life. And now it tortured him. As it tortured me, here in this moment.

Good fucking times. One day we'd look back at all this chaos and laugh. Right?

"Let's go." I turned to head back the way we'd come. "There's not much time left before sunrise. She'll be forced to hide out somewhere. First thing tomorrow night, we look for her."

Staying in a secluded area with Gabriel right then was too dangerous. I didn't trust myself not to fuck or kill him. Or both. As Arys had wanted to do to me just hours ago.

Gabriel stewed in silence behind me as we backtracked through the trees to the city streets. There weren't many vampires I trusted entirely at my back, but I felt pretty confident that his guilt would hold any wicked temptations in check.

Yep, he'd messed up alright, in a bad way. But it wasn't anything I hadn't done myself. My own vampire creation was a federal agent turned mad scientist. I'd cut the kid a break after I let him sweat about it a bit. I needed to be confident he'd never make this mistake again.

We met up with Jez and Smudge outside the nightclub where the body had been found. They'd been in the area scouting a lead given to them by a patron. They too had turned up nothing.

"So this chick can do black magic too?" Jez laughed in disbelief after we'd filled them in. She eyed Gabriel, then me. Red lips twisted in mock judgment. "You vamps shouldn't breed, you know that? You pick the worst possible people to turn. Except Willow. He's amazing." She laughed right over Gabriel's frown. How she found amusement in this I'd never know, but then again, she was on the outside looking in.

Golden hair piled atop her head in a sexy, messy bun, green eyes sparkling, Jez looked happier than I'd seen her in a long time. The pain was still there behind her eyes every now and then, the loss of Kale we both shared, but she'd thrown herself into moving forward.

From her neck hung a tear drop-shaped black obsidian amulet. It had been made for her by Gabriel himself. After Kale's death Jez's nephilim power had burst free, revealing itself. Necromancy. The woman could simply walk into a room and suck the life force from anyone breathing with her mere presence. Jez had been working with

Gabriel, as well as Spike, a badass nephilim whose name was starting to make waves in the underworld. But Jez's power was new and intense. Control was precarious and touchy. It would take time to master. So Gabriel had created the amulet to subdue her power. As long as she wore the amulet, she couldn't accidentally suck anyone dry.

"Willow is amazing," I agreed, sneaking a glance at the moody vampire scuffing his boot against the ground. "I guess, if you two don't have anything else to go on tonight, there's not much we can do but wait."

Smudge gave a toss of her inky black bangs. They fell right back into her eyes. "I've got people all over this city. If they get a visual on her, I'll know the second it happens."

Dressed all in black, the dark to Jez's golden light, Smudge was one person I'd liked right away. Since getting to know her, that feeling had grown. She and Jez had hit it off too. They'd been inseparable for several weeks now. It was adorable really. Jez deserved to be happy.

Smudge was part of The Circle of the Veil. A watchdog, she knew everything that happened within the supernatural community in just about real time. We all had our jobs in The Circle, but I believed hers to be among the most difficult. Yet she made it look so smooth.

"Sounds good," I said, eyeing the sky. Sunrise would force three of us to seek shelter in about an hour. "Keep me posted."

Before I could leave, Jez hooked her arm through mine and pulled me away from the others.

I'd been meaning to ask Jez if she'd decided to sell Kale's house or not. He'd left it to her. I'd gotten the Camaro. Of course. Which is all I would have wanted. This didn't feel like the right time to bring it up. So like every time I decided it still wasn't the right time, I kept my mouth shut.

So it surprised me that, when we reached the end of the block, she turned to me, her smile gone. "I decided to sell Kale's house," she blurted, like it couldn't be contained. "I called to have it listed earlier today. And I feel so fucking guilty about it. But I just can't live there, Lex. Renting it out would just be a constant reminder. Am I making a mistake?"

Apocalyptic

"No, of course not." I pulled her into a hug that filled my nose with jasmine perfume and wildcat. "Do whatever you need to do. It's just a house, Jezzy. He barely spent any time there anyway. You can let it go. It doesn't mean you're letting him go."

I'd gone through this myself when making the choice to clean out his room at The Wicked Kiss. Like he'd never even been there. It hadn't healed any wounds though. I still had to walk past that room every night. Memories like that, they don't fade.

She hugged me tight enough to squeeze a squeak from me. "I know that. It's just so hard. I know it's hard for you too."

"It will be ok. You can do this. Let me know if you need any help with anything."

Jez pulled back, and her brilliant red smile fell in place. "Since you mentioned it, I could use a hand cleaning the place out. There's not a lot in there, but there's a bunch of boxes and stuff in the basement. I'm going to donate the furniture."

Eyes narrowed, I assessed her coy smile. "You baited me into that one."

"I have no idea what you're talking about." Arm in arm, she dragged me back to where Smudge and Gabriel stood awkwardly, doing their best to look at anything but each other.

Jez and Smudge went on their way, leaving me and Gabriel to stand awkwardly. His energy made the atmosphere rife with tension. It felt sharp. Negative and annoying.

"I'll find her, Alexa. I know a few places I can check. The second the sun sets, I'll be out there." He dragged his gaze from mine, like he didn't want me to see something in his eyes. "I might even have a spell I can try, to locate the energy signature of her spell and break it."

"You can do that?" Knowing he didn't want me to see something, I searched him. His dark gaze revealed nothing. His energy, however, ran in frantic leaps and jumps. Anxious and desperate.

This kid became more interesting every time he revealed something new about himself. No, not a kid. Twenty. A young man in his prime in so many ways. He'd already been powerful in his own right as a black-magic, precognitive witch. Arys had made him a masterpiece of darkness.

"I can try." A half shrug. A frown tugged his mouth into something pouty and sensual. "I can't promise anything."

"And when you find her?" I asked, curious. Testing him. "What then?"

I expected him to make a bold claim to kill her. To do away with the mistake he'd made as I'd been tempted to do with Briggs. As I was still tempted to do.

But Gabriel wasn't easy to read, and there was no anticipating his reactions. He continued to take me by surprise. "Whatever you want," he said, passing the test with flying colors.

It wasn't the answer I'd wanted or expected, but it told me all I needed to know about Gabriel right then. Sure, he could be playing me. He'd gone to the dark side once, and that kind of thing couldn't be forgotten. But my gut said he was genuine.

Cutting through the swath of strange hanging between us, I advanced on him. Like a predator on the prowl. Extending a finger tipped with a claw, I ever so lightly stroked beneath his chin.

He stared into me like a deer caught in the headlights. Eyes wide, pupils drowning black. The high-strung energy thrumming around him warmed at my touch, growing softer. Malleable in my hands. A pulse from me to him, a shot of pure succubus. He didn't resist, instead opening himself fully to my seductive vibes. And he didn't resist when I brought my lips to his.

The dark voice had abandoned its chant for me to kill him. Now it wanted me to dirty him up every which way I could first. The same push and pull of sex and death that ran rampant through Arys tempted me in the worst of ways.

I had to be stronger than Arys.

I told myself that as I kissed Gabriel. Soft at first, then hungrily. I had to taste him.

He fell hard under my thrall. An incubus of his caliber could have fought the pull to some extent. Gabriel had never wanted to. He let me roll him and in return gave me that flood of lust I sought.

Everything about him felt dark. Tasted dark. Like shadows and sin. I could drive him wild. Blow his fucking mind. And God how I wanted to. I'd have loved to blame it on Arys's hungers, but this was all me.

Gabriel kissed me back like a man who knew what he wanted. He teased me with the tip of his tongue, darting it against mine before pulling away. Feeding my hunger. His hand on the side of my neck held me close as he devoured my mouth. Though he may have been content to follow my lead on a hunt or a kill, he had no such intent here. Gabriel took command of the kiss, fogging my brain with his heady vibes.

With effort so great it hurt, I pulled away. I could take him right here. Nobody was around. We both wanted it.

But my control was compromised even more now than ever before. Giving in because it felt good didn't mean it wouldn't come without repercussions.

My harem of lovers was small as far as succubi and incubi go, and I wasn't too keen on adding to it without care and consideration. Flying off the handle led to hook ups like Jenner, whom I could deal with. But Gabriel? I wasn't sure how I felt about that.

I dragged my clawed fingertip over his chin, pressing it against his bottom lip. Damn did I ever want to just eat him up. All that power to play in.

Holding his deep brown gaze, I said, "Show me I can trust you. Show me you're not everything I'm afraid you are."

CHAPTER SIX

All I could smell and feel was wolf. I snuggled in deeper beneath the blankets, pressing tighter against Shaz's naked warmth. An hour after sunrise I'd stepped out of the shower to find him waiting in my bed with a fresh vampire bite and a grin. A pleasant surprise indeed.

We'd spent the better part of the morning enjoying one another. A slow, thorough lovemaking that was all about touch and emotion and not at all about blood or power. It was exactly what I'd needed. Being alone with Shaz returned me to my roots. I felt alive with the wolf inside. Curled up in my king-size bed, we absently watched daytime TV and just enjoyed being together.

"I've been looking forward to this all night." Shaz's husky whisper tickled the back of my neck. He spooned me, aligning his body to mine so he hugged my every curve.

One arm slung over me, I held tight to it, gliding a finger lightly over the thick veins in his forearm. "Nothing makes me feel like myself again the way you do." I brought his hand up so I could brush my lips over his fingertips. Closing my eyes, I soaked in the liveliness of him. The man and wolf, my true companion. My soulmate.

I'd once scoffed at such a term. But I believed it now with every part of me. Arys and I would never have made it this far without Shaz. He was our everything.

The bite Shaz bore made me wonder what had gone down between them, aside from the obvious. Arys had gone to Shaz in a moment of desperation and need. It reassured me to know that they were strong enough to face Arys's dark urges together. Because I sure as hell couldn't help him with that.

"How's Arys?" I finally asked, afraid of the answer.

"Kind of a mess." Shaz's soft answer moved the tiny hairs on the back of my neck. "Could've been worse though. He kept his shit together when he came by Doghead. I made sure he got home. I left his place at sunrise."

Hugging his arm to me, I half rolled over so I could cast a glance back at him. "We would be lost without you, Shaz. That's why Willow chose you to be our keystone. Even without his help, you kind of already were."

He kissed the side of my nose and rolled me all the way over so I was flat on my back. Raising himself up on an elbow, he planted another kiss on the edge of my mouth. "I know how this goes now, Lex. With Arys it's different than with you. Kind of like the other side of the coin, so to speak. But I know I belong with you both."

My gaze strayed to the two small punctures marring his perfect skin. I thought about Arys's confession of his love for Shaz. Something I'd sensed developing recently but looking back realized it had started long ago, even before our Vegas visit.

That was Arys's information to share, not mine. So I held my tongue. What I didn't know for certain was Shaz's feelings towards Arys.

"Does that mean you believe Kylarai's theory?" I teased, running my fingers over his side where he had a ticklish spot.

He caught my hand before I could coax a laugh from him. Pursing his lips, he shook his head in a teasing, flirtatious manner. "As much as I hate to say so, I don't think I have much choice but to believe it. I can't argue it."

I laughed at the melodramatic pout he affected. Gently I traced around the edge of one of the two small puncture wounds he bore. "No, I don't think you can. Not anymore."

Peering down at me with those serene jade eyes, Shaz appeared thoughtful. He seemed to be on the verge of saying something he also tried to hold back. I raised a brow, inviting him to just spit it out.

"What's it like when you're alone with the others? With Falon."

Ok, that I had not been expecting. Lying in bed with Shaz, wrapped up in each other, discussing my sexual exploits with the fallen angel was the last thing I wanted to do.

"Say what now?" I blurted. "I'm not quite sure I know how to answer that."

"Sorry to throw you a curveball there." A rueful grin lit up his face. "This doesn't have to be weird. I'm just curious. Is it only sex? Power? Do you get something different from all of us?"

One after the other he nailed me with questions that felt like fists. It wasn't his intent. My reaction was my problem. So I sucked it up and considered his query.

"It's different with each of you," I began carefully, weighing every word. "With Falon it's like taking a hit of the strongest drug I have access to. It's all about the escape with him. When things become too much…"

A lump lodged in my throat. That's what it had started as. It had evolved. Encounters with Falon had taken a strange turn. We still ran from the ghosts of our past in each other's arms, but it had led us to a place we couldn't turn back from.

Clearing my throat, I continued on before my pause could convey more than I felt ready to share. "With Arys its love and hate. Violence and tenderness. The place where it all comes together and I feel whole for a while. Not as much these days though, unfortunately."

Shaz nodded knowingly, his eyes crinkling in a sympathetic wince. "I'll do whatever I can to keep you and Arys from falling apart until we figure out how to fix this. I promise, Lex."

"And you," I said with a smile, running a hand through his platinum hair. "You are where my heart lies. You speak to my soul. When I'm with you, I remember who I am and who I want to be."

He ran a hand over my shoulder, up the side of my neck. Capturing my chin in a firm but gentle grasp, Shaz leaned down to brush his lips against mine. "Happy to hear it. But you know that's not entirely what I meant when I asked what it was like with the others."

I gazed up at him, puzzled. It must have showed because he laughed hard enough to shake the bed.

"What do you want from me, Shaz? A play by play of events?" I laughed too, in surprise. Maybe a little suspicion. What was up with this line of questioning?

He pretended to consider this with genuine interest. I slapped his chest and he chuckled. "I'm gonna go with no on that one. I just meant, what's it like? Having more than one lover?"

His grin faded with his last question. Right away I saw where he steered the conversation. And why. Shaz had known other lovers in his time. When I first met him, he'd been sowing his wild oats with several women. This was not about anything of the sort. This was all about Arys.

"It's natural now." As hard as it was for me to discuss this, I had to. He needed it. So I opened up. "It wasn't always. It felt wrong, but I realized that as long as everyone involved was aware and willing, it wasn't wrong at all. Just different. Only you and Arys possess my heart. The others, my body, blood, or power. But I'll never love anyone the way I love you, Shaz."

"I know." The emotion that stole over his face set my heart free. I adored the man like crazy. But he vibrated with sudden tension. Nerves. Whatever was lurking in his mind, he wanted to spit it out. Something held him back.

"You know you can talk to me about anything. Tell me what's on your mind. Where is this coming from?"

Shaz pushed himself up into a sitting position.

Concerned but trying not to jump the gun, I sat up too. Settling myself against the headboard, I waited for him to feel ready.

After shoving both hands through his hair, he clenched them both into fists and sighed. "I've been doing a lot of thinking, trying to figure out how I feel about some things. I want to know how you feel about them too. How would you feel if I wanted to pursue a more physical relationship with Arys?"

Ka-Boom!

Yeah, I was stunned. So much so that I had to replay what he'd just said a few times in my head.

"Um." My mind was blank. Words would be helpful. I stared at him like a moron, knowing I needed to speak before he formed his own assumptions. "How much more physical?"

Truth be told, I couldn't wrap my mind around the thought of Shaz and Arys sleeping together. Not because I was against it, but because Shaz had been so clear about where the lines were with Arys.

"I'm not sure yet. I don't even know if I want to. It's just something I've been thinking about." A faint blush colored Shaz's cheeks. "We've never done anything more than what you already know about. I wouldn't. Not without your consent." His apprehension flavored the air. This was no easy decision for Shaz. He'd been wrestling with this for some time now I'd bet.

I swallowed, finding it difficult. This was tough for him, I could see that. I didn't want to say or do anything to make it worse. "Shaz, you don't need my consent to be with Arys. Just make sure it's what you want. I don't want you to have regrets." My hand found his thigh beneath the sheets. I hoped he felt reassurance in my touch.

Relief flickered through his eyes. "Are you sure? I don't want to rock the boat."

"Bit late for that I think," I joked, trying to lighten the mood. "Look, we both know Arys wants you. And you know that I of all people understand well the enigma that is Arys Knight. I get it."

Shaz slumped back against the headboard next to me, looking deflated. "I don't know what it is about that guy. Nobody else but you has made me feel the way he does. I hate that I love it."

The tortured expression he wore had me bursting into giggles. I hated the sound and wished only that Falon could hear it because he'd hate it even more. "I'm sorry, Shaz." My head lolled back against the headboard. "I shouldn't laugh. It's cute though. Sounds like you might actually like him a little." I gave him a teasing nudge and batted my lashes. It was the closest I could get to asking if he had feelings for our dark vampire. I didn't want to force it out of him.

"I guess he's not all bad." Shaz smirked and rolled his eyes, playing it off. But his aura hummed with the telltale heat of red-hot attraction. And something more. There was genuine affection there, spicing his energy with tantalizing vibes.

"Not all bad," I repeated. Gliding my hand from his thigh, up over his abdomen, I lingered to outline the taut muscles there. I angled my head to better meet his gaze. "Sounds like someone's in denial."

"Maybe," he admitted, relaxing under my touch. "I'm going to enjoy it while I can." He'd volunteer everything when he felt there was more to share.

I didn't want to push anything and scare him off whatever he felt toward Arys. Choosing to leave it at that, I stripped the sheets off Shaz and climbed onto his lap. On my knees, straddling him, I gazed down at him. His wolfy eyes drank in the sight of me.

I was glad he'd said something. On some level it was a little weird to think of the two of them together like that. And yet, it was also a hell of a turn on. If he thought I'd be mad or threatened by any further development between him and Arys, he was all kinds of wrong.

The three of us were bound together. It felt only right that they should bond.

Shaz and I had spent the morning finding love and pleasure in one another. Desires we'd both built up with Arys before coming together. He should've been there with us.

Seeing the longing on my face, Shaz wrapped his arms around my back and crushed me against him. Pressing his face into my breasts, he kissed me. "It will be ok, Lex. I promise."

CHAPTER SEVEN

SHAZ

I hated seeing that look on her face. The fear of defeat. She missed Arys. It showed in every move she made. Every word she spoke.

It caused her brow to furrow tight, creating a pinched line between her eyes. Using my thumb I rubbed it until her expression softened. "Don't worry so much. It will all work itself out somehow."

Alexa's tight rear end brushed against my groin. Holding her hips, I pulled her harder against me.

She held my face in her hands and whispered, "You save me. Every night."

We both knew she would have to be the one to save herself in the end, along with Arys. They were running out of time. I saw it. We all did. I'd been putting in overtime doing what I could to keep them balanced while taking care not to neglect my pack. The A team didn't make it easy, that's for sure. They were a handful and then some.

Since Kale's death, Alexa had changed. She was more determined than ever to save what she and Arys had. It still hurt her. Losing Kale. She tried not to let us see. But I'd seen it break her the night it happened. I watched her kill someone she loved. I saw it kill a part of her.

Personally, I'd hated Kale. I didn't care how he found his end. Until it was her. Seeing how it changed her, I'd do anything to take that from her if I could.

Alexa reached between us, finding me hard and ready. How could I not be with her hot sex nestled against my shaft? She rose up to take me inside her. I watched her face intently as she filled herself with me. In so many ways.

The frown was replaced by serene calm. Her brown eyes closed, and she let out an exhalation of breath. Releasing a demon I

Apocalyptic

couldn't see. I felt it leave her in the sudden absence of the dark cloud that stormed her.

The same storm that drove Arys crazier each night. I'd felt it with him tonight too. In the office at Doghead.

Arys was in worse shape than Alexa, though she wasn't doing too hot herself. Since she'd made Willow human, I'd watched the two of them unravel faster than ever before. But I also watched them fight through it. Being together was a battleground, as was being apart.

It scared the hell out of me that they'd had such a close call tonight and I hadn't been there. It could have all been over. If anything happened to her, I'd be wrecked. Completely annihilated. If they destroyed each other I'd be wrecked and alone.

Maybe not entirely alone. I had the pack. And Kylarai. But my greatest fear was a life without Alexa. I saw it when Shya forced us to face our fears in his hell house. And these days when I envisioned my future with her, it included Arys.

I'm not sure exactly when that happened. Back when Alexa had first turned, she'd run off with Kale. That had left Arys and me to find comfort in each other. We'd bonded over her. It was always about her.

Then one day it wasn't. It had been only about him and me, like it had been tonight. We didn't go to each other now because of Alexa. We went to each other because we wanted to.

I watched Alexa slide along my length with her eyes closed and head thrown back. One hand on her hip, I guided her motions. At random I'd pull her down hard and thrust up, making her cry out. My other hand was on her slender throat, stroking a thumb over her pulse. Down her chest to cup one of her perfect breasts. I leaned in to suck her nipple into my mouth, grinning when she moaned and moved faster on my cock.

Hedging the subject of Arys and I had been tough. It was something I'd been thinking about for weeks. Since the night he got on his knees in front of me in the parking lot and asked me if I trusted him. That night, that kiss, it had changed something. Maybe everything.

I'd been forced to realize that on some level, I did trust Arys. And that on another level, I wanted him. Maybe not with the same intensity with which he wanted me, but there was something there. I'd needed Alexa to tell me it was ok to feel what I felt. That it was ok to explore it should I ever feel ready.

"Shaz." My name was a gasp on Alexa's lips. She moved against me, setting a natural rhythm that hit all the right places. Her favorite power position, I knew, even if she thought I didn't.

Touching her face, I waited for her eyes to open. Then I grasped her waist and lifted her off me, hating the moment I slid out of her warmth. It would be brief. I got her up on all fours, taking a moment to admire the view as I knelt behind her.

She cast a glance back at me, her gaze smoldering. We'd spent the morning enjoying the softer side of things. Slow movements. Gentle caresses. Perfectly timed orgasms to make a fluffy romance novel lover swoon. We'd needed it. To be tender and savor every touch.

But now I needed to purge myself of a need that had flared to life back in the office at Doghead. With Arys's fangs buried in my vein.

With clawed fingertips I held tight to Lex's sweet behind as I entered her. All the way in one thrust. Deep and hard enough to force a growl from her. Because now she knew what this was. The beast had a carnal urge to purge.

I paused, giving her exactly seven seconds to prepare herself. She quivered with anticipation. Her claws sliced the sheet beneath her into ribbons. Our wolves reigned as our primal nature took over. There was nothing sweet and romantic about what I was going to do to her.

On my next thrust she braced for it. Rough and deep, buried to my balls inside her. She groaned and tossed her blonde hair. I didn't have to see her face to know her eyes would be wolf.

Faster and harder, I took my mate in a frenzy. She was strong enough to hold her own, taking my thrusts with soft cries and moans. Blood marked her skin where my claws dug in. I eyed the tiny slices, lost in the way it felt to finally release the tension I'd held since Arys had walked into Doghead.

Since he'd pressed me to the door and claimed me in a way just as intimate as I now claimed Alexa. Maybe more so. And here I was thinking about him while I fucked her.

I didn't know what I wanted from Arys. Not really. I just knew it was time to find out. When I let myself think about his hands on me, in places he'd never dared touch, I didn't hate it. Not anymore. I had at one time. Because I'd felt threatened by him. That had changed.

A hand on Alexa's ass, I gripped just a little tighter, scratching a little deeper. Mere surface wounds but enough sting to make her whimper. She loved it. The woman who literally survived on dominating others fucking loved to be dominated.

The wolf in me brought it out more than the man. The need to claim her in a way that left her shaking and spent. To brand myself on her body and in her memory. She couldn't be this way with anybody else, the submissive wolf allowing her mate to dominate her like the beasts within demanded. Not just allowing me but trusting me.

My other hand slid up her back to disappear into a mass of blonde locks. I moved faster, roughly slamming against her. Sweeping her hair aside to bare her neck and shoulders, I grasped the back of her neck.

The urge to mark her was instinctive. She was mine. I pressed against her, my chest against her back, and bit her. The side of her neck where it curved down toward her shoulder. A sharp snap of fangs that left four gashes that immediately welled with blood.

Her small yelp was followed by, "Damn you, Shaz." But she was far from ticked off. She shoved her ass back against me, a challenge.

The scent of her blood was strong and spicy, like nothing I'd smelled on any creature living or otherwise. She smelled like wolf and felt like heaven.

I took her hard, until she trembled and begged with a ragged, "Please." Only then did I reach down and stroke a finger over her clit. She came hard with a snarl and a moan, spasming around my cock. Unable to hold back if I'd even wanted to, I released inside her.

I collapsed onto the bed and pulled her down with me. Lungs heaving, I hugged her to me, burying my face in her hair. I fucking loved her so hard it hurt.

She squirmed in my embrace, getting comfy against me. Her lips found my jaw, and her arms curved around my neck. For a long time we just lay there in comfortable quiet.

Later, when I got up to use the washroom, Alexa called after me, "So how much of that was about Arys?"

I shut the door and from inside the bathroom said, "Sorry, can't hear you. Door is closed."

I heard her mutter, "That's what I thought."

Smirking to myself in the mirror on the way to the john, I paused, my gaze drawn to the vampire bite on my neck. Arys's bite. So maybe I did want to put my own mark on him. Maybe I even wondered how he'd respond. What it would take to make Arys submit.

I touched the tiny healing wounds. It brought back a rush, a memory.

Finding out would have to wait. Before my own personal feelings and urges could be explored or even considered, I had to keep my vampires from destroying one another.

By the time I returned, Lex was asleep. Fitfully, like usual. The crease between her eyes had returned.

I grabbed my phone from my jeans on the floor and settled back into bed beside her. Without waking, she curled in close. With one arm around her, I held the phone with the other. I punched out a slow message one damn letter at a time. I didn't hesitate before sending it. To Arys.

I marked her. But it should have been you.

It wasn't that I didn't want Lex to bear my mark. Hell yes I did. All the time if that were possible. It was that Arys never had, despite the many times I'd bore his.

Staring at the screen, I could practically feel him reading it on the other end. He wasn't asleep. Knowing Arys, he was lounging in his favorite recliner, drawing.

His reply was so typically Arys. *Gladly.*

Dropping the phone back onto the floor, I cuddled in closer to Lex and let the sound of her slumber lull me.

* * * *

"Shit, Arys isn't answering. I can't believe I slept that long." Shaking her phone in frustration, Alexa rushed around, searching for her car keys. "He could be anywhere. We have to find him. Fuck, I told Gabriel I'd meet him. Why are you laughing?"

I couldn't help it. She was too cute. We hadn't slept in that late. It was just an hour past sunset.

"I'm sure he's fine, Lex. If you're so worried, reach out to him." I fetched the keys from the kitchen table where they were partially hidden beneath a stack of mail.

She considered this and shook her head. A long blonde braid snaked over her shoulder, writhing as her head moved. "I can't handle being in his head right now."

Spying the keys I held out to her, she sighed and plucked them from my hand. Taking advantage of her closeness, I pulled her into a hug. "He'll turn up. I plan to keep a much closer eye on you two from here on out."

"Good." She gave me a squeeze before pulling away. "Me and Gabriel have a vampire to hunt, and I don't need to worry about Arys hunting me at the same time."

That was exactly what I wanted to keep from happening. Again. If I had to watch every move Arys made, I would.

We left Alexa's house at the same time. She headed to The Wicked Kiss. I swung by Arys's place only to find it empty. He'd probably left the moment the sun set. On the prowl. Arys could be anywhere, but if I knew him, and I did, he'd go where he expected her to go. He couldn't stay away from her. They would always be pulled back together.

By the time I reached The Wicked Kiss, Alexa could have only beat me there by about twenty minutes. More than enough time for her to walk in and find Arys feasting on Ebyn, Alexa's occasional willing victim. And it was certainly more than enough time for the two of them to get in each other's face about it.

When I arrived Arys and Alexa stood near the couches where Ebyn sat looking dazed. They faced off, glaring daggers. It was relatively early yet. The club had yet to reach its busiest. Arys had wasted no time getting here and getting frisky with Alexa's friend.

For no other reason than to get a rise out of her, he had come here to mess with Ebyn. Arys's strong jaw was set in satisfaction, his dark-blue eyes alight with mischief. So tightly wound they both were. It's like he wasn't even trying to resist anymore. Just giving in to his many dark urges.

"Starting to dip into the wolf on the regular now, are you? In what scenario do you see that being a good thing for you, Arys? For us?" Alexa's voice carried as she growled into his face. Hands clenched into fists, she shook from the effort it took not to slug him.

Smug and unapologetic, Arys eyed her with cool detachment. "It's keeping me from dipping into you. Is that not a good thing, my love?"

Studying them both as I approached, I quickly assessed how close they were to blows. A twitch in Arys's jaw. A flash of wolf in Alexa's eyes. Getting close.

"You have no right to come here whenever you feel like it and help yourself to Ebyn like he's on the menu," she snapped, easing forward a step.

This had probably been going for several minutes before I arrived. I glanced around for some backup. If I needed to separate them, a little help would be nice.

Arys regarded her with ice-cold hostility. As if he wanted to snap her like a twig. "Your problem, Alexa, is that you don't like to share. Time to take that stick out of your ass and lighten up a little."

Stick in the ass comment? Yeah, that shit didn't fly with Lex.

I broke into a sprint, crossing the bar in a few strides. I saw it coming seconds before she lunged at him. Arys stood there and took the fist she threw in his face. His grin widened and he flashed fangs. A shiver crept down my spine.

He stopped her next punch by snatching her wrist before her fist could bounce off his face again. He twisted it slowly, until she snarled and raised her other hand to blast him.

As I reached them Jenner rounded the corner from the back. He'd likely sensed the commotion. We shared a look and jumped in. I didn't grab for Alexa though. I knew better. I left her to Jenner and went for Arys.

Since Jenner had revealed how bad things had gotten in Las Vegas, he and Arys were on shakier ground than usual. That was really saying something. Just like siblings they were, they hated each other most of the time, but when push came to shove, they had each other's back.

Still, Arys would respond better to me than to Jenner. Both hands on his shoulders, I backed him up several feet. He tried to stare around me at Alexa, but I kept putting myself in his line of view.

"Just couldn't stay away, could you?" I slugged him in the shoulder. Though playing it cool, I readied for him to make a move. "Ebyn? Really, Arys? Could you be any more obvious? Stop trying to set Alexa off. Do I have to shadow your every move?"

That got his attention. He quit trying to shoot a glare at Lex and met my gaze instead. Something manic glowed in the depths of his sinful blue eyes. "Does that include showers and naked Tuesdays?" he asked, brow raised in thoughtful consideration.

"Naked Tuesdays? You just made that up."

"Yeah, well if you're going to shadow my every move then I'll make it happen." Arys shoved closer, almost bumping his chest against mine.

His effort to be intimidating was overshadowed by the steady pulse of sex-charged power he couldn't help but leak with every breath. Lex was running hot tonight too. I expected a lot more of this from both of them as time ran shorter. Not wanting to tempt him, I tried to keep from reacting. The text message I'd sent him made that harder.

Knowing better than to encourage Arys when he was like this, I put a hand on his shoulder and steered him toward the door. "Let's go shoot some pool or something. Somewhere that isn't here."

A glance back at Lex, I caught her eye. Her lips moved as she spewed something irate at Jenner. Feeling my stare, she looked over. Relief swept her face. She saw me herding Arys to the exit and mouthed, *Thank you*, before blowing me a series of kisses.

I'd do whatever I could to hold them together. But I was only one man. I could do only so much. We needed a solution and we needed it fast.

CHAPTER EIGHT

I watched Shaz guide Arys out of my bar, feeling both relieved and gutted as they disappeared through the exit. Walking in to find my dark vampire fangs deep in my favorite willing playmate had shattered the simple joy of seeing him after being apart all day. In a heartbeat it had turned missing Arys into loathing him.

We couldn't keep doing this. I needed to find Salem or try something without his help, regardless of the risks. I couldn't wait much longer.

Quaking with rage and seeping an overflow of energy I couldn't contain, I let Jenner slip an arm around my shoulders. "Pretty sure I can get a contact high just from touching you. Need a little help taking the edge off?"

"I'm not screwing you, Jenner. I have a vampire to track. Some of us have work to do instead of lounging around bleeding some pretty thing all night. I don't expect you to understand." Though I wouldn't say so, I found Jenner's touch both a comfort and a curse. He had a flavor so close to Arys's.

I caught myself glancing toward the back hall. Looking for Kale. I still did it sometimes. Every now and then I got a hit of honey-drenched energy that stopped me in my tracks. Then it would be gone, like I'd imagined it. Times like this, when things were at their worst with Arys, I missed Kale the most. I automatically wanted to run to him. But I could never do that again.

"Maybe if you tried it my way more often you'd be able to relax." Pressing his face to my hair, Jenner purred, "You smell like wolf and sex, but you feel like a bomb about to go off. Intoxicating as fuck. Let me help."

I wore Shaz's scent like a perfume. That too brought me comfort. The healing wolf bite on the back of my neck ached slightly, reminding me of the thrill of being taken so forcefully by my wolf.

Apocalyptic

Every now and then his dark side slipped out. Lilah had said I was drawn to the darkness in each of my lovers, and she'd been right. Shaz's dark side showed its face in werewolf death fights, dominating sex, and bite-junkie thrills.

His sudden need to mark me in every way had manifested right after he brought up the subject of Arys. Specifically, being intimate with Arys. Whatever was brewing between those two, it had gotten under Shaz's skin.

"You want to help? Make yourself useful and get Ebyn home to ride out his high." I gestured to the loopy werewolf slumped on the sofa.

"Not happening, V." Ebyn waved a hand to get the waitress's attention. "The night is young. I'm not going anywhere." When his hand dropped, he almost tumbled to the floor.

He wasn't hurt, not really. Just stupidly high and annoying, the way wacked out people can be. Both Jenner and I ignored him.

Jenner playfully tugged the end of my fishtail braid. "I meant let me help take the edge off a little. Give you a little pick me up. Why should the werewolf get to have all the fun?"

Truth be told, I felt like I was bursting at the seams. The encounter with Arys, short lived but potent, had left me feeling manic. Like I needed to make someone bleed.

I turned to face Jenner, scanning his handsome face. I supposed I could bleed him. It might be good to loosen up a bit before meeting Gabriel to track Lizzy.

Putting a hand on Jenner's chest, I backed him up until he bumped against the easy chair next to the couch. "You want to bleed for me, Jenner? Do you want to be my drug tonight?"

His ice-blue gaze fell to my mouth, then my cleavage. "I'll be anything you want me to be. Here to help, you know."

Yeah, he was here to help alright. Because he needed us to come back to Vegas with him, and if we didn't make it through this, his city was fucked. Jenner had self-serving motivations. Of course, so did I right then.

With a hand under his chin, I jerked his gaze up. "My eyes are up here. Don't look. Don't touch."

I shoved him down onto the chair and climbed onto his lap. Jenner groaned and clutched the arms of the chair. "No touching? That's just cruel."

"Did I forget to say don't talk?" I asked with a smirk, roughly grabbing a handful of his bleached-blond hair. "I meant to say don't talk."

Jenner and I hadn't screwed but the one time. That's not to say we didn't come close. Being a succubus, temptation came with the territory. I'd accepted that some time ago. Although my motivation for doing it the first time hadn't been succubus urges. It had been the need to lash out at Arys. To hurt him.

That's what we did. We hurt each other.

Jenner had his own reasons for saying a big fuck you to Arys. He'd use me to say one every night if he could. Although that may have more to do with his unfortunate addiction to me.

Using the handful of hair I clutched, I jerked Jenner's head back against the chair, pinning him to it. My other hand went to his throat, circling it like a snake. I pinned him in place, enjoying his first onslaught of desire. I'd barely done anything yet.

Succumbing to my role as the aggressor, Jenner eyed me with a cold hunger. A hunger he'd never wanted, for which he resented both Arys and me. Regardless of how he felt about it, or me for that matter, that hunger would always burn.

As I saw the streak of resentment flash through him, he saw the twisted satisfaction in me. No remorse. Did that make me a monster? I'd felt bad about Kale and worse about Willow.

It wasn't really me that enjoyed Jenner's suffering though. It was Arys. That sick joy I got out of it, that was all Arys, echoing inside me. Every time I looked at Jenner, I wanted him to hurt.

I faltered, losing my hold on the rising swoon. Jenner and I, we were both pawns to Arys's vengeance. The sudden weight of it struck me numb. I stared into Jenner's eyes, panicked. Spiralling.

Jenner saw it. He could have laughed in my face and dumped me on the floor. Probably should have. What he did was give a slight shake of his head. Without saying a word, he used a fang to nip his bottom lip. Then he kissed me.

Apocalyptic

The sudden taste of his blood brought me alive. I sucked on the small cut, running my tongue over his lip before slipping it into his mouth. He grew hard beneath me, just what I wanted to feel.

A little blood, a pull on that erotic incubus energy, and I was on my way to feeling pretty damn good. Not quite the otherworldly high of Falon, but one couldn't indulge in an immortal narcotic every night. All I needed was a little kick to bring me back to where I needed to be: calm, in control, and ready to kick some ass. I did have a vampire to hunt.

Holding his head pinned to the back of the chair, I sought out a nice soft spot on the side of his neck and bit. A little bite, just enough to splash my tongue in blood.

Jenner groaned as his hands grabbed my ass. "Fuck the no touching rule."

I laughed against his neck, basking in the power of his arousal. Pulling back, I extended my arm, willing to play fair. With no hesitation he took my hand and sank fangs into my offered wrist.

A glimpse of dark hair in my peripheral view accompanied a new werewolf presence. Juliet. What was she doing here? It wasn't like her to drop by much these days. Not since Arys had taken a bite out of her.

I met her dark gaze as it landed on us. Her brown eyes, so much like mine. They widened, pupils dilating in response to me atop Jenner, his mouth on my wrist. The acrid scent of jealousy slipped from her, like she struggled to rein it in.

Jealous? Of Jenner and me? How curious.

"Sorry to interrupt," she said, sharp enough to cut. "I'm just here to meet Briggs."

Jenner released my wrist, but slowly, ensuring to give the wound one last leisurely swipe with his tongue. Because he'd sensed that jealousy too. He'd wanted to screw my sister since he first laid eyes on her. Naturally, I'd forbidden it. Jenner was the worst kind of incubus. She'd be just another warm body to fuck and bleed. I didn't want that for her.

I climbed off him, ignoring the judgment in Juliet's stare. She was in no position to judge me. I would never apologize for who I was or what I did within my own walls.

"He's not here." I grabbed a napkin from a nearby table and dabbed at my bleeding wrist. When she started toward the back hall, I flung myself into her path. "You can't go back there. I'm sorry. It's off limits."

Doing her best to keep from looking at or acknowledging Jenner in any way, Juliet crossed her arms and cocked a hip. "Let me guess. Participants only."

"Pretty much. Just wait for Briggs out here. It's safer for everyone that way." And how. Briggs came here to fuck and feed as much as any other vamp. Juliet had to know that on some level. She didn't have to see it.

Licking my blood from his lips, Jenner patted his lap with a lascivious smile. "Feel free to wait for him right here. I don't mind at all."

Juliet turned a scathing glower on him. "Not if you were the last man alive, Jenner. Get over yourself."

He continued to grin at her like he didn't notice the poison in her expression. "You say that now, but you've had a taste of our kind. You'll want more. And I'll be here when you do." Cocky as ever, Jenner rose from the chair like he'd been poured from it. Smooth and flowing. Every movement meant to entrance.

Leaving her speechless, he glided away like a fading shadow.

She watched him go with flushed cheeks and a racing heartbeat. He was right. Juliet had enjoyed what Arys did to her, even as it had sickened and pissed her off. I wondered if she'd sought out the same thrill with Briggs yet.

Doubtful. Juliet was incredibly uptight about the whole vampire thing. Understandably.

Clearing her throat, she tore her gaze from Jenner's retreating form. "I didn't know you two were, well, whatever that was."

I caught the arm of a passing waiter and ordered a drink for my sister. Seemed like she could use one. "Don't worry, Juliet. I don't do that shit with Briggs, if that's what you're thinking."

"Of course not," she huffed, wrinkling her nose at Ebyn who was draped over the arm of the couch, sniffing in her direction. "I know he'd never sleep with you."

Before Ebyn could graze her leg with a finger, I stepped in front of the couch, blocking the intoxicated werewolf. His hand groped drunkenly at my thigh instead as I steered Juliet away.

No, Briggs would not sleep with me. Not that I wanted him to. I knew he wasn't interested either. My blood however? That he would happily take, although I preferred to save that for when I needed to coax him into posing as a good little federal agent-turned-vampire.

"What's Briggs been up to lately anyway?" I asked.

Since I let Agent Thomas Briggs go free, I hadn't seen him much, other than in passing when he came here to feed. He tried to do it when I wasn't around, because I so rarely gave him my blood that my mere presence was agony.

"I've been keeping him busy working on some cold case files." Juliet gratefully accepted the drink the waiter brought her. "I thought with his new abilities it may be worth having him take a look at them. He's been working from home. I haven't let him step foot back on FPA property."

That was a huge relief. Vampires couldn't keep their shit together in that building. Briggs had been unhinged before I turned him. Despite Juliet's many misgivings about me, she'd taken me seriously when I said he couldn't go back there.

"What kind of cold case files?" Naturally I wanted to know what kind of unsolved mysteries the FPA had stashed away.

After sucking back a third of her long island iced tea in one go, she said, "Unresolved ritual murders. Reports of strange sightings. Creatures. Shadow people. That kind of thing. Old cases abandoned by former agents."

There was more to it than she was saying. Confidential information and all. But nothing about it struck me as problematic. It didn't have anything to do with me.

"I'm glad he's keeping busy and staying out of trouble. I was worried about letting him go." Keeping Briggs as a pet was an insult to both of us. Not that I gave a damn about insulting him but who had the time to deal with a freakin' prisoner?

We'd come to an agreement. Briggs would keep a low profile and do nothing to give me a reason to kill him. His loyalty to Arys and me, should we need him for anything at all, was expected. I didn't like to throw around the vampire queen of the city crap. It made me feel weird. But with Briggs I kind of enjoyed it.

Juliet nodded and took another, smaller sip. "So was I. But I'm keeping a close eye on him, Lexi."

"Good. Are you two still seeing each other? Or is that over?" She was my sister. I had to ask.

The federal agent side of her wanted to remain tight lipped. The twenty-four-year-old female side of her wanted to share. "That's what we're meeting to talk about. We've been taking a break. I love him, but I'm not sure I can sign on for this."

This was the part where I was supposed to feel bad. For turning him and ruining their relationship. But I didn't. If they couldn't be together now, it was all on them, not me.

"I understand," I said, and I did. It wasn't easy to love a vampire, especially an incubus.

Right on cue, a good-looking vampire with dark hair and gray eyes approached Juliet. He gave me a respectful nod before introducing himself to her as Xavier. It hadn't taken long for someone to notice my knockout sister.

She blushed and fumbled her words as she accepted Xavier's flirtation but ultimately shot him down. I watched the exchange with keen interest, suppressing my laughter. She was cute and awkward. Most of all, she was interested. There was no hiding the way her pulse raced or how she drank in the sight of him like a parched woman in the desert. He was crazy hot. She'd kick herself for this later.

"I'll be around for a while if you change your mind," Xavier said with a wink before moving on.

I smacked Juliet's arm. "He's a looker. You're not interested?"

"Oh please, I'm just a snack to him. Why would I want to be part of that?" As she spoke her gaze followed him. Without giving me a chance to respond, she drew closer and ducked her head so her hair hid most of her face. "Tell me the truth, Alexa. How much action does Briggs get in this place? Does he have a steady stream of women?"

Yes, he had more than his share. Lucky me, I'd been fortunate enough to catch him in the act. I couldn't say that to her though. It wasn't my info to share, and I would not be responsible for what it might do to her.

Apocalyptic

Speak of the devil. I sensed Briggs's gritty vibe seconds before he walked in, saving me from having to answer.

"Maybe you should ask him that, Juliet."

I expected her to leave my side to go to him, but she waited for him to reach us. Dressed office casual in dress pants sans jacket, his shirt open at the collar, Briggs moved like a man on a mission. I didn't think he knew how to move any other way.

Spying us together, his expression darkened. Yeah, I wasn't keen on seeing him right now either. Already he harshed my buzz.

Once Briggs drew close enough to catch scent of my wounds, his gait stiffened. He eased to a stop, slashing a glare my way before gracing Juliet with a smile. "Sorry, I'm late. Do you want to sit down somewhere? I'll order you another drink." All smiles and friendly demeanor, Briggs morphed into something I'd never seen from him before: a decent person.

Juliet downed the rest of her iced tea and handed him the empty glass. "Sounds good, thanks. I'm going to use the restroom first."

She left us to glower at one another. When she was out of earshot, I said, "What's your angle here, Briggs? What do you want from my sister?"

Crossing his muscular arms over his broad chest, the Fed pinned me with his best stare down. "I don't believe that's any of your damn business, O'Brien. I've been playing by your rules. Leave me alone."

"Have you though?" I countered, unfazed by his hardass Fed stare. I'd seen it too many times. "She asked me if you're taking other lovers. I didn't tell her. That's on you. Whatever you do, Briggs, don't toy with my sister. Love her properly or leave her."

A shock of anger rolled through him. He took one menacing step closer. It still left a few feet between us. "Stay the fuck out of it."

Extending my arm with the bite, I let blue and gold light crackle over my fingertips in warning. "That's my younger sister. Don't for a second think I won't protect her."

He didn't press it. Backing off, Briggs glanced in the direction Juliet had gone. Certain nobody was listening, he asked, "What will it take to convince you to tell me how Willow was made?"

I didn't miss a beat. "A miracle."

"Do you have any idea the kind of soldiers we could create? The kind of power an army of hybrids would have. You'd be doing your country and its allies a service." There was the nutty federal agent talk I'd come to expect from Briggs.

Eyes narrow, lip curled in derision, I shook my head. "Not interested. It's a secret that will die with me and Willow."

I didn't mention Arys, because Briggs didn't know for sure who or what had been involved. But he'd been locked in the room adjacent, so he had his ideas.

"I might not have lab access right now, but I'm still working on theories. There has to be a way to recreate a hybrid while isolating the strengths from the weaknesses." He paused, chewing on something he wanted to ask. Something that would piss me off, based on the way his dark brows knit together. "If you won't tell me how Willow was made, would you consider donating your eggs? I'm willing to strike a good deal."

My shocked laugh died immediately. He'd reached a new level of mad scientist. It scared me. "Vampires can't breed the way humans do. You know that."

"Perhaps not, but that doesn't mean the eggs wouldn't be viable in a human host. The possibilities are endless, and the only way to know for sure is to test it." So sure he was that he had something worth pursuing, he didn't hear the insanity I heard.

Searching his brown eyes, I found him to be calm, level headed. Nothing manic or crazed at all. Which made this all that much scarier.

"I want nothing to do with your theories, Briggs. Make a play for my eggs, and I'll gut you while you watch. Just one reason to take you out. That's all I need." I saw Juliet turn the corner from the restrooms. Backing away, I snapped my fingers. The power arced from me, hitting the floor at his feet. A final warning.

I walked away before Juliet reached us, leaving them to talk. Did she know he was still thinking about this stuff? Plotting and theorizing? Did he really think he could buy my eggs? For all I knew they could be shrivelled little nothings. But what if? I could not let Briggs answer that question. For his own good and the safety of all humanity.

CHAPTER NINE

I fired off a text to Gabriel, arranging to meet. Hopefully he'd have some good news for me. His personal connection to this vampire hunt was both unfortunate and potentially helpful. If he could nab Lizzy before she did much more damage, I'd give the kid the credit he deserved.

Pulling car keys from the pocket of my leather jacket, I strode outside. And ran smack into a chest as hard as stone. I'd been looking down at my phone, but he seemed to have come out of nowhere. Just there.

Forgetting the phone, I tucked it away and eyed the beefy stranger. Correction. Demon.

I sucked in a breath and back peddled a few steps. Then I stopped, holding my ground.

Red eyes flicked over me. A scar slashed through one brow and down his cheek. He eyed me with blatant curiosity. Tall and broad, he was a mountain next to my short frame. Dark hair fell to his shoulders, wild and unruly. Like a lion's mane.

His hard face held square edges and chiselled features. Dressed in a warrior tunic and dark pants, his muscular forearms were thicker than my thigh. Skin a deep, golden bronze, he was striking. Attractive but menacing, intimidating despite not having said a word yet.

"Alexa O'Brien." Deep and gruff, his voice sent a tremor of fear through me. He had a slight accent, the way some of them do when they speak their immortal language more than the languages of humans.

Instinct kicked in, and I surrounded myself with a circle to keep him at bay. "Who's asking?"

The demon took two heavy steps, stopping inches from my barrier. He held up a hand, hovering it over my circle, analyzing my power. As I watched, he ran a finger over the circle's surface and brought it to his mouth. Literally tasting my power.

His lips peeled back in a snarl-like grin, revealing upper and lower fangs. "So the rumors are true. No wonder he's so infatuated with you. His queen of light and dark."

My world turned upside down. Nobody but Falon had called me that. I suspected that's who the demon referred to. Shock and horror made it hard to swallow.

"I'm afraid I'm not familiar with these rumors," I said, wary of the mere inches that separated me from the mammoth demon. "And who might you be?"

His grin turned downright vicious. Like it alone could tear me apart. "You, your highness, can call me Bane. There's been a lot of talk about you in the underworld since Shya went missing. Rumor has it that you're responsible for that. Among other things."

Bane openly leered as he took in my appearance. But it didn't feel sexual. It felt hungry, like he was legitimately thinking about eating me and using my bones to pick his teeth after.

"Rumors are a funny thing," I quipped. "Most of them are just that. Rumors."

Holding up both hands, Bane feigned harmlessness. "Very few people miss Shya, and I am not one of them. It makes no difference to me if you did it."

"Then why are you here?" I didn't stand a chance against this guy if he wanted to leave me in ashes. It would be a shame to go out like that after fighting to keep from succumbing to Arys.

"I wanted to see you for myself." Bane rolled his shoulders and cracked his neck from side to side. Ominous. "I wanted to see the woman capable of reaching Falon's tragically broken heart."

Say what now? Was I supposed to know who this guy was? My confusion grew. "I have no idea what you're talking about."

"Like hell you don't. It's no secret that you're lovers. You taint one another's auras. Don't lie. I've heard so much better about you. You're supposed to be a real tell-it-like-it-is type. I can respect that. It must be what he likes about you." Raising a finger, he poked it into my circle like it was a bubble.

It burst like one, falling away to leave me exposed.

My mind raced as I tried to suss out anything I might know to tip me off as to who exactly Bane was. Out of habit I reached for the Dragon Claw, but it wasn't there. Still in my car. *Shit*.

Apocalyptic

"You must be mistaken. Falon doesn't like anything about me. We're not exactly friends." Falon had warned me. He'd said trouble would come down the wire because of our entanglement. It had arrived.

"Whatever you are, it's closer than he's allowed anyone to get in an incredibly long time." Shifting his massive weight from foot to foot, Bane had to do very little to exude a constant threat with his mere presence.

He leaned in close, trying to force my retreat. To herd me away from safety. But there was no safety with demons. Standing in a parking lot that grew busier with people didn't protect me. It didn't do a damn thing.

"Who are you, Bane?" I asked, hissing his name. "Really. Why do you care so much about Falon's latest lover? I'm probably just one of many."

Tapping a foot, Bane studied me. Then he came at me fast, forcing me to defend. I threw up both hands and blasted him. The shock of energy coursed through him like lightning. Bane twitched and spasmed but didn't go down.

He broke free with a grunt. He didn't retaliate with magic. Instead he backhanded me. I went down on my ass but rolled right back to my feet. My fangs had sliced the inside of my mouth. I spat blood and braced myself.

Bane hung back. He didn't seem interested in hurting me. He was feeling me out. Also not cool. I wasn't keen on strange and terrifying demons getting too close and curious.

"You really don't know?" He looked offended. Raking a hand through his hair, he chuckled. A hair-raising, bloodcurdling sound, the demon embodied fear.

"Should I?" Fear made me angry. It was either that or scream like a horror-movie victim who's too stupid to live. Bane unsettled me on the deepest level.

Because I knew who he was. Deep down. I didn't want to believe it, but I knew.

He eased away from me, into the shadows beyond the parking lot lights. With a bent finger, he beckoned for me to follow. I didn't budge.

When he stood just beyond the light's reach, Bane dropped the glamour that gave him a human form. Two horns curled up from each side of his head. Black wings cloaked him. A black furry tail whipped about behind him. The red of his eyes had encompassed the whites, giving him an animal-like appearance. His clothing changed to that of a long blue robe tied with a black sash. Atop his head sat a crown of gold so pure it shimmered in the shadows where he stood.

"My name is Prince Bane of Rhytheria. My family rules a land on the other side." He snapped his fingers and his human guise returned. He stepped back into the light. "Falon and I were in love with the same woman."

No. Oh, please no.

I gaped at Bane, unable to comprehend what I'd already known. He was the dark prince who'd cursed Falon and Winter. He was the demon she'd chosen in order to escape the curse. The lost and tortured brokenness I'd discovered in Falon, this demon was the cause.

I snapped.

Launching myself at Bane, I threw a fist loaded with power. It cracked against his jaw, thrusting him back into a nearby car. Not content to stop at just one, I madly threw both fists. With an angry growl I drew on the light, begging it not to fail me, and I threw it in his face.

Bane's guttural cry was almost strong enough to throw me on my ass. Not quite. But the sheer shot of absolute black he nailed me with was more than enough. I hit the ground and rolled. With the breath crushed from me and a sharp pain twisting my spine unnaturally, I didn't have the air to scream. I could only watch as he approached.

Leaning down over me, Bane smiled that evil, mirthless smile. "See, you do know who I am."

"You're a piece of shit," I gasped.

"Well, you've only heard one side of the story. Whatever Falon told you about me, I assure you, it's only half true." Bane released the power that held me. Staring down at my prone form, he again had that look, like he wanted to taste my flesh.

I wasn't sure why I felt the need to clarify but I did. Tremors shook my limbs as I struggled to get up. "He didn't tell me anything. Shya did."

This seemed to take Bane by surprise. Then it became satisfaction. "Unable to speak of it after all these years. What a shame."

My limbs tingled and my face throbbed. I clutched the closest vehicle and waited for the effects of his magic to subside. "Yeah, it's a real shame that you couldn't find your own woman so you had to resort to stealing someone else's."

Yeah, me and my big damn mouth. It was going to get me into trouble I couldn't get out of one of these days.

Bane grabbed me by the throat and slammed me down on the hood of the car. His eyes were wild and animal. "I saw something I liked and I took it. I came to see if I might like you as well. I prefer my women dark haired, but I could still find a few uses for your sassy mouth."

He choked off any retort I'd have mustered. I reached for the light in my core again, sifting through shadows to find it.

"I'm impressed. Falon has landed himself another rarity." Bane didn't give me a chance to fight him off. He released me with a shove that banged my head against the hood. "But he knows how much I like rarities. He should have done a better job of keeping you a secret."

He was gone with that, leaving me to slide down the side of the car to the hard ground. Panic engulfed me. Clenching my hands into fists, I shook with fear and fury.

Silently, I pleaded for Falon. This was one issue I could not handle on my own, nor should I have to. He had to feel me.

When the air moved five minutes later, I tensed and reached for my power. Falon materialized with his usual scowl in place. It disappeared when his silver gaze took in the sight of me. On the ground hugging my knees, shaking. Face bruised and lips bleeding. I must have looked beyond pathetic.

On alert Falon glanced about the parking lot in search of danger. "Alexa? What happened? Is it Arys?"

I shook my head, suddenly cold. "No, worse than that. It was Bane. He was just here."

Falon's gaze snapped to mine. Now he really took in my battered face and wounded pride. He bent down and took my chin in his hand. Turning my face to the light, he studied the cuts and blossoming bruises.

"What did he say?" His hand was a gentle caress on my sore face. With a thumb he lightly stroked my throbbing cheek.

I leaned into his touch. "He said that you should have done better at keeping me a secret."

In the dull light I saw him pale. Dread and dismay stole over his fine features. Then it morphed into absolute rage.

Falon stood up and spun away from me. He slammed his fist into the large garbage bin at the end of the lot. It crumpled beneath his assault. Massive craters dented the metal.

After he'd unleashed all over the helpless bin, Falon returned to me. He pulled me to my feet and smoothed the loose tendrils of hair back from my face. "Are you alright?" Despite my nod, he didn't look convinced. "I'm sorry he found you. I never wanted that to happen."

"I know." Unsure of what to say, I sucked in a deep breath and released it slowly. "How concerned should I be?"

Falon pulled away, like he didn't know if he should touch me or not. Embraces of comfort and affection were not something we shared.

A frown knit his brow into knots. His face became a mask of confusion. Like he didn't know how to process the situation. I was right there with him. For the first time someone had treated me as Falon's property, rather than the other way around. Neither of us knew how to react to that.

"Don't be concerned. I'll handle it."

"What does that mean? He could be goading you into a reaction. Don't give him what he wants." The shakes eased off and the panic began to fade. For now. I wasn't looking forward to seeing Bane again.

"Don't worry about it, wolf. I've got it." He brushed the whole thing off, waving a hand dismissively. "You should probably take off. Help Gabriel with that vampire."

My initial reaction was to be insulted. Didn't he give a shit that a demon prince from his past had threatened me? "Yeah, I'll get right on that, boss." I flung sarcasm like a weapon. "Sorry my brush with true evil delayed me."

Scowl back in place, Falon had the nerve to shrug me off. "Don't let it happen again."

I bit back my next retort. Fear and anger had us both in its grip, Falon likely more so than me. One of us had to be reasonable. "He called me the queen of light and dark," I said, shuddering as I heard myself say it.

I didn't have to tell him I was afraid. Not that I'd be ashamed to admit it. Bane was just another threat of many, but I could only deal with so much at a time.

Falon's expression went blank. Emotionless. Best damn poker face ever. "I have to go."

"Just like that? Shouldn't we talk about this? Why does he even care about me, Falon? I'm nobody, but he seems to think otherwise." I put myself in front of him, grabbing his arm so he'd look at me.

Bane had said he wanted to see the woman who could reach Falon's broken heart. Why would he ever assume it to be that way?

Trying to avoid a direct eye lock, Falon pulled free of me. "Don't worry about Bane. I'll take care of it."

"Falon, wait—"

He didn't. He left me there in the parking lot cursing him.

CHAPTER TEN

"What do you know about Bane?" I demanded after discovering Willow at the bar. "Prince Bane of something or other, to be exact."

Willow smiled apologetically to the tequila-drinking lady he'd been exchanging pleasantries with. So typically his type. "The demon who cursed Falon and Winter? Not much. Our paths never crossed. I've heard things. The underworld talks. Why?"

"He was just here." I turned my face for him to better see the evidence I bore of the demon's blow. "Seems to have a weird fascination with Falon."

Willow's eyes narrowed. "I knew that asshole would bring trouble your way. Alexa, you have got to stop this thing with him before it gets you killed."

The woman he'd been chatting up wandered away, and I winced apologetically. "I think it's too late for that now. And I'm not sure I could if I wanted to."

"Because you've claimed him." Willow gazed up at the ceiling, silently imploring it for wisdom. How many times had my actions made him look skyward like that? "Of all the people, why him? You don't even like him."

"I don't know how it happened," I whispered, more to myself than to him.

He heard me anyway. "It's who you are. A master of energy manipulation in many forms. Light and dark. You didn't bond him to you by accident, you know. Intent always plays a role." Putting a hand on my shoulder, Willow gave a sympathetic nod. "You can still cut him off. Break ties."

"He called me the queen of light and dark, Willow. Falon did. The night I made you human. When he was trying to keep me from quitting. Bane just repeated it now." I wanted to hug Willow and be needy for a while. Touching him too much so soon after his change could take us to the weird place. So I didn't and that sucked.

Willow's gaze darted about as he sought out another potential blood donor. He couldn't help it. Best not to test the bloodlust. "You're one of the last Hounds and a Light Flame." The most beautiful gold-flecked green eyes met mine. They were kind and gentle, exuding reassurance. "You, Alexa, are the place where light and dark meet. Very few people command both forces. Balance must be maintained, not just between you and Arys but between light and dark as a whole. You help protect that balance. People like Bane will seek to control and harm you. But when they back you against the wall and you come out blazing, they won't know what hit them."

Somehow I felt better, even though I knew I was in danger. Not just from Bane. However, it also put me in a power position. Rolling over and running scared now would send the wrong message.

"We need to find Salem," I said. "Walking the ledge with Arys is making us weak. We can't have that."

"I've reached out to everyone I can. I won't give up. We'll find him." Willow patted my arm, doing his best to be comforting, but his attention was on the woman I'd distracted him from.

A sudden buzzing in my pocket reminded me that I was supposed to meet Gabriel. Once I'd laid eyes on the demon from Falon's past, it had slipped my mind. "Thank you for the words of encouragement, Willow. I can always count on you for that. Sorry I interrupted."

"Never be sorry. I always have time for you. That being said..." Bloodlust gave his gold-sprinkled gaze a predatory gleam. He bid me farewell with a nod and immersed himself in the growing crowd.

One day, watching Willow act like a vampire wouldn't feel so weird. It wasn't today. He emanated eroticism like it dripped from him in every move he made. My dark side wanted to go after him, to ravish him in every way.

So I beat it outside before dark thoughts could sway me. Pressing the phone to my ear, I said, "Sorry, kid. Had demon trouble. What's up?" As kid flew out of my mouth, I winced. Oops.

No time to waste, Gabriel cut right to the chase. "Brogan just texted. Lizzy is browsing around her shop right now. Meet me there?"

I made the drive in less than ten minutes. Gabriel was already there, parked down the block in one of the pricey cars from Shya's garage, a white Mercedes.

He met me on the street, and together we approached Brogan's shop, shielding so our arrival wouldn't be sensed. Gabriel had asked her to keep Lizzy there if possible. Keep her occupied somehow. The little magic shop was quiet, the parking lot dark and empty. Brogan was alone in there with a vampire who'd proven to be a loose cannon. As we neared the door, I worried about what we might find inside.

"I'll go in the front," I said, reaching for the door handle. "You go in the back in case she runs when she sees me."

Without a word Gabriel slipped around to the back.

Plastering on what I hoped passed for a normal, friendly smile, I opened the shop door. A string of beads hung on the back of the door clattered together, announcing me. My gaze darted to the young, blonde woman perusing a shelf of colorful candles. She held a basket loaded with magical items.

Brogan stood behind the counter, pretending not to watch her like a hawk. She glanced up as I entered, "Hello. Welcome to Toil and Trouble. Can I help you find anything?"

Playing along, I pretended to think about it. "Just browsing, thanks." I raised a brow to Brogan, asking a silent question.

She shrugged.

Lizzy didn't turn to see who'd entered. She couldn't feel my vampiric energy while I shielded, but I didn't feel human either so she'd figure it out soon.

In the small shop a few steps brought me close enough to scope out her basket. Gemstones, sage, a few other herbal items I didn't recognize. She added pink and black candles to her haul and moved on to the next tiny aisle housing statues of everything from Buddha to fairies to gargoyles.

She glanced over her shoulder at me, a painted-on brow arched in silent assessment. Instead of acting suspicious in any way, she moved on to a display case filled with ritual knives and daggers.

Then she did a double take. Yep. She knew I was here for her. That hadn't taken long.

Her body went rigid. This was the brief moment where she'd decide whether to run or fight. She dropped the basket and ran for the door in the back, marked for staff only. Straight into Gabriel who stood there with his arms crossed.

"Gabriel." She gaped at him, fumbling. "I was going to come see you. Have you been looking for me?" Had to give her credit for trying to turn this into a social call. Fear trickled from her. Regardless, she blinked big blue eyes at him, playing for innocence.

"You know I have. Why else would you hide your energy signature? You have to stop now, Lizzy. You can't keep killing people." Slowly he extended one hand, an offering.

We both waited, hoping she'd come peacefully. Well, that was just stupid of us.

She blinked a few more times, trying for that fluttering lash effect. It didn't work, because she was afraid and he wasn't falling for it. Her gaze darted to me. I waited, keeping my distance.

"But I did it for you, Gabe. So we could be together. The way we should be." She reached to caress his jaw, and he let her. "You know that's why you turned me. You didn't want to be alone anymore. Besides, you kill people too."

His face hardened into a mask of disgust. "I have a system. Rules. I don't run the streets."

My curiosity had been piqued. I didn't know much about Gabriel's personal rules. All I knew was that he came by The Wicked Kiss a few times a week. As far as killing, if he'd been doing any, he'd been keeping a low profile.

"Rules? Where's the fun in that?" Her hand trailed over his jaw to clutch his chin.

Her thrall slipped toward him. She went in for a kiss. It was brazen, trying to seduce the one who'd made her. Although I hadn't had a chance to feel her out, she didn't give off a vibe any stronger than Briggs. Like him, she was no lightweight, but she couldn't measure up to Gabriel or me. She had to know that.

At the slight glazing of Gabriel's eyes, I tensed. I should just tackle Lizzy. But no, this wasn't my problem. I was here as backup. If she tried any magic shit, I'd take her down.

Gabriel dodged her kiss. He shook off her attempt to enthrall him and caught hold of her arm. "Let's go, Lizzy."

"No, I came here for something, and I'm not leaving without it." She tried to pull free, but he held tight. "We're supposed to be together, Gabe, and you know it. When you disappeared the coven gave up on you, but I never did. I never stopped looking for you."

"It was just a fling, Lizzy. I'm sorry, but I don't feel the same way you do. It wasn't supposed to be like this." Gabriel genuinely seemed apologetic. His mouth was drawn and tight, his shoulders slumped.

He was learning a lesson in lovers and victims. A lesson we all had to learn at some point in some manner. Still, I felt bad for him. She'd been someone from his past who'd gotten mixed up in his present. He'd have some hard choices to make.

"You haven't even given us a chance," she pouted, her gaze frantically darting about his face. "I'll play by your stupid rules, ok? Don't tell me you regret this. You came to me, remember? You're responsible for all of this. You owe me a chance." Her plea lacked desperation or true emotion. She was playing him.

Guilt caused him to flinch. Dammit. Gabriel was a softy deep down. "Let's talk about this outside." He jerked hard on her arm, a mask of hard brutality where the guilt had just been.

Lizzy dug her heels in, refusing to budge. She flung a hand in my direction. "So you two can kill me? Why else would you bring her, Gabriel?"

"Because you need help. Killing you is not what I want. It's up to you whether that happens or not." Calm, smooth, the kid talked a good game. So subtle I barely detected it, he slipped her a relaxing pulse.

It wasn't enough. She made her choice with little hesitation, and she was damn fast about it. Shouting one word in Latin, which I did not understand, Lizzy flung black dust into Gabriel's face. It struck him full on. He froze, eyes widening in shock before they glassed over as he succumbed. If I had to guess, she'd just used a spell from his grimoire.

She pulled free of him and whirled to fling the same dust at me. Not close enough. It floated to the carpet, leaving me untouched. Two bounds and I was on her. Hands on her throat, I pinned her flailing body to the floor.

Lizzy was new, hungry, and strong. Not to mention a little crazed. Her eyes had the glossy stare of a rabid fangirl. This was more than a crush out of control. Infatuation fed by brand new hungers and sex-charged power had created a level of obsession beyond anything I'd witnessed in humans. Vampires were so easily obsessed with what they could not have. Case in point: Arys.

"You won't keep me from him," she grunted out. Raising hands blackened by sinister magic, she grabbed both sides of my head and hit me with it.

Absolute black smashed into my brain hard and fast. I screamed and instinctively tried to break free. Lizzy's magic was soul-suckingly dark. It poured through me like ebony lava, flowing and scorching everything in its path. The searing pain blinded, and I flung myself away from her.

In a blur Brogan rushed to help. A stream of Latin flew from her lips. Lizzy shrieked as a tight band of energy clamped around her, pinning her arms to her sides.

"I can't break this spell." Brogan waved a hand in front of Gabriel's face. He stared right through her, just standing there, unmoving.

"Of course not," Lizzy cackled. "It's Gabriel's spell. Only he can break it."

It was my turn to do one of those skyward stares, a plea for wisdom in the face of Arys's progeny's mistake. Why, oh why, did he have to keep a book packed with deadly black magic?

"You can break it." I was up in Lizzy's face, baring wolf fangs. "You're a dead woman if you keep this up. I can only afford so much patience for you. It's almost out."

Lizzy eyed me with a head shake of disdain. "You're heartless. Just like they say you are. Have you no compassion?"

Who the hell said I was heartless? I had half a mind to shake some names out of her but knew that would be playing into her hands. "Right now what I have is no time to deal with this shit. If you can't conduct yourself with discretion and control, I have no other option than to kill you." I made sure she saw the truth in my stare. I'd do it.

I left her bound, with Brogan standing watch. A close inspection of Gabriel revealed him to be subdued by something akin to hypnosis. He wasn't really frozen, just entranced. Held in place by a hypnotic force.

"Gabriel?" When he didn't react to his name, I laid a hand on his arm. No reaction. He continued to stare off at nothing.

Closing my eyes, I focused on the energy surrounding him. A master of energy manipulation, that's what Willow had just called me. If I could isolate the spell's energy, maybe I could break it.

The spell's murky essence coated Gabriel. Beneath it I could feel his strong vibes thrumming hard, fighting to break free. So he was fully aware, despite being struck silent and immobile. Creepy spell. Although perhaps having his own spells used against him would teach him a lesson he'd never have learned any other way.

Feeling out the metaphysical form of the spell left a bad taste in my mouth. Fibers of darkness woven together formed a strong binding around him. Each layer on its own, however, was relatively fragile. Once I focused in on each individual fragment of the spell, I was able to easily pick it apart.

A little push of power charged with both vampire and wolf, dark twisted into light, and the magic began to unravel. It retreated beneath my touch, chased away like a shadow fleeing the sun.

The final threads of magic fell away, releasing him. I saw him come back to himself, the hypnotic haze falling away. There was no doubt in my mind that he was fully aware when he kissed me.

I couldn't help that it got a little erotically charged. And I definitely couldn't help Gabriel's own desires.

Stepping in close to bring our bodies together, Gabriel captured my face in his hands and consumed my lips in a desire-drenched kiss that shook me. What the hell was he trying to prove? It almost pulled me under, but Lizzy's shriek broke us apart.

She busted free of Brogan's binding spell and went straight for her. Grabbing Brogan around the throat, Lizzy dragged her close, using her like a human shield. "Fuck you, Gabriel. Fuck you right to hell and back." Lizzy flung an erratic shot of power that shattered an entire display of glassware. It came down with a crash that left my ears ringing.

Brogan's eyes went huge with terror. She didn't struggle, managing to stay calm despite Lizzy's stranglehold.

"You used me," Lizzy accused Gabriel as she dragged Brogan with her toward the front door, pausing to fetch the basket of items she'd dropped. "I never meant anything to you, did I? You wanted an easy lay, a quick snack. But I'm just an inconvenience to you now. A loose end to tie up. Well fuck that. You won't get away with treating me like this, like I'm disposable."

As she drew closer to the door, Gabriel took a step forward, like he might rush her. "This is between you and me, Lizzy. Let her go. We can go somewhere and discuss this rationally."

"Oh, no, we can't." She chortled, but her eyes filled with blood tears. "You're just like the rest of them. Take one more step and I snap her neck." Lizzy's grip on Brogan's throat tightened.

I caught Gabriel's elbow, keeping him in place. We couldn't risk Brogan's life.

Using the frightened witch as her hostage, Lizzy shoved the glass shop door open. The beads jangled ominously. "This isn't over, Gabe." She disappeared outside, taking Brogan with her.

I counted to three and went after her. We found Brogan at the edge of the parking lot, on her knees, coughing and rubbing her throat. Lizzy had dissolved into the night. Gabriel went after her anyway, in the direction Brogan pointed. I stayed with her, reluctant to leave even after getting her back inside.

"I'm fine, Alexa. Go after her. I'll set up some extra protection wards." Brogan's pale face and speeding heartrate didn't convince me that she was fine.

"Do you know what she took with her? In the basket."

Squinting in thought, Brogan nodded, her blonde ponytail swinging. "Love spell stuff. Most of it pretty standard. Harmless in the hands of the average witch or lovelorn amateur."

"But in the hands of a black magic witch with vampire power?" I asked with a grimace. "She has Gabriel's grimoire too."

Brogan smoothed a hand over her hair and sighed. "Then I'd say she's planning on twisting something big enough to bend his will. Which is against everything most of us believe in."

Several minutes later Gabriel returned seething but disappointed. "No luck. Her energy signature is still hidden."

"We'll keep looking," I said, frowning as a strange sensation came over me.

For a split second I was in Arys's head, struck by the weight of the torment that consumed him. The constant battle that tore him apart. Then I was back in my own head, disoriented. I had to blink a few times to get my bearings. That had been happening a lot lately.

"I'm calling it a night." Brogan set about shutting the shop. She turned off the computer on the counter and some of the lights. "It's been a while since there's been any supernatural action in here. I don't love it."

"I don't blame you."

After helping clean up the slivers of glassware, we walked Brogan out to her car where I asked if she was ok one last time. After she drove away, Gabriel and I stood in the tiny parking lot. Not knowing where Lizzy would head, I'd have to put out an alert to Smudge so her watchdogs could keep their eyes peeled.

"Where should we start?" I glanced over at Gabriel who stood silently fuming several feet away. He was blaming himself. I got it. There was a lot of that going around.

Gabriel's hair hung long and loose over his shoulders. Part of it fell to hide his face as he stared at an oil smear on the ground. "Right here. With you claiming me."

It didn't take me by surprise this time, hearing him say it. It intrigued me, his request, making me look at him differently. "Why now?"

"So that she can't. She's going to use the dark love spell from my book on me." Turning to face me, Gabriel raked a hand through his hair, shoving it back. Forcing me to see the strong lines of his jaw, the angled planes of his nose.

I tore my gaze away before I could ogle him further. Arys's torment echoed in my mind. His need was my need. What I needed most was him, my other half. A tug inside me encouraged me to go to him, to find him and throw myself fully into him. Come what may.

That was the easy way out. Unable to let myself give in to that urge, I let my focus be swayed by Gabriel's request. I wanted to take what he offered. Hands clenched tight, I paced away from him, hoping distance would help. We should be hunting Lizzy, not having this conversation again.

Frustration rode me hard. In a burst of temper, I shouted at the vampire watching me from the other side of the tiny lot. "There's no point asking why you have such dangerous spells, but I'm telling you right now, if I get my hands on your grimoire, I'm burning the motherfucking thing."

"Whatever you want." A listless shrug. He didn't seem to care much about the book.

"How will claiming you keep a love spell from working on you?" Suspicion tinged my tone. What was Gabriel willing to say and do to get what he wanted?

Hands shoved into the pockets of his long jacket, he held my gaze, letting me search him for truth. "If I'm tied to you, constantly yearning for you, the part of me the spell seeks to control will already be under your influence."

How could he stand there so nonchalant and seem so sure? He was asking me to mind fuck him in the worst of ways. "I still don't think you realize what you're asking for."

"Alexa, the last thing I want is for you to feel forced into anything. But I've seen how this world works. I've seen shit I can't even give words to. I know what I'm asking. But I respect your right to refuse." He let that hang between us before adding, "We should go. Lizzy could be anywhere."

Gabriel had come close to being like the others. The night he'd first risen as a vampire I'd taunted him with my blood in an attempt to bind him to me. It had been an effort to overthrow Shya. It hadn't worked.

Now he all but begged me to do it. This was an opportunity to expand those directly linked to me. To empower us all with our growing strength and power. We might need it one day.

And did I not want to?

Arys's darkness danced through me, singing and chanting, encouraging and tempting. *Take him*, it said. *Taste him. Feel him. Claim him.*

"I'll do it." Those three words rang in the emptiness around us.

Gabriel turned to me, surprised.

With a finger, I beckoned him closer. "Just remember, there's no going back."

CHAPTER ELEVEN

ARYS

One of these idiots had put country music on the jukebox. I had half a mind to stick my pool cue up his ass. I was in a mood tonight. Some human jackass snivelling lyrics about his hard life and the girl who'd done him wrong just pissed me off.

Since Shaz had dragged me out of The Wicked Kiss, I'd been nothing but a snarling, surly asshole. Despite my attitude, he'd brought me to Doghead and shoved a pool cue in my hand. He was trying to distract me. It wasn't working.

Across the pool table Owen bent low, lining up his shot. He and Izzy were playing Shaz and me. A few guys were tossing darts across the room. Others drank and smoked, loud and raucous.

Annoying as fuck.

How the hell Shaz could put up with this crap each night?

The pack wasn't as small as it looked, based on the twenty or so wolves in the bar. Everyone else was home living the normal life, tucked into bed in their two-story houses complete with the picket fence. Useless, in my opinion. Every one of them. Playing human while a wolf lurked beneath their skin. Denying their true nature and leaving the rest of the pack to fend for themselves when the FPA came knocking.

Shaz was a better man than me. No question about it. He looked around at these sad, drunken animals and saw potential. I saw a buffet.

"Shit," Owen swore, swigging from a beer bottle. "Scratched the eight ball. Izzy, you rack."

Izzy gathered the balls and began to organize them. I watched her move them around, the colors tumbling over one another in her hands. Such lovely hands she had. Those wrists. Slender and elegant. I couldn't see the pulse in her wrist from where I stood, but if I concentrated I could pick out her heartbeat.

From her wrists my gaze traveled up her bare arms to the thin strap of her tank top. Her collarbone beckoned to be bitten. So perfectly defined, leading my gaze right to her delicate throat.

Feeling my gaze, Izzy looked up, right into my eyes, and silently snarled. A challenge.

"Try not to so obviously ogle my pack, would you?" An elbow in my ribs forced a small grunt from me. A beer in one hand, a pool cue in the other, Shaz cast an analytical glance over me.

I ogled him instead. From the bulge of his bicep beneath the sleeve of his t-shirt to the cupid's bow of his full lips. Lingering on my half-healed bite from the previous night, I drank him in. "Better?"

He eyed me warily, as he should. Using his cue, he pointed to the table. "Break."

Playing pool was a terrible way to pass time. Because time had become the enemy. I didn't want to pass it. I wanted to hunt it. Catch it. Crush it with my bare hands. Make it my bitch. But we all knew time was nobody's bitch.

I went through the motions. Line up the shot, sink a few balls. Wait my turn. Rinse and repeat. Inside an unholy itch tortured me. I'd tasted wolf blood again tonight. Still it hadn't been hers. The want had been awakened, though it rarely slumbered these days.

That taste of Ebyn had been entirely for Alexa's benefit. I needed to feel her fire. The heat of her anger grabbed me by the balls, and I fucking loved it. So I'd gone after her boy toy. It had worked. I got what I wanted when she stormed inside and found us.

So why didn't I feel satisfied with that? Because of that goddamn flicker. The piece of her that lived in me. The spark that never went out.

It wasn't me that wanted to hurt Alexa, emotionally or physically. The real essence of who I was as a person and a man, it didn't want anything but good things for her. To see a smile on her face when she looked at me instead of rage and hate. To have her snuggle in against me rather than throw a fist in my face.

Why did I continue to torment us both like this? Why couldn't I make it stop?

Because it was me. It was what I'd become. It was all I knew how to be.

That's a lie, the voice of the light whispered. *You are so much more.*

Sometimes I wished I could slam a fist into my chest and tear out the piece of me that was her. Listening to the voice while my darkest obsession ate at me pushed me from irate to downright frenzied. Alexa penetrated all of me. Every fiber of my being. The only way to tear her out of me was to destroy both of us.

Yeah, I'd been tempted a time or twelve. Who's counting? I wanted to believe I could never really do it. But I knew I could. If things got bad enough, if she ever gave up on us, I would do it. To free us both.

"Dude, I've gotta say that I am not liking the look in your eyes." Keeping his voice down despite keen wolf ears within range, Shaz held himself relaxed but ready. In case I snapped.

Humoring him, I shook my head and tried to appear anything but ravenous. "What look might that be, pup?"

"Like you're thinking about slaughtering every last wolf in here, me included. Should we leave?" Shaz wasn't taking any chances with Alexa or me anymore. At the first sign that we were slipping, he acted.

That kind of romance-novel hero crap was one of the things I enjoyed about him. Alexa deserved some Knight-in-Shining-Armor action from time to time.

Because mine was black as fuck.

But in our world the white knight didn't always win. Heroics were risky. Shaz gambled his life every night he was with us.

Raised voices drew our attention to two guys shoving each other by the jukebox. Guess I wasn't the only one who hated country music. I got the feeling these wolves couldn't get through a night without a ruckus. Throwing punches became just a way to entertain themselves.

"Yeah, I probably should go. You stay here though." I propped my cue against the back of a chair.

Shaz let his pool cue clatter to the floor in his haste to keep up with me as I headed for the door. "Arys, you know I'm not letting you leave here without me. Don't make this difficult. It doesn't have to be."

"Suit yourself then. But whatever you do, don't bleed."

The universe is a cruel mistress. It's like the powers that be were constantly finding new ways to tell me to go fuck myself.

No sooner had I spoken than the first moron sucker punched the second, breaking his nose. The blood poured. The spill of violence hung heavy on the air.

I lost it.

Shaz saw the blood, smelled it, and he knew. He grabbed me as I launched myself in the wolves' direction. Both hands on my shoulders, he shoved me back. Hard, violent almost, Shaz herded me toward the exit.

"Outside, Arys. Don't fight me on this. I'll knock you the fuck out." Shaz's eyes were drowning wolf. He was ready to defend himself and his wolves. He shouted a command for Owen to split up the fight before throwing me out of his bar on my ass.

We were alone in the parking lot. I didn't trust myself. I couldn't anymore and neither could he. "Then knock me the fuck out. Do it."

"What? Are you serious?" He pushed me again, driving me further away from the front of the club.

"Dead serious." I stood there, letting him shove me, inviting the punch that never came. "Do it, Shaz. You can't trust me right now. I'm slipping."

Shaz grabbed hold of my shirt and tried to steady me. He held on when I tried to pull away. The musky wolf scent of him was too much.

"No, you're not. Hold your shit together. You can't fall apart on me now." He searched my eyes, finding something that made his pulse pick up speed. "Let's get out of the city. Away from all this temptation."

"You, pup," I ground out between clenched teeth, "are temptation."

"I can't let you go off alone. You'll go right to her." He wasn't wrong. He let me pull free of him, but he didn't let me get far.

In my head the light and dark battled for control. They talked about me, like I wasn't even there. Each staking their claim on what was left of my mind. Then they spoke to me.

Taste him, the dark invited. *You know he wants it.*

Touch him, the light suggested. *You know you need it.*

"Better let me have it." A sharp pain in my stomach almost doubled me over. The price I paid for feeding my obsessions. They simply grew. "I'm in rough shape tonight, pup. I'm gonna come at you, and it's not going to be pleasurable for either of us when it's over."

I focused hard on Shaz to keep seeing him as anything other than dead. That near-white shock of hair that I loved to slide my fingers through. The strong hands I'd watched caress the body of the woman we both loved. The sensual mouth I'd come to long for. All of it was Shaz. Just a few of the many things I'd come to know and love about him. But it didn't matter. Not when I slipped into the kill zone.

"Being apart is breaking you both down faster." Shaz sighed and fisted his hair. "Being together makes you want to kill each other. This is the world's biggest fuck you of a catch twenty-two."

"It's not your job to save us, Shaz." It pained me to watch him suffer. Alexa and I, we were victims of chance. Shaz, however, he chose to suffer with us.

The white wolf had his own demons. Being unable to save Alexa was one of them. It didn't stop him from trying with his whole heart though. He would do anything. Die for her without so much as a second thought.

Playing the anchor for us had taken a toll on Shaz. It was there in the hunch of his shoulders. The way he pressed a hand to his eyes and muttered beneath his breath.

In a fit of temper he threw a punch at a private property sign in the middle of the parking lot. The metal bent beneath the impact, splitting. A jagged piece sliced his knuckles.

That's all it took. One gash on the back of his hand. One fat drop of blood splashing the asphalt.

The kill zone engulfed me. I was just there. Aware of nothing but the bleeding wolf, I attacked.

CHAPTER TWELVE

SHAZ

"It's not your job to save us, Shaz."

I'm not sure why it set me off so bad when Arys said that. Maybe because I knew that he was right. I couldn't save Alexa back when Raoul emotionally tormented her. And no matter how many times I kept her and Arys from killing each other, I couldn't fix what was broken between them.

So I lost my shit and punched the sign. Stupid mistake. The second I felt my skin split and saw the blood well, I knew Arys didn't stand a chance. He was already too close to the edge.

I watched it swallow him. The same darkness I'd watched take Alexa too. It came over him fast. A blink and a monster lurked behind his eyes. It was always there, in mischievous glints and sly smiles. But Arys was there too, keeping it in check.

Not anymore.

He rushed me with fangs bared and murderous intent. Having little time to react, I surged forward to meet him. Catching his middle with my shoulder, I flipped him up and over my back. He hit the ground hard, kicking up a cloud of gravel dust.

Both fists up, I backed away slowly, giving him space. Giving myself space. I really was going to have to knock this idiot out.

"Come on now, Arys. You're stronger than this." Staring into his feral eyes, I felt the need to speak. To try to bring some semblance of humanity back to him.

With precise, careful steps, Arys glided toward me. Like a snake in the grass. Creeping toward its prey. Screw that. I wasn't prey.

"Stronger than death? Lust? The need to simply be what I am? Sorry, handsome. I wish I were." He ran his tongue over the tip of a fang, capturing my attention far too easily with that simple motion.

The detachment in his voice left me with a sense of dread. Like he was giving in. Not fighting at all anymore. "You don't want to do this. I know you don't. But if you want to force me to knock your ass out, then I will." Reasoning with him wasn't going to work. He wasn't in a rational place.

It had been a while since the two of us had really gone at it. Despite the transition in our strange relationship, I was still more than happy to kick his ass. The grin that lit up his face got my adrenaline pumping. So this was happening. Well, better here with me than elsewhere with Alexa.

I didn't wait for him to make the first move. Arys was too unpredictable like this. Rather than letting him get the drop on me with that smoldering stare, I slammed my fist into his face.

It wasn't the first punch he'd taken tonight. Wouldn't be the last either. Arys's snicker didn't do a lot for my confidence, but I'd be damned if I'd show it. I hit him again, my gut sinking when he didn't so much as block. Arys took every hit, as he'd done with Alexa. With that devious grin plastered on his face. It was probably the most crazed I'd ever seen him, and that was really saying something.

Tiring myself out so I was an easier target didn't jive with me so I eased off, forcing him to come to me. This was just a game to Arys. One that he had no intention of losing. This goddamn vampire was going to be the death of me.

Tapping his chin, he invited another hit. "Don't stop now. We're just getting started."

I dropped my hands, leaving myself defenseless. "You know what? Fuck it. I'm not doing this with you. It's what you want. This isn't a game, Arys. I'm not fighting you. Because I don't think you'll really kill me."

His brow furrowed. A storm brewed within his eyes. "Don't be a fool."

It dawned on me. In the way confusion shook him, rattling his confidence. By succumbing to his darkness, Arys relied on me to keep him from doing something he'd regret. He didn't believe he could fight the dark, because he believed he was the dark.

Time for a change. The only way he'd get through this was by embracing the truth. That he was more than death. "Stop running from yourself, Arys. Stop believing this is all that you are." Hands at my sides, I fought the wolf's defensive instinct to shift. That wouldn't achieve anything good.

The storm surged, a downpour that possessed the vampire quaking before me. Hands clenched tight, like he struggled to hold himself back, he begged me with a look. And then a word: "Don't."

It was all he could manage. But I was done fighting with him and watching him fight himself. There wasn't a lot I could do for him, but I could do this. I could surrender.

"You won't kill me," I repeated, holding my ground. Remaining vulnerable.

Those magic words set Arys off like a bullet. I never saw him move. The world spun, and the breath was crushed from my lungs as he slammed me against a pickup truck. "What makes you so fucking sure?" he snarled, face inches from mine. Nothing about this was sensual. Violence shook him, his hands trembled as he fisted my shirt.

Knowing the risk, I stared into the face of a cold-blooded killer and said, "You would have done it already."

Grabbing me by the throat, Arys slammed my head against the truck. "That's a pretty risky game you're playing. Do you know what I am, Shaz? What I'm capable of." Arys's gaze slid down my body, dragging with it a scorching heat. He squeezed hard enough to threaten both my air and blood flow.

Blacking out was not an option.

Seeing as I was seconds away from losing consciousness, I probably shouldn't have been rocking a raging hard on. There were much worse ways to die, no doubt about that. Still, I didn't believe he had it in him.

"Of course," I gasped out, struggling for breath. "But do you know what you are?"

He eased off so I could breathe but didn't let go. Anguish racked him when he all but shouted the words in my face. "I have been death and darkness for three hundred years. Until her. She made me this way. She made me feel again. And now all I want to do is die."

Pain so bright it blinded flashed across his face. Arys Knight, all around badass and vampire extraordinaire, had a weakness after all. He'd lived a long life of mayhem and murder with zero remorse. Until Alexa.

She made him remember what it was to feel. To love. To exist for more than the kill. And it was breaking him down.

I couldn't pretend to understand his agony. I saw it though, and right then, that was enough.

He buried his face in my throat. Fangs pressed to my artery. He'd kill me if he did it. This was no playful bite. It would be death.

Alexa would destroy him if he killed me. We both knew that. Was this crazy bastard that far gone? I couldn't let myself believe it.

Dread prickled the back of my neck. Not fear though. I had chosen long ago never to fear Arys. Even with his fangs hovering over my carotid. "I trust you," I whispered, my body rigid between Arys and the truck. I looked forward to the night when it would be him trapped by me.

Now those were the magic words. I wasn't prepared for the reaction they brought forth. Arys jerked his head back, grazing my skin with his fangs as he did. The storm relinquished its hold and he collapsed at my feet. His entire body shook. Hunched in on himself, Arys rocked on his knees, staring at his hands like he wasn't sure who they belonged to. Seeing three centuries worth of blood.

For the first time in a long time, I didn't know how to handle him. This broken version of him sitting at my feet, shoulders shaking silently while blood tears spattered the ground.

Arys had been strong for too long. Staying in darkness so as not to feel. Now it overwhelmed him to the breaking point. I guess maybe that wasn't strength but fear. Fear could drive the strongest people mad.

I sank to the ground beside him, rubbing the raw skin of my bruised neck. He didn't look at me, just stared at his hands in silence. So I sat with him, knees drawn up, hands clasped. Staring at the night sky, trying to pick out the few stars I could.

After some time passed, Arys reached over and took hold of my cut hand. Sliding his fingers through mine, he brought it to his mouth and kissed my bleeding knuckles. The wet touch of his tongue followed. He clutched my hand tight. Desperate. His ragged sigh cut to the bone. It was the sound of defeat.

We sat there saying nothing while the night crawled by. Hands clasped. The only parts of us that touched despite how close we sat. My gaze dropped to our joined hands.

Arys didn't touch me the way he touched Alexa. Like she was desired, delicate, and something to be adored. Worshipped even. He touched me like I was a lifeline in a hurricane. Like I was strength. Not just wanted but needed.

A flicker in my chest shook me. A twinge of something I wasn't sure I was ready to feel.

CHAPTER THIRTEEN

A swell of agony ripped apart my insides. Sudden and sharp, then gone as fast as it had come.

It was Arys. Wherever he was, he was suffering. Like I was suffering. But worse. Breaking down faster. His torment echoed within me. I wanted to go to him, but it could be suicide.

I watched Gabriel approach with eager expectation. The emotional upheaval going on inside me didn't hinder what I was about to do. It encouraged it.

Holding my power in check, I gave Gabriel one last chance to decide this was stupid of him. But whatever it was that he knew, the things he'd seen that I hadn't, it was stronger than any worries he might harbor.

He stood before me, his aura swelling with a sudden rise of anticipation. "I'm not changing my mind. Why are you so hesitant? Is it because nobody else has been willing?"

Holy shit, the kid nailed it. Had he always been so insightful? Yes, of course. Because he could see things about everybody. I'd lost count of how many potential visions of me he'd had.

"Yeah," I admitted with a rueful smile, "I think it is."

It changed the entire dynamic. Willow had been willing too but that had been different. He wouldn't have lasted long as human. For him it had been a small price to pay.

I held up a finger, needing to lay down these rules for myself as much as Gabriel. "Let's get a few things straight first: Tonight it's blood only. My lovers are as inner circle as it gets. I prefer to keep that circle small. That's not to say I'm not interested in adding you to it. Just gotta make those decisions carefully."

Yeah, because my lovers became addicted to me, if one was to believe Falon. Not to mention that Gabriel had yet to give me what I needed, to show me I could trust him. Only then would he get what he wanted from me.

"Fair enough. Can I say something as well?" Gabriel waited for my nod. "I'd be lying if I said I didn't want to sleep with you. But I have no interest in anything more than blood and sex. Just to be perfectly clear."

More than fine with me. The pieces of my heart had all been given away. One of them died with Kale. The others, they belonged to Arys and Shaz. I had nothing left to spare another man. Body, blood, and power though… well that was different.

Gabriel had watched me kill Kale. I suspected that might have motivated some of this discussion. It was good to lay our expectations on the line. No sense doing this with anything but complete openness.

"Good. Then we're on the same page. Come on." Perhaps the best time to make such a decision wasn't while afflicted by such tumultuous feelings. I couldn't be where I wanted to be, with the man I craved most and our white wolf. And I could sure use the distraction.

I led him back to where he'd parked Shya's white Mercedes. Hopping onto the trunk, I loosed a subtle pulse of my thrall. "Just a warning. I'm going to roll you hard."

Gabriel's gaze fell to my lips. "I should hope so." He kept his distance, waiting for me to take command.

Which I did. One leg crossed over the other, I eyed him with growing predatory intrigue, my foot bouncing. I let the thrall trickle from me like a slow leak that steadily grew toward a flash flood.

I watched it take him. Gradually his eyes glazed until he saw only me. Nothing else in the world existed to him right then. His desire rose with a sudden ferocity that I found pleasantly surprising. It teased my hungers.

Blood only. That's what I'd said. I had to stick to my own rule.

Relinquishing the last of my hold on the allure, I let it run rampant through him. The night air grew hot with the spicy aroma of Gabriel's lust. I wanted to eat him up.

Completely under my spell, he no longer held himself back. He came at me, and I didn't stop him from kissing me hard, a bruising crush of our lips that nicked my lip on a fang. His or mine, I couldn't be sure. He sucked my lip into his mouth, tasting the tiny drop of blood.

Being an incubus, Gabriel naturally grabbed hold of the power I drenched him in and feasted on it, rolling it around in his mind. He pushed back at me with his own seductive vibe.

My hands found their way into his inky black hair. It was softer than I'd expected. Sensing the rush of heat and moisture between my legs, Gabriel nudged my thighs apart so he could stand between them.

The bulge in his jeans was bigger than I'd expected, not that I'd been expecting this at all. Again I had to remind myself that this was blood only. Rules. For some reason I couldn't comprehend them just then.

Gabriel held the back of my head in a passionate grasp as he kissed a hot path down my jaw to my throat. His aura vibrated with his yearning for me, a near audible shriek in my head.

Letting him press me against the car's back window, I enjoyed the weight of him atop me. It was new and strange. Exciting. I wrapped my legs around his waist, grinding myself against his straining erection. Gabriel groaned, palming a handful of my ass, pressing us tighter together.

The frequency of power spiralling around us caused a high-pitched keening in my ears. He was under my thrall entirely, eager for my blood and body. Against my skin he murmured, "You smell like sex and death and sunlight."

Even caught up as I was in the temptation of him, it still struck me as an odd thing to say. Although I had heard some pretty strange things from victims under the thrall. It took their mind somewhere else, opened it up to other things.

Sex and death, I'd heard that before. Sunlight? Odd word choice. Gabriel was different though. He saw things. Did he see something now?

I couldn't ask. Claiming him meant keeping him enrapt. Bleeding for him.

His fangs scraped over my flesh, and I shuddered. A steady throb between my legs urged me to rebel against my own rule and enjoy a little anarchy all over Shya's Mercedes. The only thing that kept me from doing so was needing Gabriel to prove himself first. He was dangerous. That had to be more important than my power-driven sexual desires.

Gabriel didn't drag it out. He wanted to see this through for his own reasons. The sharp sting of his fangs came sudden but smooth. His experienced bite pierced my jugular, spilling my hybrid blood into Gabriel's mouth. More pleasure than pain, the kid knew what he was doing.

Sucking at the wound, he drew on my blood and power, drinking me in. Becoming mine. Strategically speaking, this could be a good thing for me. I could already tap Gabriel's power through Arys, but this would strengthen my link to him. Should Gabriel ever prove more dangerous than he already had, God forbid, I'd have some leverage over him.

I bit my lip hard, tasting my own blood, trying to keep myself grounded. I wanted him inside me. Everything dark within me demanded it.

His tongue swirled over the bite. Arousal burned between my legs, and I moaned when he rubbed against me. Sex and power could not make my decisions. If I was going to hold my own as queen of this city, I had to be able to separate power and pleasure from logical decision making. Which wasn't nearly as easy as I wished it was.

When Gabriel's mouth found the swell of my cleavage, I knew if I didn't stop him, I never would. "Gabriel," I whispered, summoning my willpower.

"No sex. Got it. Hell, I won't even touch you with my hands." His words were lost in my breasts as he tugged my shirt up to bare my middle, which his lips quickly found. Pausing, he gazed at me with a drowning, devilish incubus stare. "Let me serve you."

Confident and smooth, Gabriel slid my pants and underwear down, and I let him. He propped my legs on his shoulders, and my breath caught. Head thrown back against the car's window, I closed my eyes and tensed in expectation of what was coming.

A nip at my inner thigh. Warm breath teased my core. The tip of his tongue followed, the slightest touch. From bottom to top he licked me, a feather light sensation meant to make me needy for more.

It worked.

Every lick teased. Each flick of his tongue a taunt. It wasn't like an incubus to leave such an encounter without making their partner climax. Multiple times in most cases. I found Gabriel's need to please neither surprising nor unwelcome.

When he began to lick me with greater intensity, my claws left deep gouges in the car's paintjob. My shaky moan made him grip my ass tighter, holding me in place. I had to bite my lip to keep from demanding that he screw me right there on the side of the road.

Goosebumps broke out on my skin. An overflow of sensual energy had me soaring. Gabriel might not have had decades of experience pleasuring a woman like some vampires, but he was doing damn fine so far. His touch was delicate but intense, explorative and eager. My body quivered for him.

He brought me fast, never touching me with anything but his tongue. Just as he'd said. Pressing his mouth against me, Gabriel rode out every wave before gently easing my legs from his shoulders.

"Son of a bitch," I sighed to the watching night sky. Tugging my clothing back into place, I sat up, head spinning slightly as the high of claiming him rode me.

Gabriel held out a hand to help me off the trunk. He held it a moment longer. Flashing me a fangy grin, he said, "I really hope you can stop calling me kid now."

"Not gonna make any promises, but I'll see what I can do." I gave him a playful shove and smoothed my hair down. Maybe it would feel weird later, maybe it wouldn't. Right then I was too high to give a damn.

I fished for my phone in my dropped bag. "Guess all we can do is wait for Jez to update us if they get anything and wait for Lizzy to make her next move. No point wandering the streets aimlessly if we can't track her." No recent updates from my watchdogs. "I'm going to head back to the Kiss. Come with? I could use you."

It wasn't what it sounded like. The more vampire power Arys and I had to keep us apart, the better. If Gabriel wanted to prove himself, he could start now.

Gabriel nodded, brows knit together in contemplation. Before I could get away, he said, "Alexa, wait a sec. I have to say this. When I took your blood, I saw something. Just now. A vision."

Of course he did. I'd given him shit before, warned him not to tell me what he saw. I couldn't handle the pressure. Something about the expression he wore said I didn't have that luxury now.

"What did you see?" I asked, swallowing hard. Wary.

He glanced up and down the empty side street, like he thought that perhaps we were not alone. My skin crawled when, in a hushed tone, he said, "You can't trust Salem."

CHAPTER FOURTEEN

I took my sweet time getting back to The Wicked Kiss. Like I was out for a leisurely drive, I steered the Charger through the city streets, lost in thought.

Gabriel had put me in a tough position. Warning me not to trust Salem meant that my only alternative was to trust that he spoke the truth. Under Shya's influence he'd done some shady shit. But I knew Shya had threatened his mother's life, using anything he could to bend Gabriel's will. He'd apologized and all but begged Arys and I to give him a chance. To spare him. So far he'd proven trustworthy despite Hurst's warning about him, despite this whole Lizzy situation.

Sure Salem was an angel. That should make him a good candidate for trustworthiness, but it didn't. Linked to Lilah, he was tainted with darkness. I'd learned not to forget that every demon was once an angel. The temptation was always there. For all of us. All the time.

With a frustrated curse I turned the radio off. I couldn't hear myself think. Probably because there were already so many voices in my head.

The white Mercedes sat in the parking lot when I arrived. Beside it, the blacked-out SUVs driven by Briggs and Juliet screamed federal agent. Those morons. I was curious as to how their little chat was going.

I got out of the car and had to pause to take in the audible buzz that surrounded the building, emanating from within. It reverberated through me, into my bones. The nightclub was a blazing beacon of power to anyone with the ability to see, hear, or feel it. The humans standing out front smoking and talking remained oblivious.

Four vampires from our bloodline lurked inside. I felt each of them, knowing their personal energy signatures. I imagined how I could pick them apart from here was how Falon could feel me as well when seeking me out. On a much grander scale of course, due to that whole truly immortal thing he had going for him.

As I stepped through the front entry I wondered how the presence of so many of us would affect those inside. A few seconds later, I had my answer. A sex-charged vibe laced the atmosphere. Like an airborne aphrodisiac the entire place had been seduced. People were dancing closer, grinding harder. Any vampires not of our bloodline were just as caught up in the charge.

Two of my vampires were tapping power at this very moment, feeding the current. Jenner and Briggs. I felt them. The skin on my arms prickled all the way to the back of my neck. Shielding tight beat back the onslaught of energy, but I couldn't block it completely. I was too tightly joined to these vampires.

The worst part was that I wanted to feel it. To let it all roll over me and catch me in its hold.

But I had to make sure an orgy didn't break out on the dance floor. And more importantly, figure out why the hell Briggs was rolling my sister. What else could he be doing?

A sharp stab in the gut doubled me over, followed by one in my head. Momentarily blinded, I reached out for the back of the nearest chair. Failing to stay on my feet, I hit the floor on my knees. A hand on my head, I bit back a screech.

Arys's anguish tore through me like a knife. Cutting through my deepest parts. My heart and soul. He was suffering. So I was suffering. The weight of his absence hit me suddenly, like a rock crushing my lungs.

The link between us opened without either of us reaching out. We were just there, inside each other's heads. I saw Arys's hand clutching Shaz's, their fingers entwined. Holding desperately to one another.

"Alexa?" Gabriel's voice next to my ear pulled me back into my own head. His arms went around me, and he lifted me to my feet. "Are you ok? What just happened?"

My yearning for Arys hit hard and cut deep. I missed him. Every second it hurt more. It would continue to grow until it drove us together and we killed each other. How much more of this could we take?

"It's Arys," I said, my voice shaky. "Things are bad, Gabriel. I don't think we have much time."

He nodded, his expression pinched. "I'm sorry. I'll do anything I can to help."

Aware of the erotic heat creeping among us, Gabriel released me when I proved to be steady. Good idea. Even though everyone acted as if they'd done copious amounts of ecstasy, for the most part everything continued as it should.

Giving him the benefit of the doubt, I said, "I know you will. Keep an eye on things out here, will you? I'll be back in five."

I slipped through the crowd to the back in search of my sister. If Briggs was defiling her, I'd decapitate him.

The back hall was rife with the essence of blood and sex. Not unusual. Ambling along at a casual pace I headed toward the room near my office. The one Briggs usually occupied despite it no longer being his prison. I think he just liked to be near my office. I wouldn't doubt that he'd snooped around in there. Not that I was dumb enough to leave him anything to find.

Before I reached his room, the door swung open. I froze, then forced myself to continue on as if heading to my office. Sure I was. They couldn't prove otherwise.

Juliet stepped out first. She stared back into the room, a smile on her face. A dopey smile. Son of a bitch. Right away my gaze found the small bite on her wrist. I was going to kill that motherfucker.

Briggs appeared behind her, pulling her in for a kiss. I tried not to see it. She was my little sister, and he was a man I loathed beyond all reason. She might love him, but I didn't have to love that.

He felt me, because he couldn't not feel me no matter how bad he wanted to. So for my benefit he turned up the heat on their kiss. A hand on Juliet's ass tugged her against his groin while he plundered her mouth with his tongue.

Gag me.

They broke apart as I reached his doorway. Juliet blushed and pulled away from Briggs, embarrassed at having been caught despite doing it in my club. She turned her bitten wrist inward, out of view, like that would keep me from knowing. I wanted to slap her and ask if she was new.

A swell of darkness rippled through me, grabbing hold of my ire and running like hell with it. I didn't even consider fighting it.

I grabbed Briggs by the throat and slammed him against the open door, knocking Juliet aside in the process. With wolf fangs bared, I snarled into his face. "You've got a lot of fucking nerve."

"Alexa, what the hell? Stop it." Juliet grabbed my arm.

Mistake. She realized it too late. A snap of the fingers of my free hand and I'd pasted her against the hallway wall across from Briggs's room.

Briggs sneered, but despite his fearless front, he couldn't hide the way his constant craving for me slammed him like a Mack truck. His gaze fell to Gabriel's bite on the side of my neck. It was just one of three bites I wore, from three different men. The scent must have been driving him nuts.

"We're consenting adults, O'Brien. Mind your own fucking business. I didn't hurt her. I would never hurt her. Screw you for thinking otherwise." He tapped his power but didn't use it. Couldn't really. Not without me kicking his ass all over the place.

"Alexa, please," Juliet pleaded, fear in her voice. Fear for Briggs and what I might do to him. "I was willing. I swear."

Keeping Briggs pinned in place, I glanced at Juliet. "Why? Tell me why the hell you want to be a bite junkie."

She strained against the force pasting her to the wall. Rage shook her pretty features into something close to ugly. "You think I want to be a bite junkie? Your goddamn vampire did this to me."

Fuck. The worst part was that she was right. Unable to keep my face from falling, I looked away, down the hall at my closed office door. Arys and me, we fucking sucked at not hurting everyone around us.

Beside me, straining against my hand on his throat, Briggs grunted. "You're both addictive as sin and evil as fuck."

I jerked him away from the door only to slam him back against it. The hinges groaned and wood splintered. "That doesn't sound like someone who enjoys freedom. Try again."

Neither of them were wrong. I didn't have a damn leg to stand on when it came to arguing their accusations. All truth. Arys and I made slaves of those we touched, even those we loved. And especially each other.

For me, it was my blood. For Arys, his bite. But always it was rooted in the power.

There is no saving us from this curse.

Lilah's words, uttered to Salem when he'd taken me to her. I couldn't let her be right.

"Damn, woman." Jenner's voice came from behind as he appeared in the hallway several doors down. "You're a real spitfire tonight. If Arys is running as high and hard as you are, I'm thinking neither of you should be left unattended anymore."

Releasing both Briggs and my sister, I stepped back and turned to face Jenner. "Are you offering?"

"Anything for the queen." Bare chested, clad in only sweat pants, Jenner made sure Juliet got a good, long look at his firm, tattooed torso. Pretty sure he flexed a little too. It hadn't taken him long to find someone happy to relieve the tension I'd left him with.

His flippant remark served to further prove Briggs's accusation right. So I might have a handful of vampires and one angel bound to me. At least I wasn't cruel about it. I gave of my blood to keep them from succumbing to hunger-obsessed madness. Even Briggs.

Admittedly, I gave him blood while hurling warnings and threats, but I gave it regardless. Albeit less often for him than the others. Couldn't make it too easy for him. The man had tried to kill me, replicate me, and God only knew what else. Probably clone me if he could.

"Helpful, Jenner," I huffed a loose tendril of hair out of my face.

It had been though. He'd interrupted before I tore Briggs's head off his shoulders in front of my sister.

Juliet devoured the sight of Jenner like she didn't just mess around with a sexy man. Yeah, I hated Briggs with an undying passion, but the guy was a Fed who'd stayed in damn good shape. I noticed. But not with near the intensity Juliet noticed Jenner.

With a further reddening of her cheeks, she averted her gaze. Not before Briggs had seen her gaze eat Jenner up. Without a word she stalked away, speed walking toward the exit at the other end of the hall. Briggs followed hot on her heels, calling her name.

"She wanted me. She settled for him." Smug as all get out, Jenner eyed my sister's retreating form with delight.

"You're an arrogant thing, aren't you?" I observed, not for the first time. "Get over yourself, Jenner. Get over your dick too. It's nice but it's not God's gift."

He smirked, sliding that ice-blue gaze over me like an explorative hand. "You loved it."

"I liked it," I was quick to correct. "Don't get carried away."

Unable to handle a slap to his ego, Jenner jerked a head toward my office door. "Give me a chance to change your mind about that."

I laughed, enjoying myself. "You had your chance."

As I sauntered away with a sashay to my hips, I could feel his stare. "It takes a lot more than one fuck to experience all of me, Alexa. You've barely scratched the surface."

I didn't look back. Chuckling to myself, I turned to go back into the club. In the dimly lit corridor where the restrooms are located, a body suddenly materialized before me. With a startled shriek I ran smack into Salem.

"Holy crap," I shouted. "You can't just pop out like that."

The warrior angel was disheveled and dirty. His hair was unkempt, his clothing torn. Like he'd been fighting. Gold eyes wide, he grabbed my shoulders, almost pulling me off balance.

"We have to act now," he said, frantic and afraid. "Before Lilah finds out that I'm here."

CHAPTER FIFTEEN

I pulled away, suddenly needing him to not touch me. His frazzled energy tried to leap to me, and I didn't want any of it.

"Is everything alright? What's the emergency?" Being alone with him in a dark corner didn't feel safe. So soon I had to decide whether to trust Gabriel or not. Searching Salem's wild eyes, seeing the unbalance that I saw in my own eyes, I knew he walked a dangerous line.

"Lilah forbade me to help you. She wants nothing to do with mending the twin flame rift." Salem glanced around like he expected Lilah to appear. It made me fear the same. "She's been tracking my every move, forcing her way into my head. Making sure I don't come here."

Uneasy being alone with him, I nodded toward the lust-drunk nightclub of people. "Let's go find Willow. I don't want to do anything without him."

With a tight nod Salem followed me through the throng, shouting to be heard over the music and voices. "I left her asleep after a vigorous round of lovemaking. It's hard to say how much time I have before she awakes."

Vigorous round of lovemaking? Such an angelic way of saying he screwed her to the point of exhaustion. A demon with nothing to do but think of ways to sabotage Salem's desire to help me wouldn't need a whole lot of rest. I couldn't help but be curious at the state of his appearance. Twin flame love could take a pretty violent turn, however.

Driven by the sense of urgency Salem exuded, I picked out Willow's energy and followed it. Right to a booth in the back corner where he'd cozied up with the tequila-drinking, pink-haired girl.

I was the worst. I felt horrible for having to interrupt him yet again.

Apocalyptic

Thankfully Salem slapped a heavy hand on Willow's shoulder, busting in without hesitation. "Sorry, brother, but it's now or never," Salem said, wincing apologetically.

With a few words to his lady friend who pouted in disappointment, Willow slid out of the booth and followed us. He was still talking to her? No action at all yet? It had been a while now since Gabriel and I had first left to go to Brogan's shop, leaving Willow here. Was he trying to make a snack out of this girl or date her? He was so unlike the other men of this bloodline. I adored him so hard for being so pure of heart.

I let Willow lead the way to my office. Falling back, I scanned the place for Gabriel. He felt close. Spying him in a small group near the bar, I glided close enough to catch his eye. With a tilt of my head I invited him to follow me. Then I pulled my phone out and called Shaz.

"Something is going on with Salem," I said in a rush, afraid of how little time we had. "He's running scared of Lilah, and I'm not sure we'll get another chance. You guys better get over here."

Trepidation filled me as I returned to the quieter back hall where the music was muffled and the occasional shriek or climactic cry rang out. What if Gabriel was right? What if I couldn't trust Salem? If anything went wrong, if the balance was severed completely...

I couldn't even entertain the horror it brought to mind.

Maybe we shouldn't do this. Maybe we shouldn't mess with the balance at all. But would we ever get another chance to fix us?

On my way by the room Jenner occupied with what sounded like multiple women, I rapped on the door a few times. "Heads up, Jenner. Arys is on his way and shit might get messy."

I didn't wait for a response. He'd heard me. In my office Willow leaned on my desk, watching the restless angel flare and resettle his wings repeatedly. The angel had anxiety. This did not instill confidence.

Watching him pace around, unable to stand or sit still, made me ill. Salem continuously glanced down the hallway through the open office door. His impatience rubbed my nerves raw.

Within ten minutes a cool storm swelled inside me, and I turned to find Shaz and Arys striding down the hall. I wasn't prepared for the onslaught of emotion that took me. Desire, anger, love, and sorrow. But the greatest of these was love.

It launched me down the hall and into Arys's arms before I could even consider holding myself back. It wasn't possible. We'd been forced apart, but we were always drawn back together. Every time stronger and more deeply entwined than the last. Making each separation hurt that much more.

Arys enclosed me tight in his embrace. I wrapped my legs around his waist, my arms around his neck, and kissed him. Pouring out the fear and desperation in the only way I could. It echoed in Arys, in the way he claimed my mouth in a bruising assault on my lips.

For a brief moment of time, we were whole again.

So easily we lost ourselves in each other. Shaz had to grab hold of each of us, breaking the spell. "Let's try a little moderation on the touchy-feely stuff, shall we?" he teased. "We all know how fast that can go south."

"And how," Arys murmured, flashing a flirtatious smile at our wolf.

"You know what I meant." Shaz kept a serious face, but when he looked at Arys, his pulse ticked up a notch. I wondered what they'd been up to while away from me. Together. I always wondered.

Reluctantly Arys and I disentangled from one another. We joined the others in the office, and the pressure in my head rose. Too many powerhouses in one room.

Arys only had to enter the room, and he knew. Leaning in to brush his lips over my ear, he murmured, "What possessed you to claim my progeny?"

"Let's call it a contingency plan," I said, low, unable to explain further. "A strategic play."

Not that Arys opposed my claiming of Gabriel. He never had been. If he had it his way, he'd bind every powerful person we knew to us. He nodded, accepting my answer.

I followed his gaze to where Gabriel sat on the couch, calmly observing the rest of us. In small, casual glances, he took everyone in. How much did he know about us from visions he'd had that we weren't privy to?

Feeling my stare, he met my eyes. I wanted to ask him if we should shut this entire thing down and send Salem away? Could he be trusted at all? Gabriel hadn't had those answers. All he'd been able to tell me was that Salem would go dark. He didn't know when or how, only that it would happen.

That knowledge had burrowed itself into the marrow of my bones, becoming part of me in a way that felt like it might split me apart. I had to tell Salem what I knew, didn't I?

Or did I? Would it give him a fighting chance or encourage him to give in? Half the people in the room were all people I was dying to tell this to. I couldn't. Not yet. Not with Salem here. I needed more time to think about this.

Willow and Salem discussed the details of how to repair the rift. Salem talked a mile a minute, rambling fast, afraid. Knowing that Lilah might force her way into his head at any moment did lend a greater sense of urgency to the situation. However, I feared urgency would lead to error.

Holding my gaze, Gabriel gave a slight shrug and settled back against the couch. Not much help but he didn't seem alarmed. I'd like to say I trusted the angel. He was an angel after all. Joined to a demon though, which kind of disqualified him from implicit trust.

I was taking a chance trusting Gabriel. Between two evils, choose the lesser. Gabriel was dark as sin, no doubt about that. He wasn't a demon though and could never be one. That gave him the win.

"She has to find the core, isolate the tear, and bind it back together." Salem directed this at Willow who rubbed a hand over his faintly stubbled jaw.

"That sounds way too simple," Shaz remarked, a skeptical brow raised. He lingered close enough to keep an eye on both Arys and me.

"It is," Gabriel added, drawing Salem's attention. "For one, isolating their power core will require an altered state experience. Second, there's no way she can mend a break in an immortal power core without being immortal herself."

Leaning against the wall near the door, I tried not to let the packed room make me claustrophobic. "Altered state experience? How altered are we talking?"

"Ideally, you'd reach a heightened mental state," Willow supplied. "A third eye view if you will. It will enable you to see the intricate design of your power. The idea is that you'll see the weak point and be able to mend it with immortal power. Salem's power."

Channel Salem's power through me and use it to repair a damaged twin flame core created by powers beyond my full comprehension? Right. Piece of cake.

"Easy peasy," I muttered, head back against the wall, staring at the ceiling. There was a stain up there. From the Harley days. Disgusting. "Willow, do you think I can do it? More specifically, do you think I *should* do it?"

His opinion mattered the most. He knew what I was up against, and he knew what I was capable of. "I do think you can do it, yes," Willow said, confidence in me shining through his voice. "My concern is Salem. My brother, do you think you can do it?"

Everyone looked to the angel for a reaction. He'd never been anything but cool and collected in my presence. Even when he lost his temper on Falon, he'd been in control and unafraid.

Salem squared his shoulders and drew himself up to his full height. "I'm here because I want to help. Will I get another chance? I don't know. Not anytime soon with the way Lilah's been going on about it. If we don't try this now, I can't say for sure when I'll be back."

Silently I sent out a plea to Falon. *Come on, you motherfucker. Hear me. Feel me.*

The immortal power had to come from Salem. He was a twin flame. Still, I preferred to have Falon there. He understood immortal power in a personal way. I told myself it had nothing to do with the way he'd left after Bane's appearance.

I looked to Arys who stood next to me with arms crossed. He eyed Salem with the same suspicion I'd felt since Gabriel's warning. Funny that he of all people was warning me about someone else being dangerous.

"If we only have one shot," Arys began, pausing to glance at Shaz. "Then we have to take it."

Our wolf didn't seem convinced. He shook his platinum head, worry creasing his brow. "Is it worth the risk of having it all go horribly wrong? If you only have one shot, should it be under these circumstances?"

"I don't know," I whispered to nobody. If Gabriel was right and Salem would go dark, then this might be the last time I'd even see him as an angel. It might be our only chance.

With a frustrated cry I shoved away from the wall and paced to the other side of the room, as far as I could get from the rest of them clustered in the middle. I didn't feel like I had a choice. It was now or never. Try to save us like I'd promised Arys I would or keep watching us unravel.

I whirled around to find them all watching me with varying degrees of expectation. "Ok, let's do this."

CHAPTER SIXTEEN

Five minutes later I sat on the floor in the middle of the room, surrounded by six powerhouse men. A succubus dream come true to be sure. Too bad it wasn't that kind of group setting. That would have been a lot less terrifying and a whole lot more interesting.

Who was I kidding? Even I wasn't succubus enough to take on the role as the center in a circle this big. Kudos to the ladies who happily did.

The coffee table had been shoved against a wall. I sat in its place in front of the couch, Arys on my right and Salem on my left. Across from me sat Willow. Shaz and Gabriel hovered close enough to watch everything that went on.

Jenner leaned against the doorframe, keeping his distance. He didn't like this kind of magic. Admitting it gave him the creeps, he hung back. He'd ditched the ladies in his room to have our back here, so I could forgive his unease. I felt the same.

Willow nodded to Salem. "Give her the sun star of protection before we do this. I'd do it if I could."

"The what now?" Curious but trusting, I sat there, cross legged on the floor, while Salem angled himself toward me and began to draw on my forehead with a finger.

"It's a symbol of angelic protection," Willow explained. "It will protect your mind. Altered states of consciousness open one up to many dangers."

Salem's finger glided over my skin, loops and swirls that made no sense to me. There was a faint tingle as the power of the mark came alive.

"Ready?" Willow asked.

My stomach plummeted in a sickening freefall. No, I was not ready. Unfortunately, I'd been forced to learn that some things I'd never be ready to face and that didn't mean shit. I'd have to face it anyway. Why prolong the inevitable?

"Yeah." I grabbed Arys's hand in a bone-crushing death grip. He'd been eyeing up my carotid since he got here. I had to do this for us. "Ready."

Arys didn't reflect my apprehension. Calm next to me, he caught my jaw in his hand and tipped my face up to his. "I know you can do this." He searched me, wanting to see that I believed him.

I wanted to. I tried. "Arys, whatever happens, don't forget how much I love you."

"That's fucking bleak, Alexa" Jenner barked from the doorway. "This isn't goodbye. Get on with it. You're making me nervous."

But what if it is? My heart only had so many pieces left. I couldn't stand to lose anymore.

"Shut the hell up," Shaz snapped, his short patience a clear sign of how he felt about all this.

"Simmer down, boys." I waved a hand to shut them both up. Then I nodded to Willow. I trusted him to oversee this entire process. Never would I have attempted anything without his guidance.

The room fell quiet. Almost too quiet.

I knew what I had to do. Find the rift, channel Salem's power through me, and pour it into the rift, making it whole again. At least that was the plan.

"It's going to happen fast," Willow said, reaching to give my arm a comforting squeeze. "Salem will use the sun star to pull you into an altered state of consciousness. Somewhat of an in between. Not quite out of body, you'll still be here. Trust yourself."

I held tighter to Arys and closed my eyes. There was no calming the rise of nerves. A spark in my palm linked us together. It reassured me.

When Salem touched the mark on my forehead again, he spoke a few words in his immortal language. And I went under. Over? Out? Whatever.

The room fell away and me with it, falling backward. Shaz's hands suddenly cradled my head, easing it gently to the floor. I felt him, smelled him, but it was all background sensation. My raw awareness had been awakened.

I was very much still in my body. I could feel it there, heavy and numb. But I was also outside of it, viewing the entire room. Every man's aura shone brightly, each a different color. I'd always been able to physically see some elements of power, but this was a whole other view.

Shaz glowed with the brightest light. Being the only one present with a proper mortal heartbeat, his energy was a dizzying green, lively and full of life.

A brilliant amber outlined Willow. It held me captive as every few seconds a streak of pure white light darted through his aura. Other than Salem, Arys and me, nobody else but Willow had more than one color to their aura.

I wanted to ogle each of them in turn. Urgency shook me, reminding me that I didn't have time for that. Focussing on Arys and me, I studied the bindings of blue and gold twisting around and through us. Standing back and viewing our power from the outside, the yin-yang arrangement became evident. What I noticed immediately and with alarm was how unbalanced we were.

A proper yin-yang has that even split with a splash of light in the dark and vice versa. We may have started out that way, but right away I saw why we were such a mess now. The streaks of yellow light breaking through Arys's dark blue were tiny, a small candle in the middle of pitch black night. Barely there. Whereas the splash of deep blue that stained my golden yellow had seeped well beyond the dark splash it should have been.

More than half of my energy ran dark.

There was no even balance in either of us or between us. It was so off. Arys was dangling on the edge of total darkness. I was now more dark than light. It was growing. Taking over.

How did I fix this? Was it supposed to be obvious? Because it wasn't.

I knew the guys were speaking in low tones amongst themselves, but I couldn't hone in on what they were saying.

The twin flame rift, the growing abyss between us, it was darkness. Slowly eating away at us. Consuming. If it succeeded in taking us, it would unleash total mayhem.

Through our joined hands the energy flowed freely, sparking every so often.

Apocalyptic

A silver thread danced between us, bouncing around in response to our chaotic energy. The twin flame soul thread. Immortal and unbreakable. That's what kept us from ever being able to walk away from each other. A true til death do us part.

Could I even do this? It felt beyond my experience. Maybe we could find another way to hold off the darkness. To keep it from spreading further. Another keystone perhaps. Fixing the rift meant driving back the darkness.

Frustrated with how little time I had to do something, I reached out with a hand that wasn't physically there and touched our joined hands. It was easily one of the weirdest things I'd ever done.

Concentrating on the flow of energy, I let it take me. I followed the current of light and dark, feeling the way it swung wildly between us, from one to the other. Erratic and unpredictable. A proper balance should feel smooth and fluid, the flow uninterrupted. The power that ran rampant through Arys and me felt hard and rough, like it had jagged edges. It was strong, a true force to be reckoned with. But it wasn't what it should be.

The darkness gripped Arys, feeding his illicit hunger. The light battled it back, meager as it was, refusing to go quiet or gentle. Within me the two sides warred, battling for dominance.

Not knowing where to even begin, I panicked. Then I heard Willow's kind voice repeating, "Trust yourself."

Making a conscious effort, I focused on my tie to Arys, drawing on the power we shared. I tapped as much as I could. If needed I'd reach beyond us to our vampires.

My lungs inflated and my body vibrated with the sudden surge. I was both in and out of it, making precise focus a challenge. Trying not to get caught up in the physical sensations, I kept my mind's eye fixed on the darkness. I'd have to force it to retreat. Having a keystone had kept it at bay. Without one, it seemed to be spreading fast.

Tapped into Arys, I reached for Salem. His power came in like an explosion, both blinding and deafening. I struggled to catch hold of it, but once I did it responded to me. To my light. It recognized me as kindred. Yes! That's what I needed.

Studying the midnight-blue force that was our darkness, I concentrated on forcing it to retreat until there was nothing else in my mind. Then I pushed the cocktail of twin flame power into it. Channeling the power of others got easier every time I did it.

Nothing happened. At first.

I refused to believe the power of a light flame who just happened to be a freakin' angel wouldn't give me the boost I needed. There was nothing but resistance.

Then something began to happen. I might have gasped. Pouring nothing but focused intent and light into the dark looming within Arys and me, I willed it to respond, and it did.

My greatest fear was doing something to make it worse. As I looked on the dark began to move. A reluctant gradual shift, like dark waters receding with the tide. I said a small prayer and poured forth everything I took from Salem.

What would it take for it to overrun us completely if this didn't work? Another attack from Arys? A meltdown from me? Violence that Shaz couldn't always be there to stop? It was a chance we couldn't take.

I drew harder on Salem, channelling everything I could into forcing the dark back. So bad I needed to see it balanced. As it should be.

Ever so slowly the shadows succumbed to my command. Bit by tiny bit it eased back.

Chasing the dark back to where it belonged was the only way to mend the rift. The abyss that spanned from Arys to me, tormenting us every night, it would only close when each side returned to balance.

The effort demanded more focus, stronger intent. It demanded all I had to give and then some. Using Salem's immortal vibe to guide my intent, I willed it to keep moving. Demanded it. Nothing else mattered more to me in the entire world right then than seeing that gold and blue in perfect balance.

With each tiny smidge of progress, I felt my fears lessen. Had Falon been right? Maybe I could do this after all.

And I would have. If Lilah hadn't been so hell bent on sabotaging us all.

We'd all gone into this knowing she'd try to stop it if she could. Because if I succeeded in fixing the unbalance between Arys and me, then I could do it for her and Salem as well. She wasn't taking that chance.

Apocalyptic

The sharp slap of dark flame power came out of nowhere. It blindsided me. The attack was specific, directed at the light flame that burned in my core.

Lilah's fury screamed through my link to Salem. She didn't just burst into his head. She took over.

Immortal power guided by the anger of a pissed off demon queen struck me. Without pulling any punches she used her tie to Salem to channel her hate and rage into a weapon that she then kicked my ass with.

My link to Salem turned darker than the most absolute of black. It reeked of brimstone and decay. Her target was my light. All she had to do was feed my darkness, undoing the progress I'd just made.

Through her twin flame Lilah poured darkness into me. The dark flame she hit me with recognized itself in me. It stirred up the darkest parts of me. Lust for blood, power, and to tear things to fucking pieces. Every wicked desire that dwelled in Arys and me grew and swelled at her manipulation.

She fed it. Forced it. Doing all she could to bring forth full darkness in both of us. Snuffing out our light. That was her end goal.

It snapped me fully back into my body. I sat up with a shriek to find Salem staring at me with orange eyes. Lilah's eyes.

She was here with us, present within him. And she didn't fight fair.

So neither could I. Lilah had forced every monstrous hunger I possessed to rush me, tempting me to give in to shady hungers. Had she forgotten that included arousal for powerful men?

Knowing she watched, I targeted Salem and unleashed a torrent of sex-drenched allure. At this point he was more of an innocent bystander caught in the crossfire than anything else. Although I'm sure he battled her inside his own mind, it didn't stop me from pulling him under.

Confusion crossed his face, followed by understanding, and then nothing but lust. I climbed onto Salem's lap, knowing that seducing him was my only way to get into his head and disrupt her hold on him.

"You want a piece of me, bitch?" I hissed, finding her within Salem's wide eyes. "How does it feel to have your lover get hard for me?"

Pandemonium broke out. Willow and Gabriel realized what was happening. The darkness that took me, it took Arys too. In my peripheral view I saw Shaz and Jenner tackle him as he made to lunge at me.

"Alexa," Salem gasped my name, the struggle evident in his eyes. "Run."

Even as the guttural plea left him, he brought up a hand and nailed me with a point-blank attack. It was all Lilah. Pure demon magic struck me down, pinning me to the floor. Using Salem to do her dirty work, Lilah took down both Gabriel and Willow with precise blasts of pure evil. Then Salem was on me.

With claws I slashed at him, fighting to keep him back. I drew on my vampires and struck back with a blast of roiling power that threw the angel back. Wings flared, he grabbed me roughly and jerked me to my feet.

My back slammed against the open doorframe, the metal latch digging into my spine. Throwing attacks at him did little to harm him in any way. It didn't help that my power ran darker than ever before. It made battling Lilah next to impossible. Which was her goal.

I couldn't beat her without the light.

Pinning me in place, Salem shook like he resisted every move she forced him to make. His eyes flashed back to his usual gold. With a sheen of unshed tears, he whispered, "I'm sorry."

Then he was gone, taken over by his dark half. She looked out at me through his eyes and smiled. "Tough luck, Alexa. You can't always win."

Salem's strong hands gripped each side of my head, forcing me to meet his eyes. Lilah's eyes. An angel and demon twin flame duo proved formidable. Being the queen of light and dark didn't mean shit against two immortals. Not when my light withered by the second.

Lilah fed the darkness into me as I fought to dislodge her hold. What light I'd had left was quickly being devoured by shadows. Arys, who'd had so little already, stood no chance.

Apocalyptic

The demon bitch wanted to drive us both to total darkness. It's what she wanted for her and Salem, and the threat of me being able to stop that had driven her to take us with them.

I pushed back against her, pulling all the power I could from my vampires. But as the light inside me dwindled, I had nothing to channel it through. Throwing dark power at her did absolutely nothing. It wasn't enough.

It was the light that gave me power over dark creatures. It flickered and struggled in my core, refusing to bow to the shadows. Still it shrank to a tiny glow.

No! This can't be happening.

We were going to lose. But how? How could this be? The bitch was locked away and yet still able to reduce me to a begging mess.

Blood tears streamed down my face. "Please, don't," I begged, having no shame. All I knew was that Arys and I couldn't end this way.

Jenner and Shaz fought to subdue him. He was making them work for it. It killed me to see the rabid glint steal in as the light faded from his eyes, replaced by shadows.

"It's nothing personal," Lilah said to me through Salem. "Just self-preservation."

A final surge exploded from Salem. This was it. He and Lilah would extinguish our light flame, ruining us forever.

Refusing to go down without a fight, I reached a shaky hand down and drew the Dragon Claw. After my run in with Bane, I wasn't being caught without it. Shya had promised it would destroy the physical form of any dark creature. Filled with Lilah's immense essence, Salem fit the bill.

I stabbed the dagger into his side as deep as I could. His startled cry hurt my ears. Lilah was forced out as Salem clutched the unexpected wound. Seconds later he vanished.

Their Godless power fell away.

Dropping the dagger, I clutched the door frame in an effort not to collapse. Although I could no longer intricately see our energy fields, I knew our light had been all but obliterated. Only the barest trace remained. I felt it inside me. Burning bright and hot, albeit tiny and pathetic. A match in a midnight storm.

So close the bitch had come to destroying us. How the fuck would I fix us now?

The urgent and irresistible need to slake my wicked desires obliterated that question. They ran rampant through me, freed from the barrier the light had imposed. I saw through a haze of black.

Moving in sync, Arys twisted free from Shaz's hold at the same time I grabbed Jenner and flung him from the room. He hit the carpet in the hallway with a grunt. Arys wrenched Shaz's arm behind his back and tossed him after Jenner. The two men collided in a heap of limbs and shouts.

I slammed the door in their faces and turned to my other half. This must be the part where we kill each other. It loomed. I sensed it. Strangely, I was ok with it. So off balance, it didn't occur to me that I should still be fighting it.

Arys and I, part of us, we just wanted the struggle to end. Our eyes locked. No longer did I see all of him there. Something was missing. Humanity. The spark that returned to him when we bonded had been snuffed out.

We weren't alone. Willow and Gabriel were a groaning mess on the floor where Salem had left them. That was fine. They could watch. It was Shaz who shouldn't see what was about to happen.

Coming together we moved as one, a perfect mirror of one another. Suddenly my hand was on Arys's throat. I threw him against the closed door, using his weight to keep it shut against the guys beating on it from the other side.

"I'm sorry." I heard myself say in a broken voice. "I tried."

Arys stared down at me with grim amusement, like our imminent doom was the goddamn punchline of a sick joke. "You did what you could. But we both knew it would end this way."

My hand tightened on his throat. Power, so dark I choked on it, ruffled my hair. Arys spread his hands wide, inviting my best shot. I didn't want to take it, but I knew he wouldn't waste the first one he got.

There was no rationale left. There was only bringing this all to a close. The way the darkness wanted us to.

I crushed my lips to his, needing to feel him again before it was all over. We owed ourselves that much. The door bounced and rattled in its frame. On the other side Shaz shouted that he'd tear the fucking thing down.

Do it, a small, quiet voice pleaded somewhere deep in my psyche. *Don't let us end like this.*

Arys took my face in his hands, far too gentle for the sinister force guiding his every move. The passion in his kiss was haunting. It reeked of death and his lust for mine.

Behind me Willow called my name. He sounded far away, muffled like he shouted through water. It was unfortunate that he'd have to bear witness to our destruction. He'd fought so long and hard for us.

Arys tore his lips from mine and, with a ragged groan, backhanded me. The force spun me around and threw me off balance. I stayed on my feet, tasting blood.

"I didn't want to love you," he said, strangled, like he tried to hold the words back but failed. "I didn't want any of this."

Worse than any physical blow, Arys's scathing words cut deep. He sounded like Lilah.

Soul crushing pain had me clutching my chest. It hurt in so many places. "I didn't ask for this either," I shouted back at him, tripping over a sob. "You came after me, remember? You could have just stayed away."

Not true. I knew that. He couldn't have stayed away any more than I could walk out of here right now and never see him again. But right then the dark rode me, and its words flew out of my mouth. It stole Arys's guilt from my memories and threw it in his face.

"You changed me," he accused, catching the fist I swung, "into something I didn't want to be." Squeezing my forearm, Arys dragged me against him.

My body blazed in remembrance of all we'd shared. I still wanted him, still loved him with every part of me, despite wanting to unleash my pain all over him. "You made me a monster," I spat, raking my gaze over his tense jaw. With each hateful word, I craved him more. "A coldblooded killer, just like you."

"I made you a work of fucking art." He smirked into my face.

A stand-off. Those precious few seconds before all bets are off and shots are fired. The shitstorm of darkness engulfed us.

Our attacks came at exactly the same time. Power exploded between us, dark meeting dark. The collision threw us both in opposite directions.

Gabriel and Willow put themselves between us, readying for our quick recovery. Latin spilled from Gabriel, erecting a massive floor-to-ceiling energy barrier in the middle of the room, dividing Arys and me.

The door burst open. Relief filled Shaz's face when he saw us alive. He didn't hold back. He threw an adrenaline-fuelled fist into Arys's jaw, snapping his head to the side. The vampire went down, out cold. It wasn't easy to KO a vamp.

"Help me get him out of here before he wakes up," Shaz barked.

Jenner helped Shaz to gather Arys like they would a drunk friend, letting him hang between them as they dragged him down the hall.

Both saddened and angered, I watched him go. It felt like my soul was being carved out with a cold, bony, claw-tipped finger.

Willow caught me and pulled me into his arms as the others took my lover away. It hurt me to see. The hollow pit left inside me ached. The spark of light that had once been a brilliant flame now flickered. A tiny candle in a windstorm. It was all we had left.

"Alexa? Talk to me. Say something." Willow slapped my face lightly, trying to get me to focus on him. Worry filled his enchanting eyes.

The sounds of the heavy metal door at the end of the hall reverberated as the guys removed Arys from the building.

"It's over." Ragged, breathy, I could barely get the words out. Defeat overwhelmed me.

"No, it's not," Willow insisted. "Not as long as you have even the smallest spark. Because that's all you need. Don't you dare give up yet."

The voice of the dark boomed so much louder now. Insistent and convincing. It wanted me to taste Willow. Temptation reared its ugly head. Why the hell shouldn't I? What else did I have left to exist for now other than blood, sex, death, and staying high on all of it until my final showdown with Arys.

Apocalyptic

The thought had barely finished flitting through my head when Willow sensed it. He stiffened, jerking back so we weren't touching. "Alexa, don't." Raising both hands in surrender, Willow shook his head. "I'm not what you really want."

Splashing him with my allure, I shrugged and touched the side of his face. The simplest of touches that had him swooning. My succubus side had always been dark. It was right at home now with less light to battle it for dominance. My wolf wasn't a fan of this new turn of events. It sat back in silence, confused and unhappy.

"No, maybe not," I agreed, my seductive purr driving his arousal higher. "But I can't think of a better way to end the worst night of my life than by drowning my sorrows in two of the most powerful vampires I know."

Gabriel backed toward the door. Distance wouldn't help him. Not anymore. I was inside him.

"Don't do this." Despite his plea, Willow leaned into my touch. His gaze was on my mouth. He wanted to taste it.

With a finger I beckoned Gabriel closer. At the same time I dragged a hand down Willow's chest, headed lower. They were both mine, and I intended to enjoy them.

The air moved. A telltale ripple I both heard and felt.

I glanced up to find myself staring into silver eyes set in a beautiful, battered face. Splotches of purple and red decorated Falon. One eye swollen, gashes on his lip, cheek and forehead.

Bane! The demon prince had done this.

Falon shoved in front of Willow, saving him from me. Clasping my face in his hands, the fallen angel searched my eyes. What he found made his mouth draw into a tight line and his brows knit together. Falon studied me like he couldn't accept what he saw. He blinked a few times and glanced away, but not before I saw what he'd tried to hide. Utter dismay.

He pressed his lips to my forehead and exhaled a slow breath. In a tone that lacked true vehemence, he murmured, "Let's get you out of here before you can fuck anything else up."

CHAPTER SEVENTEEN

"What the hell happened?" Falon blurted the second the hotel room door swung shut. He locked it and shed his long coat, flinging it over the desk chair. "Did Salem screw you over? And he has the nerve to call me a traitor."

"No way, you first." I waved a hand, indicating his bruised face. "Did Bane do this? Why the hell did you go after him?"

The bruises had healed significantly since his arrival at the Kiss. Still, they lingered. It took an assault loaded with a fuck ton of power to leave marks on an immortal. I marveled at the sight of Falon's beautiful face marred by violence. I felt it between my legs.

"Do not say his name," Falon hissed, shoving the chair so it bounced against the desk. "Tell me what happened. You're dark as fucking sin, Alexa. Don't walk away from me."

Dropping clothing as I went, I headed for the large ensuite and turned on the water in the shower. I peeled off my bra and panties before untying my hair from its disheveled braid. I wanted to scrub the entire night away. Since I couldn't do that, a layer of skin would have to do.

Falon strode into the bathroom behind me. "What are you doing?"

"Taking a shower." I shot him a look that said 'duh' and stepped beneath the hot stream. "What does it look like?"

"It looks like you've lost whatever was left of your damn fool mind." His expression guarded, Falon disrobed.

A pricey shirt and a pair of pants with trendy names I didn't know hit the floor. They were in rough shape anyway. Beneath the fashion mag duds, he went commando. Tall, naked, and undeniably divine. I stared at the cuts and bruises that marked him. Wounds from blades, fists, and magic covered his torso. He'd gone after Bane, but why?

Falon stepped into the shower, nudging me aside so he could take over the hot spray of water. Scrubbing both hands over his silver hair, the water cascaded over him. I kind of wanted to eat him a little bit. Unable to take my eyes off him, I fumbled around for the shampoo.

"You think this is bad?" Falon gestured to his wounds. "It's nothing. I won't even feel it tomorrow. You'll still be dark as fuck. What exactly did you do?"

He swiped the shampoo bottle from my hand and squeezed way too much into his palm. Slapping it into his hair, he worked up a huge lather. Taking his sweet time dominating the spray.

"I failed," I said, tone absent and detached. Spying a fresh bar of soap on the ledge, I rolled it around in my wet hands. "It doesn't matter. It's too late. I don't want to talk about it."

No, I did not. If I thought about it, I would break. And if I broke there was nothing and no one to put me back together. Not anymore.

Rather than give myself a chance to think about it, I ran the bar of soap over Falon's abdomen. It glided over his taut muscles. I massaged it into a lather, careful around the uglier wounds. Why had he let this happen? He'd gone after Bane without a second thought. Reckless.

"Too bad," he grunted, rinsing his hair, trying to ignore my roaming hands. "You're telling me everything if I have to beat it out of you."

"Ditto." My soapy hand slipped lower. He sucked in a breath. My hope had just died. I needed to drown my sorrows. I needed all my fallen angel had to give me.

Falon caught my wrist before I could wrap my hand around his swelling shaft. Still he watched me with that guarded expression, like he wasn't sure what to expect from me. "Fine. We'll talk about it after I fuck you like I own you. Brace yourself. I'm not in the mood to be nice about it."

Someone was in a mood. I didn't need to ask why.

"Good," I fired back, raising a brow in a naughty smirk when the soap slipped from my hand. "I'm not feeling so nice myself tonight."

We'd both faced personal demons tonight. Literally in Falon's case. And we'd both come away beaten down. It drew us together. More so now than ever before, I felt his brokenness. It called my name.

My craving for him had taken a darker turn, as had everything else about me. So when Falon roughly shoved me against the hard, wet tile, a devilish laugh spilled from my lips. I wanted him to hurt me in the best and worst of ways.

He shoved a hand between my legs, roughly rubbing me. Sweeping my dripping hair aside, he gave it a sharp tug. "No power. No manipulation. Just you and me. Oh, and no foreplay."

I nodded, saying nothing. Waiting with a rise of apprehension and longing, I anticipated his rough entry. Without warning, Falon thrust into me in one hard motion. It still took me by surprise. Hands splayed on the slippery tile, my face almost hit the wall from the force. No warm up. No easy build. Falon had some serious aggression to unleash.

But so did I.

Thick and commanding, he filled me. My body opened to him, holding him deep within me. So forceful were his thrusts that I clenched my teeth as it bordered on painful pleasure.

Whatever had gone down between Falon and Bane, it had left him needing to prove something to himself. Maybe even to me. It was evident in the way he took me, rough and with total abandon. At one point I wondered how much of him was there with me, aware of who it was he took his pain and aggression out on.

Of course he knew. That's what we did together. We used each other to purge the pain.

My forearms shook from bracing myself between Falon and the wall. His hands on my hips held my ass end in place but did little to keep my head from smacking the tile. The sound of our wet bodies slamming together was loud despite the rush of water. My moans became cries and small shrieks.

It encouraged Falon. Harder he thrust, his ragged groans sending a rush of moisture to my core. There was something to be said for having a lover so lost in my body without so much as the slightest touch of succubus thrall. We may have started that way, but now we genuinely wanted one another. A tough humble pill to swallow for sure.

An especially vicious thrust brought my wolf forth. Claws scratched the tile beneath my fingers. Four large fangs filled my mouth. Inside I was a mess of confusion. Wolf. Vampire. Woman. Every part of me.

What was I now without the light? I presumed it wouldn't be long before the final spark snuffed out, crushed by the spread of dark fire. It burned me, consuming all that was left.

God, why did it have to hurt so fucking much? I slammed a fist on the tile, watching it crack and split beneath my assault. A strangled sound that was both a growl and a sob hung heavy on the steamy air.

I couldn't numb the pain. The escape I found in Falon eluded me. For the first time.

Falon wasn't so lost in his wild need to purge his anger all over my body that he didn't notice what was happening. He didn't slow his pace, nor did I want him to. If anything, my sob encouraged him to drive the demons from me the only way he knew how.

Deep inside me, he hesitated just long enough for me to savor the way he felt before withdrawing. A hand slid up my body, gliding over the ridges of my spine, around to my chest. Slipping his forearm up between my breasts, Falon pulled me close against him, his chest pressed to my back.

"Let me have your pain, Alexa," he whispered in my ear. "Leave it all here with me."

I came undone. Between moans and sobs, everything burst out in an emotional volcano, spewing my shattered soul like lava. Just as surely, it would destroy everyone in its path.

When the sobs overtook the moans, Falon stopped, turned me in his arms, and pushed the soaking hair back from my face. I hated myself for crying my heart out in front of him. Again. Of all the men in my life, he was the last one I wanted to see me so vulnerable.

But the bloody tears wouldn't stop. The overwhelming realization of what had really transpired tonight ran amok through the remaining fragments of my sanity.

Frustration darted through Falon's eyes, like he didn't know what to do. Taking a deep breath, he pulled me into his arms and slowly sank to the floor of the shower, drawing me with him.

The hot water pelted us from above. He held me in his lap, so our faces avoided the spray, and let me cry. The water around us ran red as the tears splashed down. So hard I'd tried to keep it together for Arys and me. I'd let myself believe we'd be ok, defying the odds. That we were here for a reason so much bigger than we'd discovered so far.

I'd believed a lie.

Like those twin flames who'd come before us, and those who would come after, we were destined to fail. Falon himself had said so. Destiny for the twins was destruction.

It wasn't Falon's fault that I'd failed. His theory had worked. Lilah had helped fate.

Gradually, the sobs lessened and the tears slowed. I repositioned myself atop Falon, straddling him on the floor of the shower. I needed to feel him. A few strokes of my hand and he was ready for me again. With a few stray tears rolling down my cheeks, I took him inside me.

Falon's arms went around me. He pressed his face to my breasts and decorated them with hot kisses, letting me set the pace. Needing to step out of my head and fully into the moment, I closed my eyes and focused on the heady sensations of him: His arms around me, strong and gentle at the same time. The scent of him, masculine and musky but so much more. Something poetic and airy, like a summer breeze on the most amazing day. Like a flower I had yet to smell or a fruit I hadn't tasted.

The need to taste him gripped me, and I reached for one of his hands. Bringing it to my lips, I ran my tongue over the veins in his wrist. A slight nick of a fang and a tiny drop of blood welled up. Just enough to give me that explosion of Falon that I sought. I rushed to capture it before the water could steal it away.

I rode the hard length of him in slow, deliberate strokes. He felt like life beneath me. Inside me. Touching me beyond the physical. Reaching a place he never should have been able to reach.

My eyes snapped open to find Falon watching me with lust but curiosity as well. He kissed me, and I knew it was to keep me from searching his eyes. Tearing my lips from his, I gazed into him, seeking what he didn't want me to find.

Falon glanced away, down between us. Watching me slide down him, over and over. Hands on my waist, he pulled me down harder, groaning each time his shaft disappeared inside me. When I felt the warmth of his release, I came with a quivering climax.

Ten minutes later I stepped out of the shower to find myself alone in the bathroom. Falon had finished showering quickly and vacated, leaving me a few minutes to properly condition my hair and scrub the debris of life from my soul.

Oh right, that's not possible. That shit sticks with you for-fucking-ever. Wishful thinking again.

I exited the bathroom to find Falon sprawled naked on the king size bed, licking chocolate from the tip of a spoon. He frowned at the plate of chocolate-drizzled brownie. Guess it wasn't hitting the spot tonight.

"Problem with your dessert?" I asked, wondering how much he'd tipped the room service this time. Falon liked to go overboard. But what did he care? It was my money.

He glanced up, silver gaze raking me in. "Um, yeah. It's wearing a goddamn bathrobe. Take that thing off."

Smirking to myself, I tugged the robe tie tighter. I'd put it on just to get a rise out of him. I plopped onto the bed and leaned against the headboard. "Not until you tell me what happened to your face. Then you can have me any way you want."

That piqued his interest. Mischief lit up Falon's perfect but bruised face. "Any way I want? You realize that leaves the door open for many possibilities."

"I do." I nodded, pushing my stringy damp hair back. "Start talking."

Falon abandoned the brownie, exchanging it for the bottle of scotch beside the bed. He stared at the amber liquid for a moment before opening the bottle and taking a long drink. Looking straight ahead at the TV, which was off, he sucked in a breath and sighed.

"You want to know what happened to me?" Another swig of scotch chased this rhetorical remark. "You, Alexa. You happened to me. In abundance."

Even though he purposely averted his gaze, I angled myself to face him. I punched a couple of pillows around so I could lean on them against the headboard. "I'm listening. Tell me again how I've fucked up your existence."

"You wish it was only mine," he scoffed, snapping his fingers. Immediately the lights went out and we were plunged into darkness. "He's been watching us, Alexa. Bane. He's been watching you."

The large floor to ceiling window showed the city outside. The drapes drawn back, the city lights shone in, casting the only light. The office building across the street stood empty and dimly lit. Traffic on the street below had thinned with the late hour.

"Yeah, I kind of got that impression." Sitting stiff, I watched him lift the scotch to his lips again. Down the hall beyond our door came a woman's laughter followed by a man's hushed tone.

Our room was silent though. Just the sound of the scotch sloshing in the bottle and the mattress as it shifted beneath Falon's weight. He readjusted, sitting up straighter against the headboard. Still not looking my way. A good two feet spanned between us on the giant bed.

"Bane is dangerous. A spoiled brat prince of a demon who's always gotten everything he wanted. Even if that meant taking it using whatever means necessary." He paused, the bitter silence heavy and palpable. Another drink. The bottle was over half drained now.

Studying his silhouette in the trace of window light, I softly said, "I know. I heard the story."

"You heard Shya's version, but even he doesn't know how bad it was. Nobody does. It was a thousand years of reliving the same hell. You'd think I'd have learned after the first dozen times or so to walk away. Break the cycle. But I didn't have the balls. I loved her too fucking much." A vicious laugh fell from Falon's lips. He clutched the liquor bottle in a white-knuckled grip. "And still, I hated her when she was the one strong enough to do it."

Pressing my lips tight together, I didn't dare make a sound. Not yet. He had yet to speak her name, but Falon didn't talk about Winter. Not to me, not ever. I was hanging on his every word.

"I don't doubt that it was no less than we deserved. It was forbidden right from the start. We both had a duty to protect and serve the light. We chose each other instead. It couldn't be both ways." He bit back whatever was about to come next, cutting himself off. After another shot of liquor, he continued with clenched teeth, like it hurt him. "I promised myself I'd never love again. Honestly, I don't even think I have it in me. I've kept my flings with women brief, never letting it go on long enough for anyone to get attached. And it's worked. Until you."

Was I supposed to apologize or something? This had taken me by surprise too. Choosing to continue in silence, I studied the rigidness of his spine. The subtle tremble to his bottom lip marked a man battling a memory.

Falon drained the remainder of the bottle, set it on the bedside table, and turned toward me. The light from the window fell behind him, casting his face in shadows. Having keen night vision allowed me to see the inner turmoil etched on his face.

The pungent aroma of alcohol wafted around him as he moved closer, stopping right in the center of the bed. A foot now between us. Mere inches. Nerves tickled my stomach beneath the weight of his gaze.

"I don't care about your twin or your wolf or anyone else whose bed you're in. None of that has anything to do with me, nor do I want it to." His pause was painful and angry, loaded with emotion I could feel seeping from the cracks in Falon's emotional armor. "But this... Bane. *That* I care about. He wants what's mine, because taking the only person I ever loved from me wasn't enough for him. Now he wants you."

My tongue lay heavy in my mouth. I stared at him, dumbfounded. The underworld had its own set of rules. To the majority I was nothing but a pest, an unnatural with power I didn't have the right to possess. Ownership and claim had always played a large role in the supernatural world. But to have a demon view me as Falon's possession, something to be coveted, well that scared the living hell out of me.

Of course seeing as Arys and I would surely destruct in no time, perhaps I had little to fear from Bane.

Careful, wary of the strange change in the mood, I tried to keep my alarm and confusion from manifesting in my eyes. Whatever he was working up to here, he'd needed a bottle of scotch to do it.

"What are you saying?" I asked, a husky murmur in the quiet hotel room.

Drunk on whiskey and territorial urges, haunted by memories and foes, Falon slid a hand along the back of my neck, into my damp hair. He pulled me close and kissed the corner of my mouth. Lingering.

His hands were on the robe tie, untying and removing it in swift, deft motions. Shoving the robe down, Falon's lips were on my bare shoulder. He grasped the back of my neck, holding me tight, his touch possessive in a way that my wolf recognized as predatory. Carnal. Territorial.

"I'm laying my own claim on you, wolf." Falon's breath came hot against my skin as he made this declaration. "You might have marked me as yours, but in the underworld, you're mine too."

Dragging his gaze to mine, Falon let me see it all. The walls came down, and for a brief but poignant moment, he let me really see him. In those silver orbs lay a thousand secrets. And even more memories. Pain. He carried so much. Thousands upon thousands of years' worth. The things he'd seen and done, so much I'd never know. Lifetimes that he'd lived long before me and would continue long after.

An angel, holy and pure, once. A divine servant. A warrior. Yet not infallible. A fighter, lover, and killer. A traitor. Or so they said. Yet not impenetrable. Falon too carried wounds that shattered the heart and stained the soul.

Falon's silver eyes locked with mine. There was this flicker there, a viciousness I hadn't seen before. Suddenly he grabbed me and tossed me down on my back in the middle of the bed. "You hate it, I know. Trust me, I'm not loving it either."

Tossing the bathrobe to the floor, Falon nudged my legs apart. He wasn't kidding about the whole 'no foreplay' theme tonight. Luckily, it wasn't a problem. The wicked expression he wore was enough to flood me with excitement.

I couldn't help myself. Captivated by the strange turn this had taken, I opened up to him, slinging a leg over his hip. When he hesitated at my entrance, I bit my lip, the anticipation killing me. Not for the moment he took me, but for what he was about to say next.

Falon traced a finger down the side of my neck, swooping back up and around, a pattern I couldn't make sense of. No, not a pattern. A symbol. He was marking me.

I should have been alarmed, but somehow, I trusted him. The realization hit me like a ton of bricks. On some level, I trusted Falon.

Huh. Never saw that coming. Or maybe it was simply the press of his cock against me, clouding my head.

"But you know it's true. And I need Bane to know it too." Falon leaned down to bite the lip I'd just bitten before sucking it into his mouth. Then he filled me with a swift thrust that made me gasp. "You. Are. Mine."

Those words, they reverberated in my ears. Had I heard correctly? Did he really say that?

He was on top of me, pinning me with his weight beneath him, a position I tended to avoid with Falon. Because it was so damn intimate. He knew that. So now it was his power position.

Moving inside me, though gentler this time, there was no mistaking the declaration he made with each thrust. Falon's past had surfaced and threatened his present. This was him protecting it. This was him staking his claim.

Expectantly he watched me. Probably waiting for me to lose my shit. Wanting to mess with him, I smiled up into his face and rose up to match his rhythm.

"Where's your snarky response?" Falon growled, grasping my breast, his thumb flicking my nipple into a taut point.

"Do you want me to argue?" I gasped on a moan. "Want me to tell you that you're an arrogant asshole, and I don't fucking belong to you?"

With a groan he kissed me hard, plundering my mouth with his tongue. "Yes," he whispered against my lips. "Tell me to go fuck myself. Tell me it's not my place to protect you from Bane."

See, now that was something I couldn't say. Bane was his past. His foe. Why the hell should I have to worry about the demon breathing down my neck? I was up to my eyeballs in darkness. Literally. I had my own battles.

Falon's ragged plea was more about him than it was about me. He'd just marked me so all immortals would see me as his. Pretty fast turnaround time for second thoughts.

His name was a sigh on my lips. Legs wrapped tight around his waist, I met his thrusts with frenzied enthusiasm. With clawed fingertips I raked my nails down his back. He moaned in my ear, sending a shudder through me.

"I don't fucking belong to you," I managed to get out around moans and sighs.

His tongue on my earlobe made me pause, trying to remember what the hell I'd been saying. Right. Telling Falon what he wanted to hear. I could call him on his bullshit, but that wouldn't keep this train on the track to orgasmic bliss.

Grinding his pelvis against mine to rub my clit with each stroke, Falon grabbed my chin and forced my head back. Moist, messy kisses adorned my chin and throat. The occasional scrape of teeth sent electric shocks to my groin.

An especially powerful thrust forced a cry from me. Falon buried his face in my neck and muttered, "If only that were fucking true."

Eyes wide, I stared at the lights that scattered across the ceiling from the window. Wrapping both legs tight around him, I held him deep as I came. So many things had changed tonight, including here in this room.

When it was over, Falon didn't say a word. Hooking an arm around my waist, he dragged me beneath the sheets and tucked me in against him, baffling me beyond comprehension. What in the frickin' hell was happening here?

Out of curiosity, I tested his embrace, squirming as if to get away.

His forearm stiffened, rock solid. Immobile. He held me in place, trapped against his body. Against my temple he murmured, "Tell me what happened with Salem."

CHAPTER EIGHTEEN

"Are we fucking cuddling right now?" I hissed into the darkness. There were a lot of things I'd managed to overlook with Falon, but this was not one of them.

He pressed his still hard erection against my ass and muttered, "Do you need my cock inside you just to have a conversation? We're talking. Naked. In bed. Live with it."

Usually we both managed to stick to the mostly unspoken rules of the playbook: Get in. Get off. Get out. At least I liked to get out pretty much the moment we'd finished. Laying there in his arms felt all kinds of wrong. We didn't do this.

I clamped my lips shut tight against the insult that threatened to leap off the tip of my tongue. So he wanted to lay here touching me while I told him about Salem and Lilah. No big deal. Perfectly normal as far as lovers go. Ha. Sure.

Swallowing down the small dose of panic, I tried and failed to relax fully in Falon's embrace.

He pinched my ass, chuckling when I yelped. "Talk, dammit. Don't make me beat it out of you."

So I told him everything. A full recap of events featuring Lilah and Salem. Falon listened attentively, absently dragging a hand up and down my side. He never stopped that simple, repetitive motion, not even when I faltered in the retelling and had to stop to choke down a swell of emotion.

"I'm not surprised that Lilah made such a move," Falon said when I'd finished speaking. "I am surprised that Salem allowed it. There's no way he didn't see it coming."

"It doesn't matter now anyway." My chest deflated under a heart-wrenching sigh. "It's over. She wins. I lose."

A hand on my shoulder, Falon rolled me over to face him. "Is that what you think? That it's over? As long as you have even the smallest speck of light, it's not over."

I wanted to believe him. Willow had said the same thing. They should know, right?

Shadows fell across half of Falon's face, a pale glow of streetlight bathing the other. His wounds were almost completely healed. On the outside anyway.

I touched a faded bruise on his cheek. "What about you? You never really told me what happened with Bane after you left."

He gave a lazy half shrug. "I confronted him on the other side. Found him in his favorite watering hole talking shit. Told him to stay the fuck away from you. A fight was had. We were split up and sent our separate ways. Until next time. Nothing else to tell for the most part."

"For the most part?" I frowned, uncomfortable with the warm twinge in my chest at the thought of him trying to chase Bane off. "Spill it."

A smug smile spread across Falon's face. "I'm glad you asked. During our exchange of witty repartee and jibes, mine far more clever than his of course, Bane happened to mention something. He said once you realized who he was, you attacked him."

Oh, Falon just loved that. Our faces were inches apart. There was no lying or denying. He could already see it in my eyes.

"Yeah…? So?"

"Defending my honor, were you? I'm touched." His smile turned into a full-on smirk.

I wanted to slap it off his face. He was loving this too much. Yet I couldn't lie. I had snapped and gone at Bane. Playing it off like no big deal, I gave him a shove and said, "Oh, don't get hard over it. He's a piece of crap demon. Nobody should have had to go through what he did to you both."

Falon's mischievous chuckle made it hard to keep a neutral expression. He pulled me in against him, face to face this time. My automatic reaction was to sling my leg over him, lining up our groins.

"I'm always hard around you, succubus. You don't make it easy to stay clear headed." He went in to kiss me, but I turned my head, giving him my cheek, a playful avoidance.

Rubbing the warmth between my legs against him, I teased, "The funny thing about that is I've barely used the slightest bit of thrall tonight. Your little show in the bathroom, the missionary weirdness on the bed. That was all you."

"Fuck," he cursed, grasping my chin in a hand, forcing my lips to his. "You are toxic, Alexa. I wish I'd never met you."

A hand lost in his tousled silver hair, I mumbled against his mouth, "Such sweet things you say."

Reaching down between us, I wrapped my hand around his shaft and pressed the tip to my entrance. Every encounter with Falon went like this. Every climax, every wild fuck, it didn't ease our hungers for each other. It fed them.

That pretty much summed up my entire existence.

I teased him by sliding the head of his cock against me, not yet taking him inside. Falon's ragged groan in my ear made me crave more. When at last I took him inside me, he kissed me roughly, a kiss filled with loathing and twisted affection.

Falon wasn't alone in his anguish. I too felt the discomfort of where our fling had led us. This was not love. It never would be. And yet, it was just as friggin' complicated.

Slowly he fucked me. Movements unhurried, like a leisurely Sunday stroll. So much time face to face had me itching to avoid deep eye contact. I buried my face in his neck, breathing him in, tasting the perspiration on his skin.

When it was over, sunrise began to draw near. I started to roll out of the bed only to be held in place.

"Just stay for a few minutes. It's ok not to rush away the second I pull out."

I settled back in the bed, relaxed this time against him. A few minutes wasn't much to ask. What surprised me was when five minutes passed and Falon had fallen asleep. No wonder he'd managed to stay quiet for that long.

Huh. I risked a glance at him. Asleep, chest rising in even breaths, face almost peaceful, Falon embodied a strange serenity. Such a tarnished beauty he was.

He'd fallen asleep next to me. It screamed trust and comfort. Did I want Falon's trust? Had I earned it? Had he earned mine? Should we be this comfortable with each other?

The sudden urge to leap from the bed gripped me. Trying not to rush and disturb him, I disentangled myself from Falon and slipped from the bed. I paused to study him. Sprawled out, the sheets gathered around his lean waist. A work of art broken beyond repair. Tainted now, a product of his environment.

Aren't we all?

Sunrise was less than an hour away. I had to get moving if I wanted to make it home with time to spare. In the bathroom I dressed with the careful silence of a predator who knew how to move with stealth.

A glimpse in the mirror stole my breath. The mark Falon had placed on me was visible. Like silver paint on my skin. Flicking on the light, I leaned in for a closer inspection. A silver feather marked my skin. On the side of my neck but close to the front, easily seen by all. It spanned from just below my jaw to my collarbone.

I ran a finger over the feather, feeling the thrum of immortal energy within its design. As the light moved over me, the silver etched in my skin lit up with a metallic sheen.

Should he have marked me this way? Should I have stopped him? If so, why didn't I feel concerned?

Falon was a guy who came with many warnings from those who knew him. However, most of those people weren't exactly upstanding do-gooders themselves.

Gathering my things, I headed for the door. When my fingers touched the handle, Falon's voice cut through the room. "I'll see you at sunset, wolf. I'll be sticking to your ass like glue until this all blows over."

I didn't know if he meant Arys and me or Bane. Or both. It didn't matter.

Opening the door so the hall light streamed into the room, I nodded. "Falon, if this mark brings more trouble my way than it deters, I'll gut you with my bare hands and feed your insides to vultures. Catch you later, lover."

CHAPTER NINETEEN

The dark over the horizon had just started to thin when I pulled into my driveway. Beating sunrise had become second nature, a combination of instinct and timing. Having several minutes to spare, I stood in the front yard for a minute, staring at the house.

I could feel him in there. Arys. A mass of black inside my head, my heart. Reaching out to draw me in.

For just a second I faltered, wavering on my feet. I flung out a hand to stay upright as vertigo spun me upside down. Maybe I shouldn't have come home. Spending the day alone in the hotel wouldn't have necessarily been safer. Not with so many humans in the building. If I lost it and went on a bender... Ugh.

No. I couldn't run from Arys forever. If we were going down, then it had to be together. That's what I told myself when I opened the door and walked into the house.

Only to be met by an eerie silence. I kicked my boots off and closed the door, loud enough to announce my arrival. Wherever Arys was, he didn't need an announcement. He felt me too.

Following the vibration of my dark flame, I descended the curved staircase to the basement. I reached the bottom, passed the laundry room, and turned the corner to find Shaz and Jenner standing outside the large unfinished room. The heavy-duty metal door that used to hold me in there during a visit to Shya was closed and locked from the outside.

"How the hell did you manage to get him in there?" I nodded to the metal door, eyeing the small slot where one could see through. It was slid closed.

"With great fucking difficulty." Jenner swiped a hand over a gash on his brow.

Both of them looked me over with open scrutiny, seeking and finding. Jenner prodded my energy, sampling it for himself. Tasting how dark I was now.

Shaz searched my eyes for inner wounds. For the bleeding soul within. I threw myself in his arms, letting my wolf weep her pain to his. So tight I held him. Just feeling the warmth of his skin. The wolfish scent of him. The best friend who'd become the love of my life.

He stroked my hair and murmured, "It's going to be ok, Lex."

He didn't have to say anything else. Shaz just let me cling to him. The scent of Arys's cologne faintly lingered on his clothes. It made the ache downright crushing.

When I'd soaked up as much comfort from my white wolf as I could, I turned to the door. I could feel Arys there, on the other side, waiting for me to open the tiny window. I shouldn't do it; I should go upstairs.

"How bad is it?" I asked in a hushed tone. "What are we dealing with here?"

The two men exchanged a look. Jenner spoke first. "He's not rabid or crazed if that's what you're thinking. It's worse than that."

"Worse? How so?" Confused, I glanced at Shaz for clarity.

"He's like a concentrated form of incubus," Shaz said. "Everything he already was, amplified. We almost lost him when he mind fucked both of us on the way down here."

Jenner glanced uneasily at the metal door. "Nobody should be alone with him."

"I need to talk to him." I fidgeted, unable to stand still. Being this close to Arys had me vibrating. No mere door between us affected that.

"Can I just ask," Jenner began, "what is on your neck?"

Oh, right. There'd be several people wanting to know. I started to touch the feather, then stopped myself. "It's a mark that will either protect me from a demon with a hard on for Falon or make me that much more appealing. Guess we'll see." I didn't mean to be so flippant, but with my other half so close and the dark fog swirling in my head, I couldn't give much thought to the silver feather.

"That sounds risky," Jenner commented.

Shaz said nothing. He merely brushed my hair back to better see Falon's mark. His eyes revealed nothing. If he thought it was a mistake to allow the mark, he knew this wasn't the time to say so.

"Everything is risky." Reaching for the metal slider, my hand shook. I drew it aside quickly, then stepped back, afraid to be too close to the door.

The slot was too small to even put a hand through. It wasn't a grab I feared. It was looking into those eyes.

All I could see was a pile of blankets and a mattress on the floor, left there from my brief time suffering under Shya's curse. I waited, tense, knowing that Arys had a flair for the dramatic.

"How lovely of you to come, my wolf." That velvet smooth voice oozed sinister intentions. Still he hadn't stepped into view of the door. "It wasn't so long ago that we discussed this very thing, was it? One twin caged by the other. It's fitting, I guess."

I swallowed hard and said, "It wasn't supposed to be this way. We were supposed to be different."

A pause. He wanted to make me squirm and it worked. My spine prickled. My gut clenched.

"I guess we're not so special after all." Suddenly he was there, in front of the door. "Come inside, my love. Let us finish this once and for all, hmm?"

Behind me, Shaz stiffened. Like an aroma, Arys's ink black vibes wafted forth to envelope us like a cloud of smoke. The hypnotic pull drew me closer.

I met his midnight blue eyes through the tiny window. "It's not over yet, Arys. I still have a link to the light. I'm not giving up."

Gaze narrowed, he studied me. No, there was nothing rabid in his eyes. Quite the opposite. Instead he was calm and cool. Smooth as sin.

"You've been with Falon. I can feel him all over you." Absolute wickedness flashed across his face. His sexy grin bared fangs. "I bet you still taste like him, don't you? Let me taste you, my wolf. Let me taste him on you."

That dirty request sent a shockwave of heat to my groin. It didn't matter that I'd just screwed such urges out of my system with Falon. The power in that incubus command made my blood hot.

"Stop it," I hissed, shoving away from the door.

His sinister laugh followed. It reached inside me. My head. My soul. All around. I got the sudden irrational urge to dig him out of me with my own claws.

"Don't play coy with me, Alexa," Arys admonished. "I get off on knowing you've fucked another man, and you love that. Get your sweet ass in here so I can ravish you."

Was my hand moving toward the door? Yes! I snatched it back and reached for Shaz. He took my hand and held it tight.

I choked on a swell of desire. Arys exuded it like a toxic oil spill. It poured over the atmosphere, soaking it. "Look, Arys, I need to know that you're still with me on this. You promised not to give up, but I don't see you fighting this."

He eyed me through the slot, back far enough that I could see most of his face. So I didn't miss the telltale twitch in his jaw. "For the first time since I first took you to bed, I don't hear that annoying fucking voice in my head. The light. And I've got to say, I don't miss it."

Panic stabbed my heart. "Arys…"

"It's over, my love. We lost. Do us both a favor and end it already." Cold and hard, his expression became a mask of indifference. The person looking out at me through those familiar eyes, I didn't know that person. It scared the hell out of me.

Wounded, a tiny part of me wanted to crumple. But the part of me that wanted to bitch slap the look off his face was bigger and angrier. "I'm the one who links light and dark, and I still have them both. If anyone is going to figure this shit out, it will be me. So I'll damn well decide when it's over."

A stare down ensued. The dark had made Arys it's bitch. Not me. Not yet. Oh it crashed through me like a storm now more than ever before. Having no beginning and no end, just a constant flow circling through me, patiently wearing me down. I refused to let it have us both. As long as it didn't, we had a chance.

A monster lurked in Arys, staring out at me. Refusing to allow me even a glimpse of the man I knew inside the killer, the dark sought to take me too. It raged in me, demanding that I play its game. I wanted to. Of course I did. The murderous intention in my dark lover's eyes was enough to keep me fighting.

"This is me, Alexa. This is who I am. Who I've always been. The darkness." Low and menacing, Arys spoke through clenched teeth.

"No, it's not," I argued, straining against Shaz's hold on my hand. "You are not total darkness."

The intensity in his intimidating stare grew uncomfortable. Love and hate lived there. "You know me. You always have."

My jaw dropped. I remembered the night he'd said that to me. When the darkness raged in us both one night while reading his journal. That same night he'd told me that he wanted to see terror in my eyes.

So badly I wanted to tear my gaze from his. He'd see the wound he'd just caused. I didn't want that. Too late.

"I'm going to fix this," I promised, voice raw with emotion I couldn't rein in.

An ugly scowl twisted my vampire's face into something I didn't recognize. "Maybe I don't want you to fix this. Maybe I'm just done with it."

Cold. So damn cold.

Knowing a fight was what he wanted, I turned away and fled up the stairs. It wasn't really him speaking. That's what I told myself. We'd flung barbs at each other before. This was nothing.

It felt like everything. It felt like the end.

* * * *

Hours passed. I lay in my bed staring off at nothing. Blackout curtains kept the sun's light outside. Shaz lay beside me, struggling to stay awake despite my insistence that he get some rest. Arys and I took a lot out of him.

The man could only take so much. Eventually he succumbed to slumber's demand. I glanced over at him, studying the outline of him next to me. His deep, even breathing comforted me. I wanted to be able to snuggle in against him and pretend that we didn't really have my lover locked up in the basement.

Thanks to constant dark urges, I also kind of wanted to tear his throat out.

Shaz and Jenner had followed me upstairs after Arys chased me off. He needed some time alone with himself. Or maybe that was the last thing he needed.

Jenner had lingered on the main floor. Heavy curtains kept the main floor dimly lit but free of direct sunbeams. He'd volunteered to make sure Arys stayed put. Shaz and I had gone to my bedroom where we'd talked for a long time.

We both agreed we needed a short-term plan, a new keystone perhaps? Something to keep the spark of light I still possessed from being engulfed entirely. Still, that would only buy us a shred of time.

I cursed Lilah and Salem, hating them both. Hating her for being exactly who she'd always been. Hating him for loving her anyway. For letting her ruin Arys and me.

I'd cried to Shaz. He'd tried hard to be the rock, letting me fall apart. But I could see the cracks in his exterior. He was wearing down too.

The entire time we sat on my bed holding each other and talking, all I could think about was Arys. Two floors below. Surrounded by concrete walls, stewing over how much he hated everything we were. Just like Lilah.

Just thinking about it made me sick. It also made the incessant tugging in my fragmented heart that much more insistent. Unbearably so. That silver soul thread joining us rippled and shook. It gave me a headache.

I needed to see him. Which was ultimately why I'd waited for Shaz to fall asleep. So I could slip from the bed in silence and go downstairs. Of course, I still had to get past Jenner on the main floor. Maybe he'd be passed out on the couch.

After tugging on a pair of comfy, loose lounge pants and Shaz's t-shirt, I left the bedroom without a sound. I paused at the top of the stairs, listening for Jenner. Voices from the TV drifted down the hall from the living room.

Slow, picking my steps carefully, I eased down the stairs to the main floor. The basement was near the front door, the opposite direction from the living room. As long as he wasn't in the kitchen, he'd never see me go down there.

I reached the last step and kept going. My movements were sly and smooth. Soundless. I rounded the corner to the basement and came face to face with Jenner at the top of the stairs.

Apocalyptic

"Where do you think you're going?" Arms crossed, he came at me, bumping me with his forearms in an attempt to herd me back down the hall.

"Get out of my way, Jenner. I have to go to him, and I'm not going to let you stop me." I let him back me up a few paces before I planted both feet and held my ground.

When I moved to go around him, he moved with me. "No can do, Alexa. I need the two of you back in Vegas. Yeah, that's selfish. I know. But it is what it is. If you go down there, neither of you will come up alive."

To be fair, Jenner was probably right. Also, yes, he was a selfish dick. I doubted he cared all that much about Arys and me. His biggest concern was saving his own ass back home. No, that was unfair. Jenner had been there for us back when Arys had killed me. He wasn't all bad.

Too bad for him, my dark side didn't give a shit. I didn't think, just acted. Throwing a hand in Jenner's face, I guided the power with intent and dropped him like a sack of bricks. I tried to catch him on his way down so he wouldn't smack his skull on the floor. Then I stepped over his unconscious body and took the basement stairs two at a time.

Outside the heavy metal door, I stopped. I just stood there, staring at the tiny window, now closed. Feeling him there on the other side.

Opening the door would be suicide. I just wanted to be close to him. With a hand against the cold metal, I sank to the floor. Drawing my knees up, I leaned against the wall next to the door and sighed.

Hand pressed to the door, head dropped back against the wall, I let the despair take me. On the other side I felt him. A sudden shock of electricity zapped through my hand and up my arm. The door chilled beneath my touch, cooled from the other side.

Arys's hand was there, pressed to the door against mine. Just a few inches of metal between us. A single red tear rolled down my face.

This couldn't be us. Reduced to desperate caresses through a goddamn door. Because death awaited us both when we next touched.

He couldn't help himself. Not anymore.

Without Salem's help, I just couldn't puzzle out how to repair the damage done. I didn't want to give up the fight, but I couldn't help the inner voice that wondered, *Is it really over?*

"I need you," I whispered.

It felt like I was now in this fight alone. I couldn't imagine how we'd make it through the next twenty-four hours, let alone beyond that.

"I miss you." Arys's declaration coaxed forth a few more tears. First I heard it inside my head, his seductive whisper in my mind.

Then it came from above. The window slot was open. Willow had warded the door when I suffered Shya's curse. Falon had reinforced the ward since. Arys couldn't use power to get out. The door had to be opened from the outside. It didn't stop him from getting inside my head.

He sounded like himself again. I wanted so bad to believe he was still in there. That it wasn't just a devil wearing his face.

"Please don't leave me," I begged, my plea ending as my voice cracked. On the floor, emotionally spent, I begged my twin flame not to give up. "I can't do this without you."

"I'm right here." A pause. "We should be together. I need to feel you."

The longing for him grew strong enough to make me nauseous. We had to be together. It wasn't optional. We'd go mad without each other.

We couldn't be alone together either. One touch shouldn't have been so risky. Was it a risk worth taking?

I jerked my hand from the door. Listening to his alluring tone encouraged me to go to him. To open the door and fling myself in his arms. To hell with everything. If destiny wanted us, it could take us. I was done fighting.

No, that wasn't me. I didn't give up. Not until it was over.

This was not over.

When I didn't respond, Arys said, "Come to me, my wolf. Let me love you."

The simplest of requests uttered with sincerity and want. As if I were hypnotized, I reacted. So easily he'd gotten in my head. He lived there. I was too dark to resist him now.

Pushing to my feet, I grasped the door handle. My fingers worked the locks. First one, then another. There were half a dozen.

Before I could flip the last few, Shaz flew down the stairs in a blur, shouting my name. He body checked me, knocking me away from the door. He relocked every lock I'd opened, slammed the window shut, and grabbed me none too gently.

A commotion on the other side of the door got us both moving. Arys melted down, pissed off that his attempt to be sweet and manipulative had been thwarted.

Shaz dragged me along with him up the stairs.

Jenner sat on the floor at the top, rubbing his temples. He glanced up with a scowl as we passed.

Once we were back on the main floor, Shaz crushed me against his chest, stroking my hair. "Lex, what the hell were you thinking?"

"I was thinking that I can't stand to be away from him for another second, and I don't care how it ends anymore." Apathetic and listless, I stared at my white wolf, wondering why I couldn't bring myself to care as much as he did. "I'm tired, Shaz. Tired of all of it."

"No. It's not ending that way." He shook his platinum head, hands shaking with adrenaline as he held me. "No fucking way. Not on my watch."

CHAPTER TWENTY

"Alright already," I snapped. "I'm going."

Temper short, I threw my phone into my bag and glanced about for the Dragon Claw before questioning if I was in the right frame of mind to have it on me. I might stab it through just about anyone at this point.

"Lex, you know you can't be here with him. We just spent the entire afternoon talking you down from the ledge. Go to Willow and decide with him what our next move should be." Ignoring my angry stomping about, Shaz grabbed my shoulders and turned me to face him. "I'll come with you."

"Like hell you will." Perched on a stool at the kitchen island, Jenner shook his bleached blond head. "Nobody should be left alone with Arys at this point. If you both leave, I'm leaving too."

I had to agree with that. Arys was too dangerous to be alone with. So was I. Which was the main reason I couldn't let Shaz get in a car with me. If Jenner hadn't been with us all afternoon, I'm pretty sure I'd have taken a bite out of my wolf.

Not the good kind either.

When I nodded my agreement, Shaz relented. "Fine. I'll stay with Jenner. Keep in touch. If you don't check in, I'm coming to find you."

"Ok." I accepted his kiss, both ashamed and delighted by the sudden urge to throw him down beneath me and drain him dry in more ways than one. When we pulled apart I averted my gaze so he wouldn't see the darkness in my eyes.

Shaz walked me to the door and waited in the open entryway while I descended the front steps. "You're going to make this right, Lex. I know you will."

His confidence put a genuine smile on my face. I only wished I could be so sure. Pausing near my car, I said, "The only reason Arys and I made it this far is because of you, Shaz."

Apocalyptic

Driving away from the house, from my dark flame, it killed me. I hit a train crossing through the middle of town. Forced to a stop as it flew by, I considered turning around and going back.

Back to my house, to Arys. To whatever lay in store for us.

A glance in my rear-view mirror showed a few cars behind me. No problem pulling a U-turn. Everything inside me demanded that I go back to Arys.

"Don't even think about turning around." Falon's voice from the passenger seat startled me. At my screech, he laughed. "Why so surprised? I told you I'd be stuck to your ass once the sun set."

"Do not startle me like that." I punched him in the arm with the strength of my irritation. "I'm walking a very fine line tonight."

He winced and rubbed the spot below his shoulder. "Then I showed up right on time. Where are we headed?"

The train came to an end. I stared straight ahead, focusing on the road in an attempt to tune out the inner demand to return home. "The Kiss. To see Willow. I need a new plan and I need it now. Arys and I may not last another night."

"I'm a little surprised you made it through the day actually. How did that go?" Totally nonchalant, Falon adjusted his seat, getting comfortable.

The sense of chill he projected didn't quite make it into his question. It sounded too genuine. Like he actually cared.

"Don't do that," I huffed, fingers tightening on the wheel. "Don't pretend to care."

Out of the corner of my eye, I saw him turn to look at me. Since I didn't want to drive off the road, I couldn't make out the expression he wore. I felt studied. Assessed. I did not like it.

"Maybe I do care. Would it bother you?" A challenge in that loaded question but also curiosity, Falon taunted a beast with teeth who would use them.

I scoffed, forcing some extra disgust into the sound. "Of course it would bother me. Since when do we care about each other?"

Merging onto the highway increased our speed, keeping me from having to glance his way. I busied myself with shoulder checking and following all road rules like a good little license-toting werewolf. Anything to play off the uncool, serious vibes the angel brought with him tonight.

"I don't know, Alexa," Falon said after a moment of contemplation. "You tell me. You'd never have gone off on someone like Bane if you didn't care."

Now that was a ballsy thing to say. It tripped me up. Kind of ticked me off too. Falon was asking for a world of trouble.

Murderous thoughts flitted through my mind, bringing a devious smile to my face. "Have you ever had your heart ripped out and shown to you, Falon? Think I could pull it off before you disappeared back to the other side?"

His sexy chuckle reminded me of a king size bed in a four-star hotel with a killer bathtub. "You're a riot, you know that? Giving a shit whether you live or die doesn't mean I loathe you any less. In fact, the more I give a shit, the more I loathe you."

I thought about that for a moment. "Yeah, that sounds about right."

The rest of the drive into the city center to The Wicked Kiss was spent with Falon needling me every chance he got and me threatening every colorful form of violence I could dream up. By the time we arrived, he'd succeeded in coaxing a genuine laugh from me.

The second I walked into the nightclub, I was hit with the harsh reminder of how dire everything had gotten. As I entered with Falon at my side, every vampire in my path all but flung themselves out of my way. Even Justin gave me a wide berth as I passed through the lobby.

"What's that all about?" I wondered, worried they all knew something I didn't.

"Are you kidding?" A fine brow arched in disbelief, Falon looked at me like I'd said the stupidest thing he'd ever heard. A look I received often from him. "I'm shocked you aren't spewing black fire out your fingertips. You reek of darkness. Your eyes are blue and your hair has a black streak. If I were a vampire, I'd be getting the hell out of your way too."

I jerked to a halt, causing a waiter following us to do a little jig in order to avoid spilling the tray of drinks he carried. "There's a black streak in my hair?"

In a panic I flipped my hair over a shoulder and sifted through it. There was indeed a chunk of black mixed in with my ash blonde. I followed it up the side of my head, an inch or two back from the front.

Apocalyptic

When did I last look in the mirror? This morning? I'd been in such a rush to leave the house with Shaz ushering me out the second the sun sank out of sight. Wouldn't he have said anything if he'd seen it? The blue eyes, ok that had been happening for a long time. But my hair? No deal. That's where I drew the line.

"I can't fucking believe this," I muttered, staring at the black strands twisted in with the blonde. The same raven shade of Arys's hair.

Salem came to mind, and the lock of Lilah's hair braided into his hair. At least, I'd always assumed it was her hair. Maybe it was just her darkness, taking over him. *Son of a bitch!*

"Don't sweat it. Let's go talk to Willow." Taking my elbow, Falon forced me to get moving to avoid being dragged along beside him.

Willow watched us approach, his face so perfectly neutral that I knew it was fake. Whatever he thought of my current state, he was keeping it to himself. With a word to the familiar woman at his side, he left her to join us.

Two nights in a row with the pink-haired lady? Interesting.

"I've been worried sick about you," Willow said, keeping his distance. When our eyes met, his pupils dilated. I'd barely breathed in his direction.

"I don't know what to do, but I need to do something, and I need to do it fast." I also needed to slaughter every human in the place. My gaze wandered as I eyed up a broad-shouldered guy near the pool tables.

Not a single vampire dared to meet my stare. They busied themselves, escaping to a back room or the dance floor. Anywhere that wasn't near me.

Willow pinned Falon with an accusing scowl. "Was that really necessary?"

For a moment I didn't know what he meant. Right. The silver feather on my neck. Not nearly as concerning to me as the black in my hair. I'd willingly accepted the feather.

"Bane wants her, Willow," Falon shot back, venom in his retort. "Do you have a better idea?"

"Marking her like your fucking property would not have been it." Willow's temper flared the way it always did around Falon. His proximity to me seemed to enhance it.

"So what's your better idea? I'll gladly remove it if you can come up with one. It's not like you can mark her for protection anymore." Falon was all too happy to deliver that low blow.

Annoyed by their bickering, I waved a hand to cut them off. "Could we maybe worry about Bane when he's actually the most immediate problem? Because if I go full dark side, I'll probably join him just for the fun of it. Priorities, guys. Leave your egos out of it."

"Just tell me one thing," Willow said, ignoring the dirty look the fallen angel shot him. "Did you allow it?"

"Yes, Willow. He did not force it on me. Otherwise I'd be standing here with his ball sack in my hand." Both men shrank back at my flippant remark and its colorful visual. "If you help me not lose myself completely, then you can rip me a new one about the mark later. Ok? But I don't have that kind of time right now."

Hell no I didn't. Everything about Willow was setting me off. His hybrid vibe created an itch beneath my skin. An itch I could only scratch by tasting him.

Gritting my teeth, I turned away, trying to put space between us. I shielded hard to block out Willow's tempting vibes, but it was like using a screen to block out smell. It just didn't work.

The energy in the building became a constant throb in my head. Too many sources and temptations. Every hunger I possessed was triggered. I shoved through the crowd for the exit. I had to get out of there. Leaving Falon and Willow gawking after me, I took off like a madwoman, tossing people aside.

I would kill them all if given the right opportunity. The potential for such a slaughter lived in me. It always had. Now there was nothing to keep it at bay.

Well, almost nothing.

As I burst through the door into the parking lot I ran straight into the hard body of a tall, tan guy who smelled of testosterone and cologne. Human. A heartbeat. It echoed in my ears, loud and insistent.

"Sorry." He smiled apologetically and tried to go around me.

On autopilot, I snatched his wrist in a near bone-crushing grasp and yanked him to a stop. He stared at me in fear and wonder, under my thrall and I hadn't done a damn thing. Hot on my heels, Falon emerged behind me and pried my fingers from the man's wrist before shoving me along to the dark end of the parking lot where neither human nor vampire lingered. Willow quickly caught up to us.

"Is your other half as much of a handful as you are?" Falon released me when we were a safe distance from the front of the building. Then he too put some distance between us.

"Worse, I presume. He's locked in my basement." Looking at the two of them keeping their distance both from each other and from me, I couldn't help the wicked ideas that came to mind.

Falon let out a low whistle. "Locked in your basement? That's some twisted Lilah and Salem-level shit."

"I'm so sorry, Alexa." A hand on the bridge of his nose, Willow squeezed his eyes shut and swore.

"Whatever. It's not like we didn't know it would come to this." Nibbling my bottom lip, I eyed them each in turn. So many ways to enjoy them. All that power. I wondered how easy it would be to get them to agree to a Falon and Willow sandwich.

Falon snapped his fingers to get my attention. "Stop looking at us like that, wolf. I'll render you unconscious before I let you rope me into a three-way with the most uptight angel I ever met."

I snickered. "We'll see about that."

Edging even further away, Willow stuffed his hands in his pockets and stared at his beat-up Vans. "Another keystone would be a temporary fix, but it's just a patch job at best. It won't fix the unbalance. This isn't something I've encountered before. You and Arys are like no other twins. I'm not sure what to do. I'm sorry, Alexa."

His remorse for something that wasn't his fault brought me temporarily back down to earth. "Willow, stop with the sorry. None of this is your fault. You did everything you could."

"For nothing," he muttered into his chest. "To watch you self-destruct. I call that a failure."

"I call it love." I took a step toward him but froze when his head jerked up and he stiffened defensively. "No matter what happens, I'll never be anything but grateful for everything you've done for me."

Falon snorted. "Is this a friggin' *Hallmark* movie? Can we skip the heartfelt declarations and get to solving the damn problem?"

A swell of irritation fueled the glare I shot him. "Well we tried it your way, Falon. I'll give you credit for being right, but Lilah ruined everything. So unless you have something new to add, keep your trap—"

"Arys has to kill you. Again." Pausing to ensure he had my full attention, Falon added, "Fulfill your destiny to destruct. See it through. You might be surprised how it's really supposed to end."

He'd stunned me into silence. Did the fallen angel want me dead? Surely he couldn't be serious.

While I pondered the implications of Falon's claim, Willow crackled with a surge of angry energy. "That's rich, Falon. You're a bigger piece of shit than I thought you were. You have no authority to make such claims."

The staff parked down at this end of the lot. I leaned against Justin's truck, needing something to support me. "That's your big solution? How is death going to save me?"

"You're the queen of light and dark, Alexa. Get that through your thick head. I'm sick of repeating it." Silver wings flared wide, cloaking Falon, they formed a warning to Willow. But his silver gaze slashed through the night at me alone. "You're the link between life and death. Only you. So go there, to the brink where they meet. Find your lost light."

I stared at him, aghast. Then I laughed. He had to be fucking with me. "Either you've lost your mind, or you just want to see me as ashes."

"Or maybe," Falon challenged, a haughty lift to his chin, "I know what I'm talking about, and you should listen to me."

"She would die, Falon," Willow admonished, horror etched onto his innocent face. "If she treads too close to death, her body could turn to ash. There's no bringing her back from that."

The fallen angel kicked an empty beer bottle. It skipped across the parking lot and shattered against a garbage bin. "In case you haven't been paying attention, Willow, these rarities tend to walk through fire and not get burned. If anything, it makes them stronger. Their calling keeps them alive until it's fulfilled. If it's not her time, then it's not her time."

Eyes narrowed, Willow rubbed the stubble lining his jaw. "Sounds like a pretty way of feeding her a load of bullshit."

Apocalyptic

The two of them eyed one another, something unspoken passing between them. I glanced from my fallen angel to my guardian, curiosity blooming.

Turning his penetrative gaze on me, Falon held out both hands, imploring me to trust him. With a rustle of feathers his regal, intimidating wings resettled around him. "You have to stop running from death. It will never stop chasing. Stand your ground and face it. If it is not your time, it cannot take you."

I looked to Willow for a reaction. If he said Falon was talking shit out his ass, then I'd believe him. "Willow?"

My former, and in some ways current, guardian paced a small circle. He had the hardest time looking at me. I tried to shut down whatever they could feel seeping from me, shielding hard myself.

"There's truth in his theory," Willow admitted, struggling like it hurt. "People like you, who are called to great power, always face trials of some kind. Many of them have stood toe to toe with death itself and come out the other side. But there's no guarantee. At some point, when faced with death, it will be the final time."

"Bleak as fuck," Falon quipped. "Good job, guardian. I'm impressed with your positive spirit and can-do attitude. Let's put that shit on posters."

"And what makes you so fucking sure it wouldn't be a suicide mission?" Emotion overcame Willow and his shout rang through the parking lot.

Tension thrummed wildly between them. I could see it if I focused hard enough. The atmosphere came alive with each man's enticing vibes. I stiffened, ready to shove away from the truck if they went at each other.

"Because it's my fucking job to know things," Falon fired back, his temper rising, wings flaring wide. "It's what I do. I deal in information, and you should know how powerful the right information can be."

Willow's head snapped up, and he prowled toward Falon. Power danced in his hand. "Nobody could possibly know for certain the outcome if Alexa was to do this. It's too risky."

"It didn't take you long to lose your faith, did it?" With a judgmental head shake, Falon held out a hand, inviting whatever Willow wanted to throw at him.

What Willow threw wasn't power or a punch, but it had to have hurt just the same. "You're no better than me, Falon. You have nothing to lose either way. What do you care if she lives or dies? She's nothing to you but an outlet for the emotional baggage you can't get rid of. A fixation. You don't love her."

Falon had worked many years to shut down his emotions, especially when it involved Winter or reference to her. I'd glimpsed the pain he still harbored in bits and pieces when it overtook him. He'd never allow someone like Willow to see that side of him, but one thing he couldn't quell was the anger. Being reminded of Winter by anyone at any time never ceased to piss him off.

"No, I don't love her," Falon retorted, taking a menacing step toward Willow. "I have my own reasons for caring, but I do care."

This wasn't good enough for Willow. He'd struck a nerve and he wanted to keep hitting it. "Why the hell should Alexa, or anyone else for that matter, trust you, Falon? There's a reason they call you a traitor. Maybe we should explore your motives a little more closely."

When the two of them started swinging and throwing psi attacks, I probably should've tried to break it up. Instead I saw my opportunity and took it.

Slipping away down the darkened alley, I let the bloodlust guide me. To the next street over, where the party crowd was drifting from bar to bar. Falon would catch up to me eventually, but the two of them should keep each other busy long enough for me to bleed some lucky human.

I didn't want to wrap my mind around what Falon had said. It terrified me, because it had felt like truth. But I didn't know if I was ready yet to stop running from death. I'd escaped it once. I couldn't help but feel that death would not let me go so easily a second time.

CHAPTER TWENTY-ONE

I mourned the destruction of Arys and me. I ached for him with every fiber of my being: body, mind, and soul. I mourned all that I knew we could be. Everything meant for us that we would never see before the darkness gunning for us consumed us entirely.

I also mourned the loss of a man I should never have loved the way I did. The one that instinct demanded I turn to in these times, to bury my weakness in the solace of his desperate desire. But I could no longer do that.

Kale was dead. God, how I missed him.

Arys and I were well on our way to self-annihilation. And me, I was staring at the bloodless corpse of the man I'd followed through an empty parking lot. Now I had a body to get rid of. The not so fun part of giving in.

"Well, that's unfortunate," I muttered, casting an irritated glance at the blood spatter on my clothes. The sudden smile that stretched across my face reeked of malice. It didn't feel like me but something rooted deeper within. Something dark as fuck and hellbent on having me.

Staring at what was left of my victim, I laughed. The giddy high left me loopy and without care. Which had been the goal.

This party was just getting started. What I needed now was a good hit of werewolf or maybe vampire. No sense ruining a perfectly good high by coming down.

The chilly late winter air moved, the atmosphere shifting in response to Falon's arrival. Scowl already in place, he took my chin in his hand and searched my eyes. "High as a fucking kite. Don't you ever get tired of being so stupid and predictable?"

I ran my hands over his chest, another hunger finding its source of satisfaction. Blood and death had taken me to great heights. Falon's fallen essence would keep me there. For hours. Even days if I rolled around in enough of his vast power.

"Don't you ever get tired of that stick up your ass? You're so uptight." Hands sliding down to his waist, I reached beneath his shirt to trace the sexy patch of hair on his lower abdomen. "Let me help with that."

Falon caught my wrist. A brow raised, he tilted his head and gave it a shake. "If your guardian wasn't out here looking for you right now, I'd fuck my name out of you on the cold hard ground like the animal you are."

Jerking my wrist free, I flicked the tip of my tongue over a fang. Eyeing Falon like he was an all-I-could-fuck buffet, I shrugged. "Afraid of getting caught, Falon? I didn't take you for the shy type."

The tiniest slip of suggestive, succubus heat accompanied my snark. I wanted to play with him. Tease him into a frenzy, bring him to the edge. Repeatedly. Until he begged. The wicked darkness slithered through me. Tempting me.

Seeing it in my eyes, Falon shook a scolding finger at me. "You play dirty. I like you dirty, but you're running too hot. You're crossing into dangerous territory."

"As opposed to the safe zone I usually play in?" I challenged, chin lifted in defiance. "Either play with me or beat it. I don't need you to babysit me."

Desire bloomed in his silver eyes. His gaze drifted from my mouth down my body. "Your idea of control is to stay drunk on blood and power as you spiral headlong into the abyss. Someone has to keep you from doing that."

"Oh yeah? And that's going to be you?" Trailing a finger down my neck to my cleavage, I hit him with a sultry smirk. It was a weapon. Aimed and thrown with precision.

"Stop that manipulative crap, wolf," Falon hissed. "Your twin is already full dark side. If you're going to bring him back from that, you have to keep your shit together."

With a hand on the back of my neck, he kissed me. A hard, bruising kiss. A taste of the power he had. I wanted it.

I was sick of being told how to deal with Arys, how to deal with myself. I was tired of having no chance to properly grieve the loss of Kale. Like Salem, Lilah, and Arys, I too wanted to give in and stop fighting the constant pull. To lose myself.

Apocalyptic

Falon caught my lip between his teeth, biting just hard enough to sting. "I'm not fucking you tonight. You need to keep a level head right now, and you can't do that with my cock inside you."

A snarl erupted from me. I shoved him away. "Why are you doing this? Saying these things about death and destiny. All this queen of light and dark bullshit. I don't know who it is you think I am, but you're wrong."

"Since when did you stop being a badass and start being such a whiny brat? Suck it up, your highness." Grabbing me around the waist, Falon jerked me hard against him. His kiss was teasing, bare touches with a slip of tongue here and there. "You're a force to be reckoned with, but that doesn't mean shit if you don't own it."

"I can't," I said softly, drawing on his heavy angelic vibes. It left me a little dizzy. "Not without Arys."

Falon kissed my jawline before going lower, biting my neck. The fangless bite didn't pierce skin, but it did send a shock of heat to my groin. "You are the link between life and death. He may be your other half, but you're the one who will save you both. Don't make me tell you again."

"Whatever you say, boss." I wanted him, and I let him see it in my hungry blue gaze. "But let's just say I do make you tell me again. What happens after that?"

"Sometimes I'm quite certain The Circle stuck me with you as a form of punishment." Brows knit together, Falon shook his head and sighed, laying the exasperation on thick. It didn't disguise the way his heart picked up pace or the uptick in the lustful energy cloaking him. "You're about to find out what happens, aren't you?"

Pushing both hands up through my hair, I affected a feigned innocence. "How else could I possibly know? If you're going to threaten me, Falon, the least you could do is follow through."

A war raged behind his eyes. Falon wrestled with himself. Just for a second.

His hands were on me, sliding down to cup my ass, pulling me into his erection. Then my phone rang. The unwelcome interruption drove us apart.

The screen displayed Jez's name.

"Jez, what's up?" I answered, wanting to throttle her for the shitty timing.

"We've got eyes on Gabriel's spawn. She's holed up at that goth club just off Whyte." Jez's voice was breathy, like she moved fast as she spoke. "The one with the creepy back alley entrance. It looks like she's making a move. Our guy thinks she's taken the entire place hostage. We're waiting on confirmation but heading over to check it out ourselves."

I bit back the choice curse words I wanted to hurl. "Call Gabriel. Tell him to get his ass there now. I'm on my way." After ending the call, I turned to Falon. "Guess we'll have to take a rain check on the down and dirty animal sex. We've got to grab Gabriel's offspring before she levels a nightclub."

Falon ambled along beside me, making wisecracks about idiot vampires breeding. I fired off a quick text to let Shaz know where I was headed. When we were in the car on our way to the goth club, Siren's Song, Falon reclined the seat, folding his hands beneath his head.

"There's a chance death will want an exchange, demand a vampire in your place," Falon said out of nowhere. "When you face it—which you will do because you have no other choice—you may want this vampiress alive."

I warmed my fingers in front of the heater out of habit rather than necessity. Spring was right around the corner. From the death of winter to the rebirth of spring, I longed for it. Although I could have done without the symbolic parallels.

"You're starting to freak me out."

A sharp stab in my gut made me suck in a breath. Arys.

Like withdrawal I ached for him in a way that made me sick. One hand tight on the wheel, I opened the window for a cold blast. Something to ground me in the here and now. The heat made my head foggy.

"Good," came Falon's lazy reply. Eyes closed, he relaxed, unaware of the agony twisting my insides. "Then maybe you'll start to take me seriously."

CHAPTER TWENTY-TWO

Siren's Song sat at the end of a busy street known for its night life. Parking was next to impossible. I found a spot on a residential street three blocks away. The walk gave me time to try to clear the constant fog from my head.

Falon didn't leave my side. Like the world's most annoying thorn. When I drifted too close to a passerby, he grabbed my arm and jerked me close. But he too was a continuous temptation.

"Back off a little, would you?" I snapped. "Everyone is a temptation right now. Especially you."

"Flattered. But I've seen how fast you can move when you go dark side. If you give in now, as unbalanced as you are, you may not come back from it. I'm not taking any chances." Annoying as only Falon can be, he proceeded to shadow me like a bodyguard, putting himself between me and anyone we passed.

"Why do you care, Falon?" I taunted him by dropping back a step and sticking a sneaker-clad foot between his slick Italian leather boots. "Because it's your job?"

He tripped but recovered so fast it was like it had never happened. Bummer. With a scowl he grabbed my hand, tightly shoving his fingers through mine. "Because this crap-sucking world needs you. Were you expecting a different answer? Sorry, same one as before. People like you are needed to maintain the balance in this shitty world. It's why your twin flame balance matters so much."

So that was all there was to it. Same story as before. I was needed. He didn't have to like me or care about me to see that. Willow's accusations that Falon didn't love me and had no reason to care had caused some concern. What we had going worked for us. I didn't want that to change. I didn't want him to love me.

"Ok, good. That's good." I muttered to myself, staring at my black Sketchers as I walked. Anything to keep from focusing on the handfuls of walking blood bags we passed as they laughed and talked on their way to and from restaurants and bars.

Falon tugged on my hand. "No worries, queen bee. I'm only interested in what's between your legs. Your vampire and wolf can have your heart."

We found Jez and Smudge outside the goth bar. They were watchful and wary, scoping out the area. Being on task didn't stop Smudge from leaning in to steal a kiss. Relief brought a small sigh to my lips. If anything happened to me, if Arys and I didn't make it through, at least I could face whatever came next knowing that Jez had someone to watch out for her.

Sensing our arrival, she turned to find Falon holding tight to my hand while I all but broke my fingers trying to pull free. "Aww, look how adorable you two are. Since when do hate-fucking lovers hold hands while walking down the street?"

"Since one of us is about one cold-blooded kill away from going full dark side." When we came to a stop next to the ladies, Falon released his hold on me. He stayed close, not trusting me for a second.

I didn't trust me either. Too many thoughts flitted through my head. Too many voices encouraging me to say fuck it.

Jez crushed me close in a hug that filled my nose with her perfume. "I'm so sorry that evil bitch screwed you over. I wish there was something I could do."

"You can." I pulled back before the beat of her heart could convince me to take a bite out of her creamy alabaster neck. "Keep being happy."

Although her heart-shaped face wore a frown, Jez's eyes sparkled with a liveliness I hadn't seen in a long time. "I will. And so will you. Everything will work out somehow. You'll get your happily ever after with your boys."

Falon made a vomit sound so unbecoming and unlike him all three of us stared at him. Unapologetic, he pursed his lips in judgment and gave his head a shake. "You all are a revolting bunch. Like an 80s sitcom's sappy ending. Constantly. Don't you make yourselves ill?"

"And Falon," Jez added as if he hadn't spoken, her tone sardonic. "I'm sure you'll be happily hate fucking each other for years to come. It must be crazy good for you to put up with him outside the bedroom."

Apocalyptic

"Well, yeah," I said with a shrug. "The Circle stuck me with him. Might as well get what I can out of the arrangement. Lucky for me, he's far from virginal. He knows things."

Falon expertly mocked our laughter before snarling, "Are you going to stand around here gabbing all night or actually do your jobs? Pretty much anything could be going on in there. Get your asses inside and deal with that vampire."

"We're waiting on Gabriel," Smudge supplied, checking her phone. "He's on his way. Lizzy sent someone out already with a warning. If we go in without him, she'll start killing people."

"Any idea what she's up to in there?" I eyed the brick building. From this side we could see nothing but darkened windows. The entry was around back, in the alley. Away from the busy street front.

Brushing her black bangs aside, Smudge shoved the phone into the pocket of her leather jacket. "As of the last update she's holding the place hostage using magic. And she's got Gabriel's grimoire."

"Speak of the blood-sucking devil." Falon announced Gabriel's arrival with thinly veiled contempt. "Nice of you to come clean up your mess, kid."

No wonder he hated it so much when I called him kid. After hearing it come from Falon's mouth, I was pretty sure I could nip that in the bud.

Gabriel sauntered up, hands stuffed in the pockets of his long black trench. He didn't waste so much as a glance in Falon's direction. I didn't know what all had transpired between them during the time they'd both worked with Shya, but they didn't seem too fond of one another.

"I'll go in and deal with her." Gabriel's dark eyes met mine. Hunger sparked within them when he looked at me now. "None of you should have to. It's my problem. I'll handle it."

Next to me Falon stiffened ever so slightly. Just enough for me to know he'd picked up on the new link between Gabriel and me. I could just imagine the accusations that would fly later. Wicked ol' me entrapping all the powerful men folk.

"We'll back you up," I said. "She's got your spell book. We don't know what we're dealing with yet."

Gabriel's gaze fell to my throat, seeking my pulse. He spied the silver feather and his eyes narrowed. "Let me go in alone first. Maybe I can talk her down."

"Or maybe you'll get your ass handed to you when she breaks out demon magic all over your ass," Falon hissed. "I'm going in. I'll stay unseen unless it's clear you idiots need my help."

Smudge scoffed. "Supervising. Like usual. You lazy fuck."

With a middle finger extended, Falon vanished. I nodded for Gabriel to go ahead and enter. The rest of us followed him around to the alley entrance but kept our distance. If Lizzy thought he'd come alone, then maybe she'd be more likely to compromise.

I needed her alive. Death's exchange.

Did I believe that? Could I?

I couldn't take any chances. With a muttered, "Shit," I sprinted ahead, catching Gabriel before he could enter the nightclub. My hand on his arm made him spin around defensively. "I need her alive," I blurted. "If death wants a vampire, I need to give it one that isn't me."

There was no time to explain further. He didn't ask me to. But knowing Gabriel, he might already have seen the outcome for Arys and me.

"No worries, Alexa. I've got this. Give me ten minutes." Stealthy and silent, Gabriel left me in the shadows beyond the entryway's meager light.

This alley made a terrible place for a nightclub entrance. The strange quiet here created an eerie vibe despite us being the only ones there. Well off the populated front street, it stretched long and dark. Gaps between buildings gave the impression that someone waited in each of them to grab those who dared to venture here. Sketchy and quiet, the club was aged and unloved, adding to the creep factor. If I'd been human I'd have never stepped foot inside this place.

I watched Gabriel ease through the night like it ran in his veins. I couldn't shake the feeling that he would surprise me yet. "You get five."

Running a hand over her golden ponytail, Jez eyed me with curious green wildcat eyes. "You feel scary dark, Lex. How's Arys?"

Hearing his name stung. It also struck me with a pang of urgency. I needed to go to him. I couldn't. Not unless I was ready for the ugly truth Falon had spoken. And it was the truth. I knew it in my soul. The ragged half that was mine anyway.

"He's locked in my basement," I said by way of explanation. I had no easier way to sum it up. "Pretty sure things are going to get a lot worse before they get better."

"Shit. That's harsh." Hands on her hips, Jez gnawed her painted red bottom lip. "You know I've got your back. No matter what happens."

We exchanged a look, one of those best friend moments that requires no words. So many things passed between us. There was fuck all she could do to help Arys and me.

"I know that, Jezzy. Ditto."

The woman was my partner and closest friend. We'd faced a lot, together and individually. Losing Kale had been the hardest, but we were pushing through, determined not to let anything keep us from becoming who we were meant to be. I couldn't have asked for a better person to have my back.

After several minutes passed the air moved before Falon appeared, chuckling deviously to himself. "And I thought you were crazy," he said to me with a snort. "Gabriel managed to find himself a woman as crazy as Lilah. He definitely needs you in there."

"What's going on?" Sharp and alert, Smudge was all business.

Entirely too amused by the situation, Falon snickered. "Baby vampire has got herself trapped inside a circle with thirteen people she plans to use as sacrifices to summon a vengeance demon to punish Gabriel for his wrongdoing. Unless he agrees to run away with her and live happily ever after. Or some such crap."

"He's not getting through to her?" Unable to share Falon's mirth, I kicked him in the shin. "This isn't funny, jackass. She's got a lot of civilians in there."

"Goddammit, Alexa." Angrily rubbing a dust mark from his pants, he gave me a shove with his free hand. "If you can call royally pissing her off getting through to her. He's not so good at telling people what they want to hear."

"I've noticed." And I had. Gabriel sucked at sugar coating and sweet talking. It just wasn't him. It probably had something to do with his precognitive abilities. Seeing horrible future events in advance must make it hard to fake a smile. "Ok, I'm going in."

Smudge hung back, keeping to the shadows. Watching the alley. Watchdogs didn't usually get involved unless necessary. Keeping the watchdogs separate from the hunters allowed us all to focus our skills where they were best used.

Both a hunter and now a watchdog, Jez fell into step with me, ready to rumble. Falon disappeared as fast as he had come, back inside to lurk unseen.

I half expected some kind of ward on the entry, but we walked right in. A dark, empty passageway welcomed us. Voices murmured in low, worried tones. Fear hung on the air, acrid and pungent. The aroma taunted me.

I swallowed hard, forcing back the blood hunger. Innocent lives were on the line. We already had one crazed vampire to deal with. We sure as shit didn't need two, especially if I was one of them. I had a job to do. Protecting the people Lizzy had taken hostage while also protecting our secret. If I went full dark side, The Circle might not keep me around. Which I suspected was why Falon stuck so close.

We paused where the passageway opened into the club. Dimly lit, painted in all grays, the place lacked any kind of personality or flare. A large metallic disco ball hung over the dance floor, flinging shards of silver light about. Beneath it in the center of a large circle complete with an inverted pentagram stood Lizzy.

Lurking in the shadows, Jez and I scoped out the place. Someone had killed the music or perhaps the DJ. Other than fearful murmurs and the occasional frantic shout that couldn't be contained, the joint was also eerily quiet.

The entire dance floor comprised Lizzy's circle. Inside it with her were the people Falon had mentioned. Outside the circle, trying to talk some sense into her was Gabriel. There were other people sprinkled about, but they seemed to be held in place, gripped either by terror or magic. Most likely the latter.

"How do you want to do this?" Jez asked, a low murmur next to me.

"Let's just watch a sec." Shielding hard to keep my energy veiled, I grabbed Jez's hand to cloak hers too.

Not that Lizzy had any focus left for anyone but Gabriel.

Apocalyptic

He held up an imploring hand, trying to calm her. "Lizzy, we don't need to go down this road. You can choose better. Just come out of the circle so we can talk about it."

"What did you see, Gabriel? What did you see of my future? Because if it doesn't include you, I don't want it." Blood stained Lizzy's face. She'd already killed. Her eyes were wide, pupils huge. Crazy eyes.

"I didn't see anything," he insisted, tone bordering on exasperated. Like he'd said this a few times already. "I don't see something every time I touch someone. It's random. So we'll both be surprised, ok? You have to stop all this first."

Did he lie about the precog touch? I'd never know. Regardless, I'd probably never feel totally comfortable with his ability.

Gabriel was strong enough to destroy her circle. But in her hands was his grimoire, flipped open to a page we couldn't see where we stood. The demon summoning ritual if I had to wager.

"I thought you were different, you know? Not like the others. The ones who just want a quick screw with no strings attached." Lizzy glided about the circle, ignoring those who cringed away from her as she neared. "But you didn't want any strings either. Did you, Gabriel? You came here to cut them."

"It's not like that. Give me a chance to explain." Frustration seeped into his demand. He cut himself short and sucked in a breath, nostrils flaring. His tone took on a sharp edge. "Just get out of the goddamn circle so we can talk."

She flinched at the slap of his command. "Screw you. We have nothing left to say to each other. You've made yourself perfectly clear."

Without another word Lizzy produced an orange dust from the pocket of her trendy suede jacket. She walked among her captives, all huddled on the floor, sprinkling the powder on their heads. A litany of Latin followed with some of the ancient immortal language mixed in.

Inwardly I cursed Gabriel and his damn grimoire. The way I saw it, it just wasn't my problem. I'd do anything I had to in order to keep her from hurting anyone else tonight. But he could get that damn book from her.

"Lizzy, if you go any farther with that incantation, I will take over and use you as the sacrifice instead," Gabriel snarled, fury turning his usually calm features into pure predator.

I tensed. If he lost his temper and forced her hand, he could make the situation worse. The woman was in the process of summoning a demon. A demon he himself had recorded the incantation for.

In response to his threat, Lizzy moved faster about the circle. When each head held an orange dusting, she whirled back to Gabriel. "Don't you remember how we talked about doing something like this? The ultimate fuck you to everyone who messed with us."

Black hair falling into his face, Gabriel eyed her with cold calculation. Seeking an opening. "That was years ago. We were seventeen. Stupid kids. Come on, Lizzy. This isn't a game."

She failed to keep her lip from trembling, but she didn't cry. She was beyond tears, on a crash course with only one end in sight. At this point Gabriel could grovel on his knees, and she wouldn't forgive him. He'd had his chance to love her, and he'd turned it down. Lizzy was going to make him sorry for it.

Jez leaned in, her scent tickling my nose. "Nothing he says is going to help this."

I nodded my agreement, holding my breath against the tempting aroma of leopard with a little kick of something more. I'd never tasted Jez's blood, and I didn't plan to change that. So I gestured for her to enter on one side while I slipped around the corner in the opposite direction. It allowed us to each come up on opposite sides of the circle.

"No, it's definitely not a game." With an enraged shriek Lizzy spun around and slashed open the throat of the man behind her. Her hand gripped a bloody ritual knife. It had appeared as if from nowhere. Damn black magic.

She didn't stop at just one. Four more people went down clutching their gushing throats before Gabriel smashed through her circle. Jez was a blur as she sprinted forward, ready to have his back. I came around from the other side, coming up behind Lizzy.

Gabriel tackled her, and they tumbled to the floor. She turned the ritual knife on him, slashing wildly. The surviving hostages ran for the door.

Apocalyptic

The unfortunate victims bleeding out on the floor were beyond help. Blood pooled in puddles. Rich and dark in the dim light, it filled my nose with each breath.

The two black magic vampires threw each other around the pentagram using both physical prowess and magic. The grimoire hit the dusty floor, and Jez snatched it up.

Every shot of magic thrown fed the growing cacophony in my head. I shrank back, a hand on my temple. Discomfort in my core bloomed into agony. Darkness threatened, hungry for the last of my light. It urged me to allow the bloodlust to take me.

I fought it back. Somehow, that tiny flicker of light still proved to be strong enough to survive the onslaught.

Until Lizzy lashed out with the blade again, this time getting lucky. It nicked Gabriel's side, drawing blood.

Blood that writhed with incubus power. Everything I wanted right there.

I must have lunged at him. I don't remember. The next thing I knew I was flat on my back, staring at the beams in the open ceiling. Silver wings flared overhead, taking over my view. Falon's hand tightened on my throat, holding me down.

Instinctively, I fought against him. Being held down and dominated ignited a whole new fire. My wolf came snarling forth, showing in my eyes and extra-long fangs.

"Settle your crazy ass down, Alexa." Falon added a little extra squeeze for good measure. "Did you not think that claiming Gabriel would affect you as well? You should know this by now. Idiot vampire."

In the pentagram behind us, Lizzy threw spell after spell, but Gabriel countered each one. She simply wasn't as strong or skilled as him. Then she caught him off guard. Pulling a black amulet from her cleavage, Lizzy thrust it toward Gabriel.

Horror spread across his face.

"Didn't think I'd find this, did you? Guess you shouldn't have recorded its whereabouts. I cracked that demon language years ago."

Gabriel backed right off, holding both hands up. He plead for real now. "Lizzy. Don't."

Confused, I struggled to get up, no longer fighting Falon, just wanting to get on my feet. The angel let me up but kept a hand on my arm.

Recognition riveted my focus on that amulet. I knew it well. Because we had Shya trapped inside it.

CHAPTER TWENTY-THREE

A wicked grin stretched Lizzy's face wide, into something creepy and clownish. She dangled the amulet from a silver chain. Wire twisted around the stone in an elaborate design, tying it to the chain. It swung ominously from two fingers tipped with chipped black nail polish.

"I can't imagine you'd want anything to happen to this little beauty." Lizzy eyed the swinging amulet, her lips curled in satisfaction. "Tell me, Gabe, what's it worth to you?"

My heart lodged in my throat. Questions bombarded me one after the other. Where the hell had Gabriel gotten that stone in the first place? It was supposed to be in Salem's possession.

Confusion furrowed Falon's brow. So I wasn't the only one wondering what the hell was going on.

"Whatever it is you want, I'll do it. Ok? You win. Please. Just give me that stone." Even calm and quiet Gabriel couldn't keep the panic from flitting across his face as he watched Lizzy swing the chunk of black obsidian.

It was a delicate stone, fragile really. Although any gemstone would break under the right amount of pressure.

Staring at the black stone, it was hard to imagine my mind trapped in there with Shya. But it had been. I would never forget those visits.

A chill came over me. If she freed Shya... If he got out... I'd be standing right in from of him. Delivered on a fucking platter, so to speak. I'd never stand a chance. Not with the meager light I had left. He would destroy me.

I jerked forward, fear driving me to do anything to stop her. Falon held me back, having to wrap both arms around me to keep me in place. I couldn't let her free that demon. I just couldn't.

But I wasn't the only one with a reason to fear Shya's return. Gabriel too would be on the demon's chopping block. And unlike

Falon, who would face his own vengeance, Gabriel and I would die a final death.

"If you want me to leave with you, I will." Hands held out in surrender, Gabriel took a careful step toward her. "If you want to kill me, I'll stand here and let you do it. All I ask is that you give me that amulet."

Lizzy swung the amulet faster, her gaze never leaving Gabriel. "I don't want either of those things anymore. What I want is to make you suffer. Like you made me suffer. You manipulative asshole."

As the stone moved faster, edging closer to the tips of her fingers, I struggled to break away from Falon. "We can't let her free him," I hissed.

"We won't." Falon jerked me hard against him, his voice a snarl in my ear. "Rushing her like a rabid animal isn't going to keep that stone intact."

I should've been glad that someone was being rational. However, I saw my fate dangling on the end of a pissed off witch's fingers, and I panicked. If that demon escaped, we were all screwed.

"Lizzy, please just—"

She never let him finish. Lizzy twirled the chain faster and faster, the speed making it creep to the very tips of her fingers. Then she let it fly off, directing it up, toward the ceiling. It whipped upward, spinning wildly.

In the same moment the chain left her fingertips, Gabriel attacked. He didn't hold back. One word of the demon's immortal language accompanied the black fire that streamed from Gabriel's palms. It swarmed Lizzy, engulfing her in seconds.

Before I could shout at him to stop because I needed her alive.

At the same time, that all seemed so trivial. It didn't matter now. Not if that stone hit the floor and shattered. Time seemed to slow right down and somehow speed up.

I watched as the black fire overtook the vampiress. She fell back shrieking as it forced its way inside her. Burning her from the inside and out, most assuredly demon magic at its best. Or worst, depending on which side you viewed it from.

Lizzy never stood a chance. In mere seconds the fire had consumed her. Her scream cut off, and her body burst into too many pieces to count. Chunks of gore and blood flew in all directions, turning to dust and ash as it hit the floor.

The black obsidian amulet also made its way downward. Landing right in Falon's waiting palm. That silly poofing trick was pretty damn handy after all.

Overwhelmed and still trying to make sense of what just happened, I reached out blindly to grasp at a barstool near the dance floor. Jez gripped my shoulder, asking if I was alright. I had no words.

Falon recovered first. Not nearly as shocked as the rest of us, he rounded on Gabriel, shaking the stone clutched tight in his fist. "Start explaining and make it good. You're about ten seconds away from joining your girlfriend in ashes on the floor."

That got me moving. I joined Falon, getting between him and Gabriel. A hand on Falon's chest, I forced him back a few steps. He didn't acknowledge me but let me move him. His suspicious silver gaze stayed locked on Gabriel.

Yeah, it was suspicious as fuck that Gabriel had Shya's stone. Had he had it all this time? I'd sure like to know.

I motioned for him to start speaking. "Let's hear it, Gabriel. How the hell do you have Shya's stone? It's supposed to be with Salem."

Gabriel's hands clenched and unclenched. He seemed shaken by what had just transpired too. "The one Salem has is a fake." He paused, either to let us absorb this or decide what he wanted to share. "I switched the stones the night we trapped Shya. You never had the real stone, Alexa. The amulet you passed along to Willow's friend was a fake all along."

Searching his eyes for signs of a lie, I found only truth. "What? Why would you do that?"

"Because he's still Shya's underling," Falon accused, wings flaring with menace. "He's probably been waiting for the right time to let him out."

"That's bullshit," Gabriel retorted, exuding anger. "I saw that Salem would come for it. I planned ahead. Asshole."

I'd touched Gabriel several times here and there. Even a few good grabs by the throat tossed in. He could have had that vision at any time. I wanted to believe him, but I feared Falon was right.

"But the stone you gave me that night, it felt like Shya. His energy. Like he was in there." I just couldn't accept that Gabriel would turn on us now. Or that he'd been playing us all this time.

Gabriel shrugged, offering me nothing but his explanation. Take it or leave it. "I imbued the stone with a trace of his energy, swiped from his feather. It was easy enough. It felt safer not to tell anyone."

"But you didn't see your girl stealing it?" Falon scoffed. "How convenient for you."

"I don't see everything for fuck's sakes!" Gabriel shouted. The air around him thrashed with the heat of his rage.

I held up both hands, silencing each of them. "That's enough. Falon, back the hell off right now. I'll deal with Gabriel. Give me the amulet."

Extending a palm toward the pissed off angel, I waited. He could refuse. He could disappear with it and release Shya himself. Part of me worried he would. Deep down, I didn't know if I could really trust Falon.

He saw it in my eyes. The doubt. Huffing in disbelief, he laughed without humor. "You still don't trust me?" Grabbing my hand, he slapped the amulet into my palm, looping the chain around my wrist for good measure. "I've fucked you until your soul bled, until mine did, and you still think I'd sell you out to Shya? Fuck you, Alexa." Falon stalked away, wings disappearing as he slammed through the doors and into the night.

Ok, I'd deserved that. He was right. We'd never have been able to bear our souls to one another, purging the constant flow of pain and suffering, if there hadn't been some trust involved. No matter how twisted or dysfunctional it might be. I'd seen him on his knees, emotionally spent, begging me for release. Still I believed him capable of terrible things.

But weren't we all?

"I'm gonna go make sure Smudge is handling the hostages ok." Jez excused herself, following Falon. At some point during the brief but intense altercation, the hostages had fled. Smudge would likely have Nova or another immortal alter their memories of tonight.

Apocalyptic

Gabriel and I were left alone. In my hand the amulet grew warm. It hummed with Shya's all too familiar essence. Heavy in my mind when I focused on it, my stomach turned.

Unable to continue touching the stone, I let it hang from the chain looped around my wrist. "Everything you just said, is it complete truth?"

"I swear it is." Looking frazzled, Gabriel shoved a hand into his long hair, raking it back away from his face. "If nobody knew about the fake but me, then nobody could blab. Letting Salem get his hands on the real one wasn't an option. I hope you can understand."

Salem's demand for the Shya stone had never felt right to me. The angel had pretty much forced me into it. Having Shya back in my possession gave me back a sense of security Salem had taken away.

"I do. I can't say I'd have done it differently in your position, but this is your only chance to tell me if there's anything you're leaving out." I held his gaze, demanding truth. "Lies are a deal breaker."

"I didn't lie about anything, Alexa. I just kept the truth to myself, to keep it safe." He flung a hand toward Lizzy's scattered remains. "I'm sorry I couldn't spare her. I just reacted. She was going to set him free."

Disappointed put it lightly. I nodded. "I know. It's just as well. If death wants me, it's not going to accept anything less."

Gabriel watched the stone swing. "If death wants an exchange, offer me."

He was dead serious. That made me uneasy. Someone with a lot to live for didn't so willingly offer themselves up as an exchange for death.

"Not a chance," I said, refusing to even consider it. "I'm done with sacrificing others to save myself. Never again. And you shouldn't be so quick to volunteer."

He huffed a short, bitter laugh. "Nobody would miss me."

"Don't say that. You have a lot to offer. Stay the hell away from demons and you might be surprised just how much." It hurt my heart that Gabriel felt that he didn't belong anywhere with anyone.

Before I could pep talk him further, my phone rang with an unwelcome interruption. Because any interruption at this point meant bad news.

Shaz's voice came frantic in my ear. "Arys is on the move, Lex. He got the jump on us. He's gone."

CHAPTER TWENTY-FOUR

ARYS

Did they really think they could contain me? All three of them knew me better than that. Well, they should have. Overpowering Jenner had been child's play. Too easy. Not even a challenge. He was just so hungry for it. Because of her.

He'd tried to resist at first. I'd gone to places he could barely fathom, and he gave himself over to the want. Once he opened the door, I'd put him on his knees with an arm twisted behind his back. Remembering how he'd screwed my wolf, I flirted with the idea of ripping his damn arm right off and beating him with it.

Shaz's appearance brought a quick end to that plan.

With the ice-cold hand of darkness filling me to the brim, I flung a hand toward each of them. They went down. One shot and I left them both in an unconscious heap on Alexa's basement floor.

Where was my wolf anyway?

Not in the house. Her absence was everywhere, hanging like a noose over my head. Being away from her was the worst hell I'd ever known. And I'd known my share of hell.

It ached like a wound that devoured my soul. Her soul. Our soul. Dear God, this was fucked. We couldn't go on this way anymore. The constant torment, the sick yearning that grew until I screamed in vain attempts to purge her from me.

She could never be purged. We were the same.

And yet not. Just enough to pit us against each other. Self-annihilation. Or perhaps release. Finally.

Didn't she deserve that much? I could give her nothing that she deserved. But I could give her an end to this madness.

Of course, I might as well have some fun with it.

Swiping Shaz's keys from the kitchen table, I'd helped myself to his Jeep. Now with the taste of blood in my mouth, I stood outside the last place Alexa would ever want me to be.

FPA headquarters. The city's old, forgotten hospital. With Juliet O'Brien inside.

Because where else would she be but playing good cop? Pretending to fight the good fight. She was going to fight alright. I wouldn't have it any other way.

I'd come to finish what I started with the younger O'Brien sister. I'd come because a human kill wasn't enough to sate me. Not anymore. But most of all, I'd come to draw Alexa out.

She thought she could run from me? From herself? She thought wrong.

The entity trapped on the property took notice of my arrival. It welcomed me, inviting me in, promising me that what I most desired dwelled inside. Without hesitation I strode onto the grounds. Right away the wickedness there celebrated my impulse.

Alexa would shit a brick if she could see me.

The place was emptier than usual. I could feel it right away. Letting myself in was as easy as walking through the main door. A wave of my hand over the security card slider and the locks disengaged.

Once inside I paused in front of the first camera I spied. Giving it a sly grin, I slipped by. Hunting a wolf.

The first agent I came across leveled his crossbow pistol at me and fired without hesitation. Smart man. Not skillful enough though. I backhanded the bolt aside and grabbed him by the throat. Seconds later his blood hit my tongue, hot and tangy with fear.

I let him drop and turned to the rubble-strewn stairs. Where would the little wolf be? Downstairs in the unsavory lab on the prison lockup level? Or upstairs in the offices, trying to justify her reason for even being here?

Looks like I was going up.

Debris littered the ramshackle deathtrap of a stairwell. Broken glass, chunks of drywall, plumbing pipes, random shit that had no business being there. The FPA had moved into the abandoned hospital because of its condemned status. In order to keep people from creeping around, they'd left it just as they'd found it.

Apocalyptic

Nobody dared to accost me in the dangerous and dark stairwell. Once I emerged on the top floor, I was surrounded by agents. Too bad for them, their manpower had decreased in recent months. Agents had been dying faster than they could replace them. I suspected at this point not many were willing to take a job in our city.

Baby O'Brien stood behind the half a dozen agents who held their weapons trained on me. Waiting for her command. That was her first mistake. Waiting.

Because I didn't.

A flick of each wrist ripped the guns from every agent's hands. A snap of my fingers and all six of them flew backward to slam against walls, doors, and one another. I moved among them, a pure physical force, breaking necks and tearing out carotids.

Until nobody stood between Juliet and me.

"What in God's name are you doing here, Arys?" Gun pointed at my head, Juliet stood her ground. But she couldn't hide the tremble of her hand or the uptick in her pulse. "Where's Alexa? Does she know where you are?"

Licking a smear of blood from the edge of my mouth, I blatantly ogled her cleavage. To be fair, since when does any federal dress code include a top with a plunging neckline and a push up bra? Alexa would kill me if she knew what I was thinking about her sister. Which was pretty much my goal here.

"She will. Any minute now." I surveyed the bodies splayed about the hall. "Is that it? I knew you were hurting for people but damn. All alone now, are we?"

In my ear came a murmur. The entity asked me to remember what she tasted like, and I did. Juliet O'Brien had tasted like forbidden fruit, sweet as sin. That hit of wolf I craved with a hint of something soft and feminine that reminded me of Alexa.

"Don't think I won't do it," she hissed, finger on the trigger. "I don't have a single reason not to."

"Sure you do," I countered, unafraid. She'd never make the shot if she took it. Not before I was on her. "You have Alexa. If you blow my head off, she'll level this place."

Juliet pursed her lips and shrugged. "Guess we'll see. If it's me or you, I'm choosing me."

Arms hanging harmlessly at my sides, I walked toward her. Slow enough for me to enjoy the build-up but fast enough for her panic to grow in leaps. It permeated the air. Fear. Woman. Wolf. So fucking close she was to being all that I wanted.

Just one problem. She wasn't Alexa. Of course, that didn't mean I wouldn't enjoy this.

"I wouldn't expect it to be any other way." The remnants of a small bite on her wrist caught my attention. Briggs. That hypocritical bastard. No different than the rest of us now.

"Why are you doing this?" Juliet demanded. She managed to hold her ground until I got just a little too close for her. Then she started backing up, matching my speed.

I didn't answer right away. My gaze traveled from her full, pillowy lips down to the curve of her collarbone. Her pulse taunted me along with the whispering voice in my ear.

"I have to. For her. For myself." Watching her squirm was starting to make me hard. I couldn't wait for her to bleed. Patience though. It wasn't time yet.

Her brown eyes widened. She risked a glance behind her, assessing how far we were from the office housing the control room. How long it would take her to reach it? Didn't matter. She couldn't outrun me.

"You've completely lost it, haven't you? Where's Alexa? Did you do something to her?" Despite her fear the littlest O'Brien seethed at the thought of me harming her sister. Yet she still hadn't fired off a shot.

"I've done many things to her, sweetheart. And I'm not finished."

The darkness in my laughter made her jump. That's when her finger twitched.

I had plenty of time to dodge the bolt that whipped past my head with several inches to spare. Before she could fire off another, I rushed her. Knocking the gun from Juliet's hand, I reached for her.

She jerked back out of reach, turned, and ran. Down the loud, echoing hall toward the bank of offices.

I gave her a head start.

A familiar sensation in my head stopped me in my tracks. Alexa.

I let her see what I saw. Juliet fleeing me, her boots smacking loudly as she went. Alexa's panic was immediate. It trilled through me, putting an extra spring in my step. I resumed my pursuit with my wolf watching as the distance between her sister and me grew smaller.

'No!' she shrieked, her voice shrill inside my head as if she'd screamed it in my ear. 'If you want me, Arys, you can have me. Leave Juliet out of this.'

'Sorry, sweet. Gotta run.' With the entity cackling in my ear, I shoved Alexa out of my head with enough force to rattle her teeth.

Now she would come.

I caught up to Juliet as she reached the control room. She slammed the door shut, but I kicked it out of her grasp before she could lock it. With a yelp she jumped back as the heavy door smashed against the wall.

One guy sat at a bank of monitors. He spun around in his chair, mouth agape. Juliet shouted at him to run, but he was too stunned. I grabbed his shirt and flung him from the room before slamming the door in his face.

Flipping the lock, I turned to the quaking werewolf. "Now, where should we begin?" Quirking an eyebrow, I flashed her a fang-baring grin. "I'm not sure how much time we have before Alexa arrives, so we better make the most of it."

Back pressed to the control board in front of the monitors, Juliet held up both hands. "I know you don't want to do this. Not really. Please, Arys. Stop."

Pausing to breathe in the fear she exuded, I said, "You really don't know shit about vampires, do you?"

If I let myself touch her, I might kill her too soon. Before I could coax all I wanted from her. Before I could have the pleasure of destroying her in front of Alexa. Restraint had never been one of my strong suits.

"I know that you love Alexa more than anything, and even though you might hate me, you don't want to hurt her like that." Voice wavering slightly, Juliet held my gaze. The woman refused to play the victim.

I could force it though. Have her on her knees before me, begging me to take her. The visual enticed me a little too much.

Pinning the she-wolf against the control panel, I got too close, forcing her to lean away. "I plan to hurt you both in a variety of ways before I'm done."

She couldn't resist. All I had to do was hold her gaze just so, and she fell into my eyes. Under the thrall with no more than a look, Juliet was a fighter, but she was still too green to take on someone like me.

Her brown eyes went to my lips. She wanted me to kiss her. Not a shred of fight left. Too easy. It sucked some of the fun out of it. Over her shoulder I searched each monitor's display, waiting to see Alexa appear.

Dragging my lips over Juliet's soft earlobe, I whispered, "Tell me what you'd like me to do to you."

A small gasp left her, and she ran a hand brazenly over my chest. "Anything you want."

Now that's what I liked to hear. I chuckled, intrigued by Juliet's inner bad girl. Curious, I wondered if she was as dirty as Alexa could be. "Get on your knees and tell me what a naughty wolf you are." I released her with that command and stepped back. A shiver of delight crept up my spine when she went to her knees before me. "Tell me how much you love vampire cock despite your squeaky-clean persona. Tell me who you really are, Juliet."

She stared at me with glazed eyes. So far under. So completely mine. So many terribly wonderful things I wanted to do to her.

I never got to hear her filthy confessions. By the time I felt the air move, Falon was already there. Already throwing a fist in my face. The immortal force it carried launched me off my feet and through the window that looked out into the main office.

Of course she'd sent him ahead. The fallen angel was so deeply enslaved to Alexa, even he didn't know the extent of it.

None of that stopped him from kicking my ass.

On me before I could get up, Falon grabbed my shirt and dragged me to my feet. Knowing better than to give me a chance to enthrall him, he smashed another powerful fist in my face.

Pasting me against a fire extinguisher encasing that jutted out of the wall, Falon snarled, "You're not finished yet, asshole. Otherwise I'd end you right here. Don't fuck this up any more than you already have."

Apocalyptic

Without waiting for a response of any kind, he hit me with a blast that only an immortal could withstand. I went down. Out cold.

CHAPTER TWENTY-FIVE

"Shit, shit, shit." I held my breath as my Dodge Charger careened through a red light, fishtailing as I narrowly avoided a collision. Horns honked, and I didn't have to see them to know several middle fingers accompanied the noise.

Reckless driving wasn't something I engaged in lightly. Nothing pissed me off like an asshole behind the wheel. But Arys had my sister trapped in a haunted hospital with an evil entity thriving on every move he made. I had to get there, red lights be damned.

I raced through the city, trying to cut as much time off the drive as possible. In the passenger seat Gabriel watched the scenery speed by. If he was concerned with my driving, he didn't show it.

After getting the call from Shaz, I'd forced my way into my dark lover's head. And what I saw shook me to the marrow: Juliet. Running from Arys. While he hunted her through the dank halls of the creepiest building in the city.

Arys had let me see what he wanted me to see. Then he thrust me out.

I sought Falon, ready to beg him to save Juliet. Never before had I been so jealous of the angel's ability to immediately move from one place to another. I found him with Smudge, ensuring the hostages lost their memories of tonight's events.

I grabbed his arm. "Arys has Juliet cornered in the FPA building." If he'd shrugged me off and told me it wasn't his problem, I wouldn't have blamed him.

He responded with a sardonic, "Of course he does," and promptly vanished.

Now I raced over there, hoping against hope that I'd find my sister unharmed. I couldn't let myself consider the alternative.

Arys had gone out of his way to force our final confrontation. It would be tonight. His attack on Juliet served as his way of ensuring I'd come. He knew I would and that I'd be mad as hell.

As my car roared through the night-time streets, I clenched the wheel and seethed. How could he do this to me? To us? Why should I continue to fight when he so readily gave in? Why should I care?

I couldn't care. Not anymore.

This had to stop. We had to make it stop. I didn't know how we were going to do that. I kept waiting for the fear to grip me. The end was nigh. Shouldn't I be afraid?

Because all I felt was done.

That feeling only intensified when I screeched to a halt across the street from the old hospital. I shoved the gear shift into park and threw my door open, almost falling out in my haste.

On the sidewalk just beyond the building's property line stood Falon and Juliet. On the ground several feet away sat a pissed off and magically handcuffed Arys.

My feet led me first to Juliet. Grabbing her shoulders, I looked her over, examining each visible vein and artery. "Are you alright? Did he hurt you?"

"He's a fucking psychopath, Lexi. He was going to kill me." Voice shrill, Juliet quaked with the aftershocks of adrenaline. She stank of terror.

I backed off as suddenly as I'd grabbed her. That smell was too much. I was too close to the edge.

"We were just playing, my love." Arys offered his calm version with a half shrug. Hands bound behind him in FPA issue cuffs, he regarded me with a devilish smile. "It was all in good fun. Just needed to pass the time until you arrived."

A surge of rage struck me, absolute in its darkness. It swelled up from within and burst out in the punch I threw at Arys's smug face. "Well I'm here now. Is this what you had in mind?"

I faltered before I threw the next hit. Arys laughed in my face, so thoroughly entertained by my outburst. "It's exactly what I had in mind. Although, this isn't exactly fair play now, is it?" He held up his cuffed wrists. An invitation.

Once they came off there would be no stopping what came next. The end of us as we knew it.

I backed away from him, from all of them, needing space. Standing in the middle of the street, I tried to see through the haze of red-hot emotion driving me. Seeking clarity, I thrust my hands through my hair and squeezed my eyes shut.

Where was the light? Where was that tiny spark when I needed it?

The streetlights hit me just right as I raked my hair back.

Arys made a noise of surprise. His smugness had weakened when he said, "There's black in your hair."

My eyes snapped open, and I knew they were his midnight blue. He was taking over every part of me. "Surprised? I can't imagine why. You've been slowly taking over every piece of me since the night we met. If only I'd been able to see then what I so clearly see now." My shout rang through the otherwise quiet street. Those who lived close enough to this building to hear anything probably knew better than to come investigate.

My attack was personal, cutting right to the bone. I saw it slash across his face only for a second before the darkness slipped back over him, hiding any semblance of humanity.

"If only," Arys agreed, tone seductive and sinister. "You played your own role, Alexa. Everything about this, about us, you wanted it. Right from the start. Don't pretend you're different. Better. We're the same. You thrive on darkness. You fucking love it. But you can't accept that you're not so squeaky clean, so you blame me for your own filthy urges. You're down here in the dirt with me though, aren't you, my love?"

An image flashed through my mind. Brief. A flicker and then gone. Salem and Lilah, in their memories. Hurling the same emotional weapons, harboring the same internal war of love and hate.

I thought we'd succeed where they had failed. I'd been wrong.

Without thinking I drew back a hand that blazed with deep blue light and prepared to throw it in the smirking vampire's face. If he wanted to end this, we'd end it alright.

A strong hand caught my forearm. Shaz shook his head, his expression imploring. "Lex, don't. It can't end like that. It would be suicide."

I dropped my hand, letting the power fall away. Across the street Jenner leaned against the car they'd driven here, the Jag that usually sat in my garage until Arys had swiped it a few nights ago.

Jenner kept his distance, but his crossed arms and tight posture revealed his unease.

Aside from Juliet, everyone here had been present the night Arys killed me. Why shouldn't they be here now?

"I'd prefer to call it self sacrifice," I half joked, trying and failing to break the tension. "It was always going to come to this, Shaz. We knew that. We were just stupid enough to think we had more time."

Shaz glanced at Arys who sat there watching us with a cool detachment. Emotionless.

"You can't just kill each other," Shaz insisted. "That's insanity."

My gaze strayed to Falon who stood several feet away, hands shoved in his pockets, looking bored and uninterested. He thought I didn't trust him. I'd lost track of how many people had told me not to. That he was a traitor. Yet he'd bared the wounded parts of his soul to me. He'd seen the ugly parts of mine as well a time or ten. There had to be an element of trust during such exchanges.

Falon had gone after Bane to protect me. So why would he wish to see Arys kill me after that? Try as I might, I just couldn't find a reason he'd want me dead.

Our gazes locked for just a moment, but that was long enough. Silver collided with blue, and something tightened in my chest. I was putting a lot of faith in him here.

"We're not going to kill each other," I said, choking on my next words. "Arys is going to kill me."

There it was. The flicker of light. Tiny as a match flame now. We didn't have much time.

Shaz searched my face, like he couldn't be sure of what he'd just heard. Capturing that black lock of my hair between his fingers, he heaved a deep sigh. "I can't lose you, Lex."

Again my gaze darted to Falon whose expression revealed nothing. It was a lie. A mask to hide his true thoughts and feelings, whatever they might be.

"You won't." Falon spoke up, drawing every gaze his way. "When she reaches the brink, where life meets death, I'll stop him from taking it any further if I have to."

My stomach flip flopped.

Juliet plopped down heavily on the sidewalk, as far from the rest of us as she could get without leaving. She listened to this with wide eyes.

Shaz groaned and rubbed his forehead. "How can this be the best way?"

"It's the only way," Falon supplied, so matter of fact.

Touching Shaz's jaw, I drew his focus back to me. "I think he's right. I command light and dark. I have to go to the place where they meet. If that doesn't restore the balance between Arys and me, nothing will."

A snicker floated from Arys. He stood, the motion smooth despite his arms being cuffed behind his back. "Is that what you've been concocting with your angel, my love? A way to restore the balance? It's too late for that."

Just looking at Arys was enough to set me off. His cocky smile was back in place.

Hungrily, he eyed Shaz, ensuring the wolf saw the killer's intent in that predatory stare.

Shaz was no longer so easily threatened or intimidated by the vampire's tactics. Putting a hand on my shoulder, he ignored everyone but me. "There's nothing I want more than for you to restore the balance. If you're sure about this, then you have my support. Just please, be sure. I love you."

I kissed him, lingering just long enough to say what I couldn't say, but not so long that it could be mistaken for a just-in-case goodbye. I couldn't let my thoughts go down that path. Too recently I'd said goodbye to Kale. I was not leaving Shaz. Not tonight.

"And I love you." I had to pull away before the twisting and churning in my gut could manifest as blood hunger. The smell of wolf and man was just too much.

Arys stretched his neck from side to side, the cracks especially loud in the quiet. "So you've got this little plan all worked out, and I'm supposed to just play my part? That would imply that I want to restore the balance."

Now it was my turn to laugh like a smug jackass. My feet were moving of their own accord. "You think you have a say in the matter? Either way you're going to try to kill me the first chance you get. The rest is out of your hands."

Arys watched my approach with growing intrigue. "We'll see about that."

With both hands on his chest I shoved him. Hard.

He stumbled backward and fell, onto FPA property. The dead grass crunched beneath him. On his ass, his jaw muscles twitching, Arys's amusement disappeared. Replaced by a cold mask of indifference and mania.

The entity had him. It had to be in his head. I could feel it lurking, seeking opportunity.

I had to make sure his killer nature outweighed his desire to destroy us. It wasn't him who didn't want to restore the balance. It was the darkness. Restoration would force it back to the halfway point, nicely matched with the light. We would be us again. Rational and in control. But better. Renewed.

Lilah may have ruined that for her and Salem, but I would not allow anyone to ruin it for Arys and me. Not her, not Arys. Nobody.

I stood over him, glaring down into my dark love's eyes. How I adored him, and yet I wanted to boot the sneer off his face. "Get up," I hissed. "We're doing this."

Shame on me. I made the mistake of turning to ask Juliet for the key to the cuffs. I wanted Arys free and able to fight.

"I was starting to think you'd never ask." The telltale *chink* of metal preceded the hit that knocked me on my ass. Arys held up each wrist, a cuff locked on each, the chain broken. "Nobody will ever be able to say we didn't end with a big finish."

CHAPTER TWENTY-SIX

The ground beneath me thrummed with the evil entity. It murmured something next to my ear, but I was too stunned by Arys's stunt to listen. Those cuffs were spelled. They'd held every vampire I'd known to wear them, me included. Only Falon had broken them with little effort.

In my peripheral view I saw Shaz start forward. Falon held him back with a hand on his shoulder and a low spoken word I didn't catch. He couldn't help when Arys advanced on me with vicious glee lighting up his face in a maniacal mask. Like someone I didn't know. Had never known.

Lies. The darkness spoke lies into me, wanting me to believe. The tiny match flame wavered but did not go out. I got to my feet with hands raised. Deep-blue energy sparked from my fingers. It jumped with the barest streak of gold, but that was enough for me.

I faced Arys, the inevitable showdown we'd always known was coming, and I steeled myself to see this through.

The wolf within wanted me to shift and tear his throat out. No part of the beast understood why I'd be willing to let him kill me. It momentarily tore me in two. A fight to the death, the wolf wouldn't accept anything less. The darkness agreed. It wanted nothing more than to consume me completely.

Yet I still had that flicker.

The entity's slimy voice muttered something, but it didn't speak to me. It spoke to Arys. The dark flame, so like its queen. Not good.

When I saw him pause and tilt his head to listen, I darted forward and slammed a fist loaded with power into his chin. The blow snapped his head to the side, and he almost went down. Recovering quickly, Arys came at me with a flick of his wrist that struck me with a pure dark blow.

Apocalyptic

My chest tightened as the power coiled around me, like a snake trying to crush the last speck of light from my soul. The suffocating sensation made it hard to tap my power. Our power. Anything Arys threw at me was mine too. When I remembered this and calmed enough to focus, I easily made the coil fall away.

"We could be here all night at this rate," Arys observed, coming at me fast enough to get me backing up.

"Then stop with the dark coercion tactics and just take me already. You know you want to." Fisting my hair, I pulled it over a shoulder, baring my neck on one side.

Arys's pupils dilated at my invitation. He bit down on his bottom lip, his gaze on my neck. "You're a wicked woman. As always, it's tempting. But what I'd really like is for you to stop fighting this already. Imagine what we could be if you'd let go of that goddamn spark."

It pierced my soul to hear him say that. Even though I told myself it wasn't really Arys. He overflowed with darkness. The entity whispered in his ear, manipulating him. Still, it hurt to see the detachment in his cold stare.

I didn't doubt that the entity was bargaining with him right now. Offering him Lilah's empire, for a price of course. Arys had no reason left not to accept.

I would not let him become Lilah.

Instigating a fight to rile him up wasn't going to work. Not in his current headspace.

The heat of our conflict had fizzled out with the near obliteration of our light. Crazy as it sounded, I knew that wasn't right. We needed the spark of fire that made us butt heads but also made us love hard and hot.

Everything about us right now was wrong.

So I used the only other weapon I could turn on him. The one he couldn't fight. Because we were all slaves to our own desires.

I drenched Arys in succubus thrall. No gentle seduction or slip of power but a full immersion. He didn't fight it, because it was in his nature not to want to. Instead he blinked a few times, awareness turning to fury, then unbridled lust. Arys grabbed for me, and this time I let him. Claiming my mouth in a brutal kiss, he jerked me against him.

The familiar sensation of his body against mine almost broke me. It was all I could do not to abandon my precarious hold on control here and fall headlong into the abyss with him.

With a frustrated snarl that was pure wolf, Arys somehow resisted. Grabbing hold of the seductive force, he twisted it into his own allure and threw it back at me. "Is that how you want to do it? You want to fuck each other into oblivion? Now that I can get on board with."

He wasn't the only one frustrated. Each angle I tried, he thwarted. We were too much the same. We couldn't outplay one another.

Clawing my way back up from the pit of desire, I growled, "What I want is for you to stop screwing around and bleed me already."

Arys had been a vampire far longer than I had. Using vampire abilities to force this situation wasn't going to work either. So I targeted what I knew best, where my advantage lay: the wolf.

An echo of my wolf lived inside Arys. I sought it out now. Letting my wolf show in my eyes, I bared four beastly fangs and came at him with claw-tipped fingers. One slash and blood seeped from four deep gashes across his chest.

Like I'd anticipated, the beast within him saw the threat and rose to meet it. Arys's blue eyes went solid wolf in a blink. Confusion warred with rage on his face.

Rage won.

He came at me, throwing a body check that knocked me off my feet. Before I could get up he grabbed my arm and dragged me several feet before throwing me. I crashed into the crumbling stone of the old hospital and dropped to the ground with a grunt.

All I had to do was get Arys to bleed me, somehow keep hold of my tiny match flame, and trust Falon to step in at the right time. Right. Simple.

Sharp pain through my side had me clutching what I suspected to be a broken rib. All in all, not a big deal. But any pain was weakness in a fight.

Needing a second to recover, I threw a hand up in front of Arys before he could grab me again. The force shoved him back, buying me a few precious seconds before he was on me.

Apocalyptic

When he seized me and jerked me close, his hungry kiss caught me off guard. It was dark and desperate, passionate and powerful. I fell into him. Remembering what we'd been. Longing for what we should be.

Then he grabbed me by the throat and smashed my head into the side of the building.

Seeing stars is an overused phrase I'd never really related to. Until now. Light burst behind my eyes like fireworks on a dark night. Blinding. Pain exploded through my skull. A scream tore from me, leaving my throat raw. Vaguely I was aware of raised voices nearby.

"Get up, love." Arys nudged me with a foot. "You wanted to do this."

So that's how it was. Alright. Gritting my teeth, I kept telling myself that this wasn't really him. I knew that deep down. Still, peering up into his gloating face made it hard to feel anything but revulsion and hate.

It's not real, I told myself. *You are the same soul. There can be no hate there. It's a lie.*

Right on the heels of my inner pep talk came the oily voice of the entity in my ear. 'You belong with us. Stop fighting your fate, lost wolf.'

"Fuck you and your evil queen," I hissed. I refused to listen to it, knowing well how easy it could get into one's head.

A quick glance revealed that Falon still stood on the sidewalk, off the property and just out of reach of the entity's touch.

I got to my feet, trying to ignore the pain racking my skull. I winced against the agony. Daring to touch the side of my head, I wasn't surprised to find my fingers come away wet with blood. The damn vampire was going to bash my brains out in front of our wolf and my sister.

Going on the defensive, I lashed out with a shot of erratic energy as Arys grabbed for me. He deflected the attack, sending it wide. Pulling me into his arms, he spun me to put my back to his chest. Gripping my chin, he forced me to face our friends who watched our struggle play out.

"Look at them," Arys demanded, fingers biting into my skin. "Smell that? It's two werewolves. Hear their heartbeats? Listen."

He shook me when I struggled against him. Arys picked through each of my senses, setting each one ablaze. The power of suggestion in his commands doused me in the erotic swell of the bloodlust.

"Remember how he feels beneath you," Arys whispered, his words only for the two of us now. "Inside you. Don't you want to feel him? Don't you want to taste him?"

The seductive pull of his suggestion, along with his hard body snug against mine, brought to mind many wicked and sinful ideas. Erotic heat set my cheeks and groin ablaze. My gaze locked on Shaz. Memories of his blood and body flitted through my head. Oh yes, I most certainly did want him.

No, I couldn't fall victim to this manipulation. I thrashed against Arys, pleading with him to stop. Hearing my desperation, I knew it wasn't going to help my case here. Yet I couldn't help it. If Arys convinced me to tag team our friends with him, I'd be forever lost to darkness.

"I'm not letting you have us both!" My shouted declaration accompanied a burst of energy that brought Arys to his knees.

I went down with him but broke free and rolled back to my feet. Bleeding. It shouldn't be hard to redirect his focus now. I hoped. Extending my blood smeared fingers toward Arys, I appealed to his bloodlust. "Come on, Arys. Don't you want to taste me?" For good measure I used a claw to open a gash on the side of my neck.

His brow furrowed and he seemed conflicted. I knew the entity spoke to him. Seeing him as the easier target now that he was full dark, it had little to say to me.

Hunger burned in his midnight eyes when they fell upon my bleeding neck. Knowing I had won his attention, I turned it up a notch, willing to pull out all the stops to make this happen. I peeled off my top and tossed it aside. Blood ran down my chest to stain my cleavage before disappearing inside my black bra.

The entity may have known darkness in its general form, but I knew Arys and his specific tastes. I was what he wanted most. More than anything else. Even he couldn't change that.

Arys went to the dark place. A place I'd only thought I knew. My actions veered far from squeaky clean. But as dark as I'd ever played, never had I been without the light to keep some kind of rein on me. No light lit Arys now.

But this was how we did things, Arys and I. All the way.

He held himself so rigid that I could see him tremble. I watched him have that final moment. The one we all have right before we succumb completely.

Chest heaving as super-charged adrenaline drove me, I dragged a finger down my chest, through the blood and over the swell of my breasts. Whatever made them all want me and my blood the way they did, it was stronger than anything else that afflicted Arys. He came at me and I braced for it.

When he grabbed me the instinctive urge to fight kicked in.

I struggled as he wrestled my arms down and pinned my wrists with one hand behind my back. With the other hand he grasped my face and kissed me. A torturous melding of mouths that made me forget what the hell I was doing. Arys's kiss was possessive, his every touch a demand. He followed the rivulet of blood that ran down my chest, licking it up with hot, moist strokes of his tongue. An unbidden gasp encouraged him.

"You want me to take you?" he asked, voice raspy with want. "Your wish is my command, my queen. Remember that you asked for this. There's no stopping it now."

Terror followed his promise, trickling down my spine like ice water.

Arys buried his face in my breasts, kissing and nipping while tugging furiously at my pants. All while keeping my wrists restrained behind me. With Arys's mouth on my needy flesh, I strained against him, seeking more of his touch.

A roar like the angriest window-rattling, storm-driven wind assaulted my ears. Power whipped wildly around us, blowing my hair about in a tousled mess.

With my pants around my ankles and Arys's mouth sucking greedily at the blood staining my chest, I lost the last scrabbling hold I had on my control and plunged headlong into the abyss. It was just the two of us there in that place. Oblivious now to those who watched, Arys took me in every way.

Unlike the first time he'd killed me here on this property, he fed every one of his hungers with my body and blood. A low growl in my ear had me moaning as he licked the wound on my neck. A rustle of clothing and his hard on pressed against my thigh. Without releasing my wrists, he turned me around and forced me down on my knees. I had seconds to take in the hard ground beneath me and the rock that dug into my left shin.

Going to his knees behind me, Arys grabbed my hip and filled me with one forceful thrust. Hard and fast he filled me. Jerky, rough thrusts. Carnal and furious. If he hadn't been holding tight to my wrists, I'd have been thrown onto my face.

A guttural snarl accompanied his aggressive possession of my body. Arys slid his free hand around my throat. Holding tight, he pulled me back toward him and leaned in to sink his fangs into my neck.

He went for the artery. Straight for a killing blow. For a human.

As a vampire, I wouldn't bleed out as fast, and it would take being sucked dry of all blood and power, and then some, to kill me. Still, the first niggling scrap of worry hit me. What if I couldn't trust Falon?

Blood spilled down my body, soaking the dead grass beneath me. Arys drew hard on my blood and the essence that lived within it. My wolf wanted to fight, but I'd already given myself to the abyss.

To my dark love.

All that I was, my entire life force, it flowed into my vampire. Filling him. Draining me weaker with each passing moment.

It took longer to weaken than the first time I'd died by Arys's hand. The pleasure of his bite and his claiming of my body subsided under the swell of gut-wrenching agony.

Arys withdrew and gathered me in his embrace, tugging me onto his lap as he collapsed on the ground. With my hands free, I flung my arms around his neck. Another arterial bite and I choked back a sob. Weakened until I could no longer hold on, he clutched me tighter in his arms.

Power and blood gushed from me. Limp, I closed my eyes and waited. Was I supposed to know when I reached the brink? Would it be like last time? What if this didn't work?

Apocalyptic

A sudden, final swell of power left me as Arys drew it in, feasting on everything he could take. I felt the tiny match flame leave me, all that remained of our spark.

He took it into himself and his head snapped up.

With wide eyes he stared at me. True recognition flickered across his face. "Alexa," he murmured, caressing my face.

I couldn't keep him in focus. My lashes fluttered closed, and I struggled to pry my lids open. "Don't stop," I gasped. "Not until Falon tells you."

The sense of his hand on my face grew dim. Vaguely, I was aware of his mouth on my wounded neck.

Everything faded as Arys killed me for the second time.

CHAPTER TWENTY-SEVEN

It took several moments for me to realize that I sat in a Paris café. How I knew it was a Paris café, as opposed to some hipster joint down the street, I wasn't sure. I just knew I was there.

Disoriented and confused, I glanced around. There were several tables littered with people enjoying their coffee, speaking animatedly in French. Surely this wasn't death. I seriously doubted the other side to be anything like Paris. But really, what did I know?

I scanned the sign behind the barista. Could I grab a latte in this strange place? No, that wasn't right. This wasn't real. I had to figure out where I was and how to leave. Did I want to leave?

Maybe I was dead. Like good and dead. And this was some kind of artsy afterlife. I could get used to this. It wasn't the worst afterlife.

"Hey, gorgeous." A familiar voice had me spinning in my seat. "Fancy meeting you here."

The scent of leather and a cologne I'd never forget struck me before I laid eyes on him. Kale Sinclair sauntered up to the tiny bistro table where I sat. Wearing his trademark duster, he took a seat across from me. Enjoying my shock, he merely smiled, letting me soak it in.

"Is this for real?" I mustered, wanting so badly for it to be but knowing better than to trust blindly. Had the powers that be really sent Kale?

"It is most definitely for real." His broad grin was free of fangs, but those enchanting mismatched eyes remained the same ones I'd always known. "Can't say I'm too happy to see you here so soon, but I am happy to see you." Kale took my hand.

He felt so warm and alive. No vampire essence. Just him. Still sweet as honey.

"Am I dead? Did Arys finally kill me for good this time?"

Kale's genuine, carefree laughter was as rich with sugar as his vampy vibes had ever been. No doubt and darkness plagued him now.

He was free of it, of me. I'd wondered if death had released him and now I knew. I could rest in peace with that knowledge.

"You're in between but you won't be staying. You've barely begun your journey, Alexa. It's going to take you to amazing places." Stroking a thumb over the back of my hand, Kale tapped the end of my nose. "Hey, why do you look so scared?"

"Because I came to restore the balance, and I don't know how." Unable to tear my gaze from his face, I let myself enjoy those eyes while I could. "Isn't death going to pop in and demand the vampire its owed?" Despite my worries, Kale's chuckle soothed me. I couldn't help but relax.

"Alexa, you're a light flame and a Hound of God. The hybrid queen. You command both light and dark, as you were called to. Death will get its vampire when you're good and ready to give it one."

Sadly I shook my head. "Just a dark queen now, I'm afraid."

"You misunderstand, beautiful." Kale brushed a hand over my cheek. His gentle caress brought many memories to life. "This isn't death. It's more of a visit. You haven't left your world. And you won't. Not tonight." The calm he exuded made me unafraid, but it didn't clear the confusion.

"Yeah, no, I really don't understand. Why am I here? And why does it look like Paris?"

I gestured to the view of a city I'd never visited, right outside the window beside our table. Sunlight streamed in, lighting Kale's eyes in a way I'd never seen before. I marveled at him, drinking it in and hoping the memory would stay.

That's how I wanted to remember him. With sunlight in his eyes and a carefree smile.

"I loved Paris," he responded, wistfully gazing out the window. "I would have loved to show it to you. This is as close as it gets. I chose to meet you here."

The streets were different. Stone instead of asphalt. Old buildings held generations of stories to tell as opposed to the young concrete jungle of the downtown at home. People passed by, some quickly, others in no hurry. I didn't have to leave the café to feel how different it was from home. If only Kale had been able to show me what he loved about it.

"What happens now?" I dared to ask, afraid this meeting would end as fast as it had begun.

Kale studied me with those oh-so-human eyes. Not a trace of predator lurked within them. They were more beautiful than I'd ever known.

"You go back," he said, confirming my fear that we would part. "But not without what you came for."

"Wait." I sat up straighter in my chair, spine rigid, chest tight. "Do you mean it worked?"

He nodded, letting me crush his hand in my excited grip. "Embracing your darkness was the key all along. You faced the absolute worst and won. Like a phoenix, you will rise."

"What do you mean it was the key all along? What about the others? Salem and Lilah? Ozzie and Rachel? Why just us?" Brow furrowed, I tried to puzzle this out.

The damn powers that be liked to throw unexpected twists and turns. At least they seemed to have sent Kale with some answers. Were the rules different for each set of twin flames? No, shit didn't work that way. But there were always loopholes and outliers. Exceptions to every rule, so to speak.

"The immortals can't die. They can never visit this place in between life and death. Humans rarely survive a trip here, to the brink." Kale waved a hand over my head, motioning for the barista's attention. "Now do you see what makes the two of you so special? Nobody else has gone toe to toe with death, twice, and returned even more powerful than before."

"More powerful than before? Ok, Kale, hold on a minute here. Let me get this straight." Flustered, I tried to make sense of this. "Letting fate play out as it may brought me here. That's the key? To stop fighting it and give in? Falon was right?"

A hand appeared between us, placing a drink on the tiny table. Whoever it was, the barista I assumed, disappeared before I could get a look.

"He was right," Kale agreed. "The problem with the solution is that, for most twin flames, it's a catch twenty-two. Except for you and Arys. Be aware, Alexa, upon your return the two of you will be the most powerful twin flames in existence. More so than even the immortals. Watch your back."

Because we'd be restored. Balanced as we should be. I took Kale's warning to heart.

Kale began to sip from the coffee cup. He was right at home here, beyond life and death. I couldn't stop staring at him.

"Are you completely free of me now, Kale?" I blurted, unable to hold it inside. I needed to hear him say it. "Did you find the peace you sought?"

Setting the cup aside, he took both of my hands in his. "I did. I'm free of every burden I carried as a vampire. That life had more than run its course for me. I couldn't have asked for a better ending than to know and love you."

He was happy. It's all I'd wanted for him.

Could one cry in the in-between? Apparently so. The tear that streaked down my cheek to splash on the table top was crystal clear. "Ok, good. All I wanted was for you to find your freedom."

"And I want you to find yours." Leaning across the table, Kale kissed me. A tender press of lips over much too quickly. "Never underestimate yourself, Alexa. Your enemies will never know what hit them."

Sensing that I was about to be sent off, I grabbed his wrist, needing more time with him. "Can't I stay longer?"

Kale winced and sighed. "I wish you could. Staying too long means never going back. You'll lose your window to get home." With great reluctance, he pulled his hands from mine.

Digging into the pocket of his jacket, he produced a large black stone. It filled the palm of his hand as he extended it to me. When it was nestled firmly in my hand, the stone erupted into flames. Blue and gold flames, dancing in a pattern, winding around one another. Like a yin yang of fire.

I gaped at the mesmerizing and strange flames. "What do I do with it?"

"Take it with you." Kale pointed to the back entry of the café. "Through that door."

He got up and I reluctantly followed suit. Nobody in the café paid us any attention. Like we weren't even there. I threw my arms around Kale, refusing to leave without feeling his arms around me one last time.

"I miss you," I whispered, choking on a sob. Dear God, how I missed him.

Kale crushed me to him in a hug. Into my hair he murmured, "Not as much as I miss you."

I didn't want to go, but staying was not an option. With the fiery stone in one hand, I grabbed for him with the other. One last squeeze.

Then I turned and opened the café door, stepping into a blinding white light.

CHAPTER TWENTY-EIGHT

SHAZ

I watched them fight, needing to jump in and have her back. My wolf wouldn't accept anything less than death beside its mate. Falon held me back.

Seeing her slip away in Arys's arms, for the second goddamn time, gutted me. Through this ordeal I'd tried so hard to keep up a tough front when face to face with her. She needed my encouragement, not my doubts and fears. But I felt anything but confident now.

As she hung limp in Arys's arms, something changed in him. He grew frantic, shaking her, imploring her to forgive him. He completely fell apart.

I went to him, kneeling next to them, helping him balance her weight. I tugged her clothing back into place, resting her head gently on the ground. Then I turned to Arys, who sat there staring at her, both hands fisting his hair, blood tears streaming silently down his face.

Adrenaline pumped hot through my veins. It was no small wonder that I managed to keep my composure. Slinging an arm around Arys's shoulders, I dragged him close and pressed my face to his. A wolf nuzzle felt like the most natural way to offer him comfort.

"It had to be this way," I assured him, praying that Lex was right about this. That Falon was right about this. "You did what you had to do."

Arys had no words, which didn't happen often. He leaned heavily against me, staring at Alexa's prone form. In silence we sat there together, waiting. For what felt like an eternity.

After several long, excruciating minutes she sat up with a gasp, eyes wide. She saw us there and reached out a hand. Ashes fell from her palm, littering the beaten earth.

Arys grabbed her and pulled her close, settling her between us. They clung to each other, each of them holding onto me as well. I sat back and stared up at the night sky, sucking in a deep breath.

She made it. She survived.

* * * *

Arys put his house up for sale and moved in with Alexa. At his gentle insistence, I also packed up and moved out of my apartment. Not willing to take any chances after the crap we'd all been through, Arys wanted the three of us to share a living space. It wasn't the worst idea, and it was probably about time for us to take this step. Alexa's house had more than enough space for the three of us. So did her bed.

Here we were one week later, all moving in together like some happy little trio. I kept waiting for it to feel strange. Yet, walking out the door to the apartment I'd rented alone for years, I didn't look back. I knew I belonged with them.

"Hey, careful now! You're going to take out my light fixture." Alexa's shrill shout pierced my eardrums.

While backing up the stairs, I managed to shift the trajectory of the heavy antique to avoid said fixture. Arys and his damn old furniture. This was the one large item he refused to part with, some dresser he'd been hauling around for a century.

At Alexa's instruction, Arys and I carried it up to the guest bedroom. There Arys and I shoved the old dresser against a wall. He paused to run a finger over a deep groove in the wood. A date was etched into the surface: *1849*.

"The year I first saw her in my dreams," he explained, spying my curious stare. "I don't know why I carved it in there. Once I did, I felt like I had to cart it around with me everywhere."

"I get it." A smile quirked my lips. Every glimpse of the man behind the vampire continued to amaze me.

Seeing my amusement, he slugged me in the shoulder. "I just have a box of art supplies to bring in. How about you? Got much left?"

I followed him from the room and down the stairs to the main floor. "Just a few boxes of clothes and video games in the back of my Jeep."

Apocalyptic

Doing something as domestic and normal as moving in with the woman I loved shouldn't have been so exciting. But it was. Even with her barking orders at us, instructing us on where to put each item we brought into the house. The woman was a control freak, but I friggin' loved her.

Since they'd had their balance restored the A team was back to how they'd been in the start. Before Lex turned. Before all of this. When they first united. They were both still feisty, temperamental vampires. But they no longer swung so far to the dark side that they couldn't control themselves.

At least, not yet.

Both of them still looked at me with hunger in their eyes, gazes straying to my throat. Only now it was with playful intent rather than a predator's need to kill. Oh, that lingered within each of them. The killer darkness. I saw it. Bound now by the restoration of their twin flame.

One would be a fool to forget that it was half of what they were.

After spending most of the night moving both Arys's stuff and mine, I was ready to unwind. I dug a cold beer out of the fridge. Popping off the top, I drank back a quarter of the bottle.

I felt at home.

"Your ugly old recliner is taking over my living room," Alexa complained as she entered with Arys behind her. "I know you love it, but maybe it's time to get a new one. And put it somewhere else. Like the basement." She said this with a sweet smile, but her tone was dead serious.

So far she'd been a good sport about her lovers' sudden move into her house. As soon as Arys suggested it, she'd been on board. She wanted us close. Of course that didn't mean we could put our shit wherever we liked.

Arys plopped into the offending chair he'd shoved into the middle of the living room. He ran a hand over the worn upholstery. "It's gonna take an awful lot of sweet talk to convince me to get rid of this chair. Maybe a little more than sweet talk."

Lex turned to me, tossing long blonde waves over her shoulder. The thick black streak stood out against the rest. She'd turned so dark that it had crept into her hair. I kind of liked it though.

"Help me out here, Shaz. Do you think this crappy chair belongs in the middle of the living room?" Long lashes framed soft brown eyes. She batted them at me, hoping I'd back her up.

"The middle? No. Maybe the corner." I ducked the throw pillow she snatched from the couch, anticipating the incoming projectile. I knew her so well.

"Screw you guys. That chair is out of here." She flung the next pillow at Arys who deflected it with a palm.

She was too damn cute when all fired up. It didn't take much to tease her into a frenzy. This time I opted to tease Arys instead. "No worries, Lex. He can't sit in it forever. He'll have to get up at some point. I'll help you sneak it out of here when he's not looking."

"Like hell you will," Arys fired back, taking the bait. "Touch this chair and I'll have it reupholstered in your white furry hide." A dark brow raised, he regarded me with an unspoken challenge.

Tipping the beer to my lips, I suppressed a laugh. "Never gonna happen. You know you couldn't bring yourself to do it. Just like at Doghead. You can't really hurt me." My tone had taken on a playful lilt.

Was I flirting with him? Maybe a little. Couldn't even blame it on the beer, having only had the one.

"Don't go there, pup," Arys warned, his seductive voice low and hypnotic. The vampire was all fun and games until the tables were turned on him.

I'd touched a nerve. Something had transpired between us that night in the Doghead parking lot. Our bond had been put to the test and survived. It had grown stronger. He seemed a little touchy about it.

"What's your problem, Arys? Not ready to admit that you couldn't kill me?" I straight up called him out. Hey, if he wanted us to live, fight, and screw together, then he could crack the hard exterior and be honest.

"Oh, I could have definitely killed you, Shaz. I chose not to." Haughty as ever, one of the vampire's strongest traits, he sat there in his crappy chair, projecting a high and mighty attitude that even had Alexa scoffing.

For some reason I couldn't leave it alone. The past week since the events of that night at the hospital, I'd spent a lot of time in thought. As if I didn't do that enough.

They say that actions speak louder than words, but sometimes all you need is words. "Yeah? So why did you choose not to?" I challenged.

By forcing him to give voice to whatever this was between us, I forced myself to do the same. A small part of me thought I should shut the hell up and drink my beer. But it was too late for turning into a chicken shit now.

Alexa watched this exchange with growing curiosity. She studied me with a brow raised in puzzlement, wondering about my point here.

But Arys knew.

He and I locked eyes. I could feel him willing me to shut up and drop it. So I said nothing, but the challenge remained in my gaze.

With a curse, Arys shoved out of the chair. Fists clenched and jaw twitching, he snarled, "Because I love you, goddammit. Does that surprise you? It shouldn't. You are hers, Shaz. So you are mine too."

He said it. Now it was out there. My own suspicions confirmed. I'd needed to hear him say it, to make it real.

Arys waited for me to absorb his confession. Now I had to decide what I really felt for him. I'd put myself in this position, needing to face this truth before I buried it completely in denial.

My fierce gaze sank into Arys like a blade. "You think I don't know that? The moment I learned about the twin flame bond, I knew. On some level. I guess I've been in denial for a while."

Across the room we stared at one another. The air crackled with tension.

Lex gripped the edge of the counter, watching with bated breath. She didn't seem surprised at his claim. I suspected she'd already known. But she didn't know how I would react. Hell, I didn't even know.

"And now?" Arys challenged.

CHAPTER TWENTY-NINE

So much emotion flowed across Shaz's face. He seemed to wrestle with himself, just for a second. Then he launched into motion. Depositing his beer on the counter, he crossed the room in a few long, smooth strides and stopped in front of the waiting vampire.

Shaz slid a palm along Arys's jaw up the side of his face into his unruly black hair. Without hesitation, my white wolf claimed my dark vampire with a possessive kiss that screamed the declaration Shaz struggled to voice.

Something had shifted between the two of them. More so in recent weeks than ever before. I sensed it. Nobody could have pushed Shaz to this point. He had to work through his feelings on his own. Evidently he'd been doing that.

Arys so rarely allowed anyone else to take the lead that it both pleasantly surprised and delighted me when he submitted to Shaz, letting him guide the kiss. A slip of tongue was visible as Shaz licked Arys's bottom lip before tugging it between his teeth.

A week ago I'd never have trusted Arys this close to either of us. I'd come back from my much too brief visit with Kale to find my hands filled with ashes.

Right away I'd felt the balance restored.

Everything inside me that had been heavy and oppressive had been forced back. The light and dark hung in balance again. It felt like a crushing weight had been lifted from my soul. Dark thoughts and urges did their best to test the limits here and there, but the light kept them in check.

A lightness I hadn't felt in months spurred my steps now when I walked. Everything felt right. Like it was all as it should be. Which naturally just made me suspicious as to what lurked right around the corner.

Apocalyptic

When Arys insisted on selling his house and moving in, my first instinct had been to resist. The last time we'd lived together, temporarily, we'd driven each other crazy. But seeing as that was kind of our thing, I couldn't come up with a legit reason for us not to share a house. Shaz's ready willingness to join us was the clincher.

Watching them together now, devouring one another in a kiss that screamed passion, it confirmed that we were in the right place together. Here. Now.

Slowly, I went to them. Taking my time. Enjoying the view.

When Shaz broke off the kiss, Arys muttered, "You're a goddamn enigma, wolf."

Shaz gave him a playful shove and reached for me. Encircling my wrist with his fingers, he pulled me between them.

Right where I wanted to be.

"I think we've done enough work for one night," Arys purred before going in for a kiss, letting me taste Shaz on his lips. "Time for some play. You're always up for some play, aren't you, my love?"

Arys would always run darker than I would. It showed in the mischievous glint in his eyes. Even after all that had passed between us, I still swooned when he looked at me that way. Like he wanted to devour me.

His hunger for me still burned hot but no longer did it tread into the murder zone. It would probably take some time for me to completely let my guard down around him. One couldn't be too careful. Not with a vampire like Arys. That would just be stupid. But it felt nice not to have to fear my other half.

This sense of peace between the three of us, it was surreal. I kept waiting to wake up. Or maybe I was still dead, and this was my heaven. But I was still a vampire so probably not.

A warm hand on my side drew me out of my thoughts. Shaz slipped an arm around my waist, pressing close. I turned between them, a hand on each of their chests. With a gentle push, I nodded to the sectional couch.

"Go sit down. Both of you," I said. "Take off your clothes first."

They exchanged a look with each other before glancing back at me. With a half shrug and a grin, Shaz kept us guessing by being the first to disrobe. Stripping his t-shirt off, he tossed it onto Arys's crappy old chair before heading to the couch.

Hands on his belt, he paused. "Feel free to join me."

Arys playfully pinched my behind before sauntering toward the couch, undressing as he went. I watched him move. Glide, really. Stealthy and sleek. Inhuman. The muscles in his back rippled beneath the golden light cast from the kitchen. My fingertips burned with the need to feel the hard lines of him and that smooth, forever-young skin.

Their obedience got me going on a little power trip. When they both went for the middle cushion I said, "Opposite ends. Facing each other."

A dark brow raised in intrigue, Arys settled himself onto the couch. Leaning back against the arm, he regarded me with a smoldering stare. Across from him Shaz sat with his legs crossed, watching me, hands hanging loose in his lap.

The middle was all mine. I stripped down to my bra and panties before joining them. When Arys reached for me, I batted his hand away. "Patience," I admonished with a naughty smile.

Not the submissive type, Arys ate up the sight of me and sat back. He'd play along for now, but once I pushed him to his breaking point, he'd snatch control away.

To punish him a little for being so impatient, I started with Shaz. I climbed onto the couch between them. On my knees, I stroked a finger along the edge of his jaw. "Close your eyes."

My command was only for Shaz. I wanted Arys to watch.

Holding my wolf's face gently with both hands, I kissed him. A soft but light touch of lips. I wanted him to breathe in my scent, to feel me so close. To crave more. When he tried to slip his tongue in my mouth, I pulled back.

Down his chin, following the curve of his neck, I savored the heady scent of Shaz's growing desire. Pine and wolf. Aromas of home. Over his chest, down the planes of his taut abdomen, I traced a path to the faint trail of hair that led to places of pure pleasure.

The weight of Arys's gaze grew heavy upon me. Resisting the urge to look at him, I kept my focus on my white wolf. Lower still my hand drifted. Each inch agonizingly slow.

Goosebumps broke out along his skin in the wake of my touch. The force of his arousal tempted my hungers. By the time my fingers grazed the soft, velvet head of his erection, he was rock hard.

A few strokes. Light at first, my hand circling him loosely. After coaxing a moan from Shaz, I gripped his shaft tighter, pumping it harder. Just a few solid strokes. Then I released him and turned away, leaving him quaking.

Turning toward Arys, I found myself peering into drowning pools of black. "Close your eyes," I whispered.

He held my gaze just long enough to make me think he'd refuse, then closed his eyes. I had yet to even touch him, but the vibration between us hummed strong and hot. And in balance. The dark part of us took our intimacy to some rough and wild places. The light part made it all mean something.

Finally I felt that it all meant something. No doubt. No dark voices taunting and tormenting in the back of my mind. Just us.

Like I'd done with Shaz, I started with a light touch. Outlining Arys's abs with my fingertips, I followed the many tight lines of him. Unable to resist, I leaned down to trace more lines with my tongue.

Arys sucked in a breath and swore softly. The energy crackled between us. Stronger than ever before. Super charged and vibrating at a frequency I'd never felt before, I fell headlong into the pull.

Hungrily I kissed Arys's abdomen, working my way lower. After watching me tease our wolf, he was more than ready. I wrapped a hand around his thick shaft, biting my lip. Holding myself back now was becoming the real tease. I wanted to eat them both up.

Gifting the smooth tip of Arys's hard on a few flicks with my tongue, I released him and with a wicked laugh, turned back to Shaz.

I knew better than that.

Arys wasn't the type to be teased. He only had patience when he was the one doing the teasing. "Sorry, my love, but it's been too long since the three of us have been together like this. I just can't play by your rules." Arys's apology preceded an abrupt change in position.

He flipped me onto my back, so I lay sprawled on the couch between them, my head in Shaz's lap. Pushing my legs apart, Arys selected the perfect position to descend between them.

"This is anarchy," I muttered, unable to muster any semblance of irritation.

Not with his mouth already on my skin. Warm, wet kisses decorated my inner thighs. I sucked in a breath and held it in anticipation.

Shaz slipped a hand into my hair. He twisted the strands of blonde and black through his fingers. Peering up at him through my lashes, I gazed into calm green eyes. It had been some time since I'd seen them so serene. Yet a jade fire burned in those orbs. He leaned down to take my mouth in a sensual kiss. His potent wolf vibes were rife with passion and a steadily growing desire.

The touch of Arys's tongue between my legs set off a small explosion in both my brain and my groin. I moaned softly into Shaz's mouth. He responded by kissing me deeper, consuming me. The palm of his hand was a sudden, warm, and welcome sensation as he cupped my breast, teasing my nipple with the pad of his thumb.

Turning the tease back on me, Arys gave me a few long licks, and then he stopped. Reaching under me to grab a handful of my ass, he dragged a fang over my inner thigh. I strained for his touch, needing him to keep going.

He made me ache for it. Two fingers slid inside me. Targeting my g-spot, Arys rubbed in slow, circular motions. I quivered under his manipulations.

Shaz held the side of my face, kissing my cheek, temple, and jaw. Adorning me with affection and devotion. I plunged my hands into Arys's hair, whimpering with the building tremors that racked me.

"On the edge, right where I want you," Arys murmured, again stopping his delicious torment. "Get on your knees, Alexa. Facing me." His command was followed by a resounding smack on my ass.

Relaxing back against the arm of the couch, the vampire regarded me with a devious grin. I sat up and pushed onto all fours. Behind me I felt Shaz repositioning. I knew how Arys wanted to do this. Such a voyeur, he arranged us so he could watch Shaz take me from behind. It conveniently left my head in his lap.

Over my head the two of them shared a look. I could only see Arys from my position on the couch, but that was enough for me to see the ease with which they communicated without need of words.

The exciting sensation of Shaz's shaft rubbing against my ass had me offering myself to him without shame. Arys watched with intrigue, nodding to our wolf who found me wet and ready. He thrust inside me and I groaned.

That snapped Arys's focus back to my face. Fisting a handful of my hair, he held my gaze. No words needed here either.

Wrapping my hand around the base of Arys's shaft, I licked it like a lollipop. Swirling my tongue around and over before sucking as much of him into my mouth as I could. I took both of my men inside me, filling myself with the two people who held me together.

I'd like to have believed that we would always have this. I'd learned enough in my time to know better than to expect smooth sailing. There would always be bumps in the road.

Arys and I were more formidable restored than we'd ever been when unbalanced. Not everyone was going to be cool with that. We had to expect some blow back. Factor in the strong circle of friends, lovers, and allies we'd acquired, and it only increased the odds of someone finding a reason to stir up shit for us.

None of that mattered right now though. I couldn't think beyond the steady rhythm of my wolf driving the moans from me. Or the taste of Arys, slightly salty in my mouth. His groans fed my ego and my desire.

Moving in tandem, reading each other with ease, the two men changed up our position. Arys spread out on the couch, pulled me down on top of him and slipped inside me. Shaz stood next to the couch, just inches from my head. I was more than happy to give him the same oral attention I'd given Arys.

The many sensations of our lovemaking teased me. From Arys's cologne tickling my nose to Shaz's ragged breaths, and the way they each felt beneath my fingers and inside my body. The power cycling between us ran with a high-pitched frequency. The lights in the kitchen flickered.

I alternated between using my mouth and hand on Shaz. He clutched a handful of my hair with clawed fingers. He was getting close, which brought me closer. I drew on my mate's lusty vibes, riding the building waves.

With both hands on my hips, Arys held me in place against the force of his thrusts. My inner muscles began to tighten around him. Arys grasped one of Shaz's hands and used it to tug him closer.

Shaz took it a step further. Gently pulling away from me, he nudged Arys up into sitting up on the couch with me still in his lap, riding him. Curious but intrigued, the vampire didn't question the request.

Our wolf slid onto the couch behind Arys, meeting my gaze over his shoulder. My breath caught as I saw what he had in mind. So many times I'd looked into Arys's eyes over Shaz's shoulder. This was an interesting turn of events.

Watching me take Arys inside me over and over, Shaz pushed a hand into the vampire's hair. Wolf fangs were visible when he put his mouth to the back of Arys's neck. First, he tasted him. A swirl of his tongue on flesh. But we all knew what was coming.

Beneath me, Arys trembled. He wanted it and he wanted it bad.

So did I. Bearing witness to the moment my wolf would claim my vampire was almost enough to make me climax from the anticipation alone. Was this really happening?

Eyes wild with wolf, Shaz bared fangs and bit deep. Arys's eyes closed in bliss. His grip on my hips tightened as he jerked me down hard onto him. The bite was messy and bloody, but Shaz kissed and licked the wound, his hand tight in Arys's hair.

His other hand descended between his legs where he touched himself, moaning softly. It was more than I could take. I came hard, squeezing Arys tight inside me. His release was immediate. He flung a hand back for Shaz who grabbed it tight in his. I let my head drop down against Arys's firm chest. Letting the pleasure waves rush over me, one after another, I smiled to myself.

Then I gave them both a playful smack and said, "Let's move this upstairs."

CHAPTER THIRTY

ARYS

I couldn't remember the last time I'd watched the two of them sleep. It felt like someone else's memories. Someone I didn't recognize as me anymore. Because that had been before.

Before we'd been forced to go through hell in search of the other side. Before we'd become the worst versions of ourselves on the downslide to destruction. Before my light half and I had found ourselves and each other again.

I sat up against the headboard of Alexa's giant bed. She lay curled on her side, pillow tucked under her cheek. For the first time in months, something that resembled peace left her face soft and beautiful. Free of frown lines and anxious furrows.

The woman had barely slept since becoming a vampire. It was about time she finally got some rest.

Shaz sprawled between us, asleep. An act of trust and affection that spoke the words he had yet to say. I needed no words though. I knew. Our relationship had undergone many evolutions in the time we'd known each other. I strongly suspected it had not yet reached its final form. All in good time.

A hand went to the bite on the back of my neck. I hadn't expected him to make such a move. Though he had yet to put it to words, I knew how the white wolf felt about me. I'd gladly bear his mark anytime.

Sensing my gaze, he cracked one green wolf eye open, the way animals do when someone draws near while they slumber. Satisfied that there was no threat, his beastly eye closed, and he settled in against me. If anyone needed the rest after the recent chaos, it was Shaz. He'd been running damage control round the clock.

His head rolled against my thigh. That near-white shock of hair was soft against my bare skin. Unable to resist, I dragged my fingers through it. I harbored fantasies of fisting that platinum hair while making him moan my name. Again, all in good time.

Killing Alexa, for the second time, had satisfied my darkest desire. This time my obsession died with her. Feeling her slip away I'd had no guarantee that she would come back. The moment I drew the last fragment of her energy, the last of her spark, the darkness scattered and I saw clear again.

Everything we'd done. Everything we'd become. It all hit me and I came apart.

If Shaz hadn't been there to keep me together, I don't know what I might have done. Holding her lifeless body in my arms, knowing it might be the very last time, it had reduced me to the bare bones of who and what I am.

A man on a monster's journey. A killer without remorse. One half of a whole, my existence meaningless without her. If Alexa had turned to ashes in my arms that night and I had somehow survived it, I'd have walked into the first sunrise after.

When she'd come back to us and opened those beautiful brown eyes, I'd profusely thanked a God who'd long ago stopped listening. I didn't deserve anymore chances.

But she did.

With my fingers in Shaz's hair, I studied Alexa. The sheets had slipped down, allowing me a nice view of her body. Smooth pale skin. Supple breasts that offered both pleasure and comfort. A slender neck decorated with a smattering of blonde and black tresses. And a silver feather.

Alexa's body bore the many marks of her lovers. Some of them temporary, like the claw marks on her hips and ass from Shaz. Others seemed to be permanent, like the streak of black in her hair.

I eyed the angel's mark. We'd be having words about that, he and I. I hadn't missed the fact that he'd been the one to know for certain how Alexa could find restoration. Suspicious? Just a little.

When I'd brought it up to her a few nights ago she'd warned me off, citing that Falon was hers and she'd deal with him. It had led to a heated exchange, a bitch slap was thrown with my face on the receiving end. It all culminated in some hot sex on the floor in the hallway.

The restoration kept us from drifting too far to one side or the other for long. What it hadn't done was affect the feisty conflict that arose between us. Though now it didn't result in murderous feelings. Just a few slaps and a good fuck.

We felt like us again. But better. Stronger.

Falon was Alexa's own personal therapy. I got it. I did. It didn't bother me that she had more lovers than I did. This wasn't a contest, and if even it were I'd blow her out of the water with my historical count of lovers.

What bothered me was Falon's past coming back and making my other half a target. What bothered me was the goddamn immortal mark on her neck. The angel had his uses. He'd proven that much. However, if so much as a single hair on Alexa's head met with harm because of him, I'd never rest until he paid for it.

Annoyed and restless, I slipped from the bed, tugged on a pair of loose fitting sweatpants and headed downstairs. I grabbed my sketchpad and a few pencils from where I'd left them on the kitchen table and flopped into my comfy old recliner.

It still sat in the middle of the living room where I'd left it, trying to get a rise out of Alexa. It had worked. Enjoying what I knew would be a short-lived victory, I flipped open the sketchpad to where I'd been working. A profile sketch of Shaz covered the page, his face turned slightly away. It was the view I often caught of him while slipping unnoticed glances his way.

The gentle scratch of my pencil on the paper soothed me. It was one of my favorite sounds. Although nothing could top the sound of my lovers in the throes of pleasure. Or a victim's moans seconds before they turned to screams.

Lost in shading the background of my sketch, I didn't sense Alexa's approach until she appeared from the hallway. She took one look at me reclined in the chair she hated and rolled her eyes.

Setting my sketchpad aside, I held out a hand to her. "Come here, my love."

Draped in one of Shaz's black t-shirts, hair spilling in disarray about her shoulders, she climbed onto my lap and settled in against me. My arms went around her, and I pressed my cheek to her hair.

We sat there in silence for several long, comfortable minutes. Just enjoying the calm and one another.

"This feels weird. Not wanting to tear each other's throats out. Good weird though. The right kind of weird." She laughed softly, tucking her head in under my chin. Tucked tight against me, she felt so small and fragile. An illusion I knew and yet maybe not so much.

My wolf had a sensitive heart beneath her tough-as-nails, in-your-face exterior. She let me see it in that moment. Curled up in my lap, on the chair she loathed, looking tiny and harmless. The packaging was certainly deceiving.

The absence of her light had robbed me of so much, and I hadn't been able to care. With its return I was made whole again. My missing half restored, I hoped to never not care again.

Hugging her tight enough to make her squeak, I chuckled. "See, this chair isn't so bad. It has its good qualities."

She reached to touch a worn spot on one of the arms. "It's hideous, Arys. I hate it. But you clearly love it. So you can keep it. But not in the middle of the damn room."

There were no small victories as far as this woman was concerned. I grinned to myself, content with the win.

CHAPTER THIRTY-ONE

Nothing about The Wicked Kiss had changed. It was the same eager crowd of willing victims. The same regular vamps who opted to keep a low profile by prowling the party crowd instead of hunting the streets. Loud music poured from the speakers. Party in the front. Pleasure in the back. Business as usual.

But I had changed. Arys and I, we'd changed. I felt more alive than I had since before the turn to vampire. In a different way though. The constant tug of war between light and dark had been subdued, from a raging inferno about to blow to a steady hot but controlled burn. Conflict naturally arose between the two sides. One couldn't exist without the other. But for the first time in pretty much ever, it felt right. Like we could handle it now. Like everything was as it should be.

Two weeks now had passed since that night outside the hospital. Two blissfully calm weeks. A few nights of calm? Sure that was somewhat normal. Weeks? Not damn likely.

So when Justin found me lounging on one of the couches with Ebyn, I knew from his grim expression that shit had been disturbed. Licking a trace of blood from my lips, I left the dopey wolf and rose to meet the hulking vampire.

He waited for me to draw close enough to hear his low tone. "There's a demon asking for you. He's willing to wait outside, but he's not leaving without delivering a gift from Prince Bane. Whomever the hell that is."

Fuck me. Here we go.

"Don't worry about it, J. I've got this. Thanks." No, I so did not have this, but I wasn't about to admit that to anyone.

A demon could have popped right into the middle of the club uninvited and unannounced. He'd asked for me and then waited. So he was playing an angle here. Maybe just to lure the hybrid queen out of her blood den for a parking lot attack. Although I couldn't see why Bane would send someone to do that in his place.

Striding through the lobby, I drew the Dragon Claw. Dagger in one hand, a perfectly balanced gold and blue psi ball roiling about in the other, I stepped outside. And almost ran smack into the demon who stood conspicuously right outside the entryway.

He wore a wormy smile and a bowler hat with suit to match. His appearance was that of an older, smaller man. Such a deceptively harmless look. Standing beneath the parking lot street light in plain view of all, vampires and humans, the demon held out both hands. A small black velvet box appeared.

"A gift from Prince Bane of Rhytheria for Alexa O'Brien, the Queen of Light and Dark." He held the box out toward me. "An apology. He hopes you will forgive his unwelcome forwardness and accept this gift."

I took my time eyeing him up. Black eyes. Bottom feeder. Not to be underestimated though. A poke and prod at his power and I was more than confident I could take him. It was rude as hell, but he'd come to my doorstep so he had to expect it.

He didn't react.

My first instinct was to laugh. The over-the-top dramatic use of our so-called titles and the fact that Bane thought I'd accept anything from him was a little hysterical. Also downright crazy. However, it also made me uneasy that Bane called me that. Because nobody else ever had but Falon.

"Who the hell are you? His servant?" I didn't wait for his response. It made me nervous that Bane had reached out to me in any way. I was just grateful he hadn't shown up again himself. Yet. "I don't want anything from Bane other than for him to forget I exist. So you can take your little gift back and tell him I'm not interested."

The demon blinked ebony eyes at me, confused. "Don't you even wish to open the box? You have yet to see what's inside."

My hand tightened on the dagger's hilt. Something about the demon's careful innocence over his malicious features raised my defenses. "I don't give a rat's ass what's in the box."

But it called to me. Whatever was inside that tiny box, it wanted me to find it. This had to be a trap. Remaining calm and composed, I refused to be intimidated by Bane without him even being present.

"How can you possibly know that if you have yet to look?" He just kept holding his hands out with that little box nestled in the middle of them.

"Alright." I raised the Dragon Claw, ready to lop his head off. "We're done here."

Before I could follow through with my swing, Falon appeared. He lunged at the demon and wrapped both hands around his throat. "Why did he send you?" Squeezing hard enough to make the guy's eyes bulge, Falon backed him up away from the doorway.

I followed, preferring not to have witnesses to whatever was about to transpire. "He brought me an apology gift from Bane," I explained when the demon failed to get a word out due to the crushing of his throat. "I told him I don't want it."

"Hear the lady?" Falon snarled into his face. "Tell Bane to stay the fuck away from her."

In a sudden burst of rage Falon squeezed tighter and tighter, twisting until the demon's head tore from his body. A fit of temper just unleashed all over Bane's servant. Just like that he was forced back to the other side and the master who'd sent him.

Falon turned to me with wild silver eyes. "You didn't see what was in the box?"

"No. Did you just call me a lady?" I nudged him with an elbow. "Have you recently suffered a serious blow to the head? You do know who I am, right?"

"Unfortunately," he said with an exaggerated sigh. "Just keeping up a front. Don't wet your panties over it."

Studying the fallen angel, I gave his energy a poke and prod as well. Frazzled. Angry. It made my skin prickle. Intrigued, I slipped him a little erotic heat. "Now, now, Falon. You know that's not the kind of talk that makes my panties wet."

He frowned at my invasive assessment but made no effort to resist my sensual pulse. If anything, it seemed to relax him. A sly grin lit up his face. "No, it definitely is not. You're a filthy little vixen. You like it dirty."

With him I sure did. I also liked to know what the hell was going on. "How did you know to drop in right when you did? Don't tell me that was a coincidence."

"Not at all," he admitted with a shrug. "I put a ward on this place. Wards can't be used to keep demons out of public places, but they can be used to alert me if any show up."

The first little niggle of fear dug at me. Falon thought Bane was enough of a threat to put a goddamn ward on my nightclub? "How worried should I be? Because *that* worries me."

Glancing about at the chattering people loitering outside, Falon took my elbow and led me across the parking lot, out of earshot. "Worry is wasteful. Preparation will save your ass. I'm just taking precautions."

"Because you think there's a reason to. Be honest with me, Falon. How likely is it that Bane is going to let this go and forget about me?" My tone was sharp like a razor, demanding truth.

He leaned against a silver SUV and crossed his arms. One hand came up to scratch absently at his chin. "Not likely at all."

"Fuck. Fuck. Fuck!"

A burst of anger, fed by my dark side, made me want to throw a punch in his face. Screw him for bringing this shit to my door. Sympathy and understanding beat the ire back, reminding me that he didn't want this either. Bane had made Falon's existence an eternal hell. Now he was back for more.

"Do you think I'd just stand back and let him come after you?" Falon snapped, his own inner emotions driving his temper. He shoved away from the SUV and his wings flared wide.

"Why wouldn't you? Two birds, one stone. Seems like the obvious way to be rid of both of us." The moment the words left my mouth I knew I'd screwed up.

He'd proven himself already. So why couldn't I trust him on this?

Falon grabbed me by both upper arms and pasted me up against the SUV he'd just been leaning against. "Let's get one thing straight. You're wearing my mark for a reason. I don't share you with anyone. Right here, right now, and every single moment we're alone together, you belong only to me." With each heated word he got closer until his lips brushed against mine.

Apocalyptic

Bane had done a hell of a number on Falon. So much so that he'd been willing to mark me as his among immortals to send his own message to Bane. Me. Someone he loathed with each breath. Yeah, Falon was dealing with some serious inner shit.

I couldn't help but get a charge from his outburst. "Is that so?"

"You're kidding yourself if you think otherwise." He dragged his lips over mine, a tease, and pulled back.

I couldn't argue that. So I changed the subject. With him pressed against me, pinning me to the vehicle, maybe I'd get an answer I'd been wanting. "How did you know what I had to do to save Arys and me? Who told you?"

Falon claimed it was his job to know things. I'd been able to accept that when all I held dear had been on the line. Now that we'd come out the other side, I needed to know more.

"You don't want to know," he murmured against my lips before dragging his tongue along my lower one.

"You mean you don't want to tell me." I playfully pulled away. If Falon thought he could use seduction to sway this his way, he hadn't learned anything in our time together. Dousing him in a splash of thrall, I touched his cheek and purred, "Tell me who told you."

With an eyeroll and an exasperated sigh, Falon huffed, "Who else? The kid told me. Gabriel."

"What?" I pushed Falon back and stepped away from the SUV. "Why would he tell you and not me if he saw something like that? And why the hell didn't you tell me that in the first place?"

Shoving his hands in his pockets, wings resettling around him, Falon gave me a knowing look. "You wouldn't have believed it. You don't trust him."

"And you thought I'd believe it coming from you because of the deep well of trust we've established? That was risky. You're not that delusional, Falon." Sure we'd managed to forge elements of trust in certain areas, such as working together for The Circle. Or when bleeding our souls into hotel room sheets. But there were limits to how much we could trust one another. There always would be.

Head tilted in a haughty assessment of my crossed arms and sassy attitude, he smirked like he knew something else I didn't. "Well, you did believe me, and it saved your annoying ass. So you tell me who's really delusional."

My sass began to dissolve like ice covered in salt. No witty comeback came to mind. He won this round. Shit. He grinned, enjoying his point.

"How long have you both been sitting on that information?" I couldn't help but be curious.

"He told me a few weeks ago," Falon explained. "Naturally, I didn't believe him right away. Not until Salem turned on you. Gabriel had warned me that he might. I had to see it for myself before I could tell you that death was the answer."

Letting this all sink in, I nodded. I wasn't sure how to feel about all of this.

"What do you think was in that box?" I asked, unable to wrap my mind around the two of them discussing my fate without my knowledge. A change of subject seemed safest.

Angling back toward the club, we headed inside. Falon's wings disappeared as we emerged into the streetlight on our way in. "Knowing Bane it could have been anything from a completely harmless jewel or as deadly as a curse that would explode in your face upon opening. Better to never find out which."

I cringed at the thought of what my unwelcome gift might have been. "Sending it back to him rejected is only going to encourage him, isn't it?"

I didn't know a lot about demons overall. My interactions with them were limited to a select few. However, I knew darkness well. It lived in all of us. It would not give up until it got what it wanted.

"Count on it. The thing about Bane, he's a planner. A patient one. He can wait days, years, centuries. Whatever it takes. Then he'll strike when you think he's forgotten all about you." Sticking close, Falon followed me through the lobby and back into the club. His words rang with personal truth.

A pang of sympathy flared in my chest. I quickly doused it out before he could see it in my eyes. Averting my gaze, I took in the club in its entirety, ensuring all was well.

"Perfect," I said dryly. "I can hardly wait."

Next to the couch where I'd left Ebyn stood Willow. He whipped about as I drew closer, panic etched all over his face. Adrenaline began to trickle through me. In my heart I knew it was bad. Beyond a mere shit disturbance.

Apocalyptic

"Can I speak with the two of you alone?" Willow jerked his head toward the back hall.

Falon and I exchanged a look. If he wanted Falon there, then it had to be bad. Worse than bad. What could be worse than that? Swallowing hard, I nodded, and the three of us headed to my office.

When the door closed behind us, Willow drew a deep breath. "I just received word through a friend that Salem and Lilah are missing."

"Missing?" I repeated, blinking rapidly as I tried to accept what that meant.

"Nobody has seen him since the night they sabotaged you. He's not with her in her prison. It's empty." Willow's usually gentle tone was like a nail in my coffin right then. A sharp, painful blow.

"No," I breathed, sinking to the couch. This could not be.

Falon took this news with a tight, pinched frown. "They've gone full dark."

Willow nodded, his concern so great that even his usual disgust with Falon was absent. Although he'd been softer toward Falon since his intel on how to restore the flame had proved solid. "It appears to be that way. Perhaps not, but we should be ready for that, should they turn up. Expect the unexpected from here on out as far as those two are concerned."

Full dark. If that were true they'd both be demons. But still two souls united as one, forever in darkness. Evil on steroids. Worse than anything Arys and I together would have ever been. That was really saying something.

I sat there staring at a smudge on the coffee table. Unable to process the latest dump of crap on my parade. Lilah and Salem. Full dark. This could only be bad for all of us.

"They'll come after me," I said, my voice hollow and detached. "Lilah will. After all of us."

Silence ensued as we all processed this horrific turn of events. Then quietly Willow asked, "Have you hidden Shya's stone? Lilah can never find it."

I met Falon's silver gaze. Together he and I had hidden it days after getting it back. A small church with consecrated ground on the outskirts of my town, a mere five minutes from my house. Ground so holy that Falon himself was unable to tread upon it. I buried it there, deep within the earth. I wanted to keep it close, where I could keep an eye on it, without taking the risk of keeping it in my possession.

Demons could easily send a human subject to retrieve such items. However, they'd have to know where it was first. The holy ground should keep any black magic locator spells from working. Or so Falon believed.

"Yeah, it's buried on holy ground. About as good as it gets." For someone with a pissed-off demon queen who hated him on the loose, Falon seemed rather calm. Maybe it was another front.

"Then that will have to do." Willow turned his encouraging green gaze my way. "Try not to be overwhelmed, Alexa. You're at your strongest. In perfect balance. They are not."

No, they were just friggin' immortals with a near endless well of dark power. One of them was on a vengeance mission.

I'd always known Lilah would escape her prison again one day. I just hadn't thought it would be so soon. She would return to claim her throne and seek revenge on those who'd wronged her.

And she would start with me.

CHAPTER THIRTY-TWO

I sat alone at my favorite booth near the door, watching Ebyn shamelessly flirt with identical twin sisters. Some people were here for vampires and only vampires. Others were open to just about anything. If any non-vampy type could smooth talk those sisters into bed, it was the playboy werewolf.

Falon had left, and Willow had disappeared with a woman. Which was fine with me. I could use a few minutes alone. Shaz was at Doghead tonight with his wolves. Arys and Jenner had left earlier to make whatever kind of trouble they liked to make together.

Pulling out my phone, I shot my sister another text. She'd ignored the last dozen. I expected her to ignore this one too. Still, I sent it anyway. She couldn't say that I wasn't trying to fix this. Arys had even offered to give her as many free shots as she'd like to take at him.

Nothing. She'd been laying low, keeping to herself. If she was still carrying on with Briggs, I didn't know about it. He'd been scarce around here lately.

She hadn't responded with so much as a 'glad you're not dead, again' message. Well, maybe she wasn't glad.

Like a cloud slipping in front of the sun, I sensed a shadow's approach. I glanced up from my phone to find Gabriel headed toward me. He smiled apologetically at a woman who tried to get his attention as he passed her table.

Slipping into the booth across from me, he set a locked briefcase on the table between us. He pushed it toward me. "It's my grimoire. I said you could have it and I meant it. I should have brought it sooner."

No need for small talk and chitchat as far as Gabriel was concerned. I liked that about him. "Let me see it."

He raised a dark brow and reached for the lock. "In here? Are you sure?"

"I just want to see it." He could've put a dead animal in there for all I knew.

Gabriel spun the numbers on the combination, and the lock popped open. He lifted the lid just enough to give me a glimpse of the thick black book. Right away I got a bitter taste in my mouth.

He opened the cover and let me see the writing and symbols on the first few pages. It made my skin crawl. I nodded for him to close and lock it back up. I surprised him by saying, "Keep it."

"Seriously? Even after everything that happened with Lizzy?" He gave me this look that was almost suspicious.

He was suspicious of me? I wanted to laugh. "Well, I'm pretty sure you learned a valuable lesson with that one. Keep it spelled. Nobody gets into it but you. Hide it. Get creative."

Doubt crossed his face. He reached for the briefcase, then stopped. "Are you sure?"

Gabriel kept expecting punishment. It baffled me until this moment. "I'm guessing that your time with Shya involved a fair amount of abuse when you screwed up."

His expression revealed nothing when he said, "You spent time alone with Shya. You know what he's like."

So yes, the demon had definitely handed out some ass kicking. But that wasn't me, and as far as I was from sugary sweet, I wasn't cruel. "Gabriel, I'm not Shya. As long as you don't screw me over, we're good. Just keep that book on lockdown."

When I made no move to take the briefcase, he dragged it off the table and onto the booth seat beside him. "There's something I wanted to talk to you about."

Yeah, I wanted to talk to him too. He wasn't getting away without answering some questions. "Shoot."

"I want to come to Las Vegas with you. If you guys run into trouble there, I might be able to help."

Now it was my turn to shoot suspicious glances. "Why would you say it like that? Have you seen something about Vegas? Don't hold back now, Gabriel. I know you're the one who told Falon how to restore the twin flame balance."

He stiffened, sitting up straighter in his seat. "He told you, huh? I would've told you, but you'd never have believed me."

"Yeah, yeah. I know." I waved off his excuse. "What I want to know is, when did you see it?" Did it really matter in the grand scheme of things? Not at all. Still, I was curious how long he'd been carrying that knowledge around.

"That night in Shya's fabricated horror house on Halloween," he began, tapping his fingers on the table's top. "When I passed the demon power I'd gathered to you. I saw it then. Just bits and pieces. It didn't fully click until I got the vision of Salem. I can't always put it together from one vision."

He'd sat on the information for months. I pondered this, constantly curious about the strange being that was Gabriel. Not long after Halloween, Gabriel had slipped up and told me that he'd seen something. I forced some of it out of him, and all he'd said was Arys and I would turn on each other one day.

Clearly, he'd left out the most important part. Both he and Falon were right, however. I would have struggled to trust Gabriel if he'd told me to let Arys kill me again. I couldn't blame him for choosing to go about it the way he had. He'd still ensured the information got to me at the right time.

"You can come to Vegas. But if I catch you withholding anything at all—"

"I haven't seen anything," he interrupted, raising a hand. "Not yet anyway. I swear."

Crossing my arms, I sat back against the fluffy booth. "Right. Well, I've heard that one before."

He started to plead his innocence again but stopped when he realized I was just busting his balls. The guy really needed to lighten up a little.

A cool breeze inside me preceded the ruckus a group of partying ladies started at their table. Their voices raised in girlish screams and drunken laughter. I sat up straighter and craned my neck to get a good look at them.

From their midst emerged Jenner and Arys, grinning and eating up the attention. Especially Jenner who lingered to enjoy it a little longer.

With his midnight eyes on me, Arys sauntered over, oozing enough sex and swagger to draw the gaze of every person he passed. A playful light danced in his eyes, but his jaw was hard set. Something was up. Because when it rains, it pours.

Arys caught my hand in his and used it to pull me out of the booth and into his embrace. Sparks flew as our hands touched. He smelled like cologne, blood, and shenanigans.

"Do I even want to know what you two have been up to?" I slid my arms around his neck and kissed his tense jaw.

His seductive laugh gave me shivers. "Playing by all the rules, I assure you, my queen."

"So you're breaking the rules and you're lying about it," I teased right back, searching his stare for what I'd sensed the moment he walked in. "What's up, Arys?"

After giving me another squeeze, which included a fondling of my ass, Arys released me so we could sit in the booth across from Gabriel whose thumbs flew furiously over his phone screen. He glanced up and put the phone down when he saw Arys's grave expression.

"Roscoe called to update Jenner on a few things while we were out." Arys slipped an arm around my shoulders. "Loric has started making some changes to the club."

The ominous way in which he said this got my imagination spinning some wild threads. "I'm guessing these changes are going to start fires we'll have to put out."

Looking pleased with himself, Jenner ambled up to our table. At first glance he seemed like his usual playful incubus self. But when he slid into the booth next to Gabriel and met my inquisitive gaze, worry haunted his icy depths.

"I was just telling them about the news you received," Arys explained, gesturing for Jenner to take it from there. "That there's been some changes made to the club."

Jenner squirmed a little. Visibly. I'd have enjoyed it if it didn't mean we'd have to clean up someone else's mess.

"Loric changed the fight ring," Jenner began. "I guess it's anything goes now. Any creature type. No rules. Nobody leaves until someone's dead. It's become a full-on, underground, supernatural fight club."

Slowly I released the sigh I'd been holding in. "The fight ring never should have existed in the first place."

Apocalyptic

"Tell that to Harley," Jenner snarked. "Oh wait, no, you can't. You killed him."

The vampire was on edge. His nightclub, his city, his home. All of it was in danger of being taken from him. I understood the moodiness. However, I didn't appreciate being its target. Although I knew it wasn't just because I'd killed Harley. Jenner gave no fucks about that. He was hurting for a taste of me.

Noting the way he eyed my jugular, I growled, "Ready to join him, Jenner?"

Beside me Arys chuckled. "Tell her the rest, Jenner. Tell her what he's done to your theatre."

The theatre? Jenner had been seducing and bleeding women for the public's entertainment in the theatre for years. I'd seen it myself. It had been undeniably sexy while almost being intimidating and horrific.

"How much worse can the theatre get?" I asked, glancing between the two of them.

Jenner shot Arys a dark scowl. Most likely willing him to shut his trap. "Loric is performing in the theatre now. He's turned it into a horror show. It's not about the seduction and tease anymore. It's just fear, bloodshed, and death."

Whoever this Loric asshole was, he seemed intent on remaking The Wicked Kiss Las Vegas from a den of pleasure into a place of terror and mayhem. I didn't have to look at Arys to know he wanted to go kick this guy's ass.

"So when do we go?" I asked, leaving it up to Arys and Jenner. It was their city. Their nightclub.

"As soon as we can," Arys answered right away. "Loric's working up to something. This isn't just vampires being vampires, business as usual. Something else is going on there. Something dark."

Fuck. I gnawed my lower lip. I'd made a promise to Arys. Now that we were whole again, I had to see it through. So we would go to Sin City and help Jenner to take back the city he and Arys so loved.

"Ok. Book the flight." I sucked in a breath, steeling myself for the news I had to share about Salem and Lilah. "I have something to tell you too."

EPILOGUE

Stepping into Kale's house was a punch in the heart of sensations. Even though he hadn't spent the majority of his time there, it still smelled like him. Leather and cologne. I paused in the doorway to take it all in.

"Perfect. You're right in time to help me with something. Get in here. I'm in the bedroom." Jez's voice drifted from down the hall.

Making my way to Kale's bedroom left me with mixed emotions. I missed him desperately. Yet after seeing him in between, I felt more at peace with him being gone.

Only Jez knew that I'd seen him there. I hadn't told the guys. They didn't need to know how I'd gotten the twin flame fire. Just that I had. The meeting with Kale was special, just for me.

And of course, Jez.

I walked into the bedroom to find her sitting on the floor outside the closet with a pile of things scattered about. Everything from clothing to miscellaneous crap like cell phone chargers. There were a few personal items in the mix.

My gaze went to the bed. Too many memories hit me at once. Kale and me, entangled in those sheets. In his arms, watching the dust motes float in the stray sunbeams that made it through the blinds. It felt like a lifetime ago.

"Tough memories, huh?" Jez's tone was soft. "You know, since you told me that you saw him, I feel so much better about it all. He got what he wanted. We can be happy for him."

"Yeah, for sure. Me too." I forced myself to turn and see what she'd called me in for. "Still hard to remember though. What do you need help with?"

She stood up from the pile, lifting a small, fireproof safe. "Think you can manipulate the lock?"

Not a problem. A little metaphysical force and the lock clicked. Jez set the box on the end of the bed and flipped open the lid. Inside were various personal items. The few pieces of jewelry looked incredibly old. Old newspaper clippings filled one envelope. Another had Jez's name on it. A hundred year old movie ticket stub had been carefully placed on the bottom of the box: *Dr. Jekyll and Mr. Hyde.*

I had to laugh. I'd been pretty Jekyll and Hyde myself during the time I'd known Kale.

Somewhat hesitant, Jez peeled open the envelope with her name on it. She sifted through the papers inside, and her heart-shaped mouth dropped open. "It's info for a savings account he opened decades ago. There's a ton of cash in there." Her eyes welled up and she shook her head. "He knew I'd never take it if he tried to give it to me while he was still here."

Jez could use the money. She worked for The Circle, and though they'd always kept us fed and housed, they weren't just handing out the cash. Although I'd heard from Falon that one could do special jobs for special perks. Regardless, this was Kale's way of taking care of Jez beyond the sale of his house.

"Hey, what's this?" The edge of a book peeked out from beneath the house deed. I grabbed the book and tugged it free. It was a journal.

Was journaling a thing for vampires? Made sense. How else would one keep track of so many damn years?

I held the worn book, even older than the one Arys had given me to read. I cradled it close to my chest, suddenly feeling closer to Kale despite not yet having looked inside.

"Kale kept a journal?" Jez pondered this. "Yeah, I can see that. Keep it. Let me know if you find anything juicy in there."

It might be some time before I'd be ready to read it. Still, I tucked it into my shoulder bag feeling a little warmer inside.

When we finished up in the bedroom, we went through the kitchen drawers, ensuring no personal effects were left behind.

"So things must be good with Smudge. You two seem really happy together."

The smile that brightened Jez's face practically lit up the whole room. "It's going so good I'm afraid to talk about it in case I jinx it."

"Good. I'm glad. She seems crazy about you." It gave me a great deal of comfort to see the way the two of them were together. So cozy. Connected. They'd bonded fast and it appeared solid.

"Honestly, Lex, I'm a little freaked out by how into her I am. It's never ended well before." With a tight, pinched smile, she shrugged and tossed a stack of old utility bills into a garbage bag.

"Well, that was then. This is now. Don't let the past keep you from loving again, Jezzy. I'd hate to see you as a dried-up old spinster, all hardened and alone." Snickering, I tossed a newspaper dated three months ago into the bag she held.

Jez went through the cupboards, checking each one. "Smudge has been a lifesaver with all this necromancy stuff. I don't think I'd be handling the day to day of it so easily without her."

"How's that going?" I watched her move through the kitchen, doing what I could to help. For just a second I swore I got that rich, honey-drenched vibe. Then it was gone.

"Better. There's a learning curve, which is putting it lightly. But being able to lock it down helps." She paused and reached to touch a finger to the black amulet that hung around her neck. "I think I'm getting better."

After everything we'd both been through recently, it was nice to have a quiet moment alone. Doing something as mundane as packing up Kale's house helped ground me in a sense of normalcy. I didn't get that a lot.

Jez wouldn't be coming to Las Vegas with me this time. She and Smudge would stay here and keep an eye on the city. Considering her last visit to Sin City had included drunken hookups and rowdy behavior, her choice to stay here revealed much about her current state.

I hadn't decided yet who we'd be bringing to Vegas. Going there ready and able to protect ourselves was vital, but I couldn't leave my city unattended. Not with Lilah and Salem MIA.

The very thought of the two of them brought a sour taste to my mouth. Had Lilah manipulated him into freeing her? Had she broken out and run? Maybe he'd gone after her. Too many possibilities and none of them felt right.

They would turn up, and from what I knew of Lilah, she'd wait until she could really screw me over. I wasn't sure if I should be more concerned with her or Prince Bane. I opted for Lilah. Her ability to carry an obsession seemed far more terrifying than Bane's. Of course, he might prove me wrong.

Apocalyptic

"Gabriel thinks you could be a real powerhouse one day. You have the power. With enough skill, you could create your own zombie horde and make them do your bidding." I teased Jez, laughing at the image that brought to mind. Probably shouldn't have. That shit could happen.

"Yeah, you laugh now," she said, rubbing her hands together like an evil villainess. "Speaking of Gabriel, are you taking him to Las Vegas? Seems like he's been seeking a way into your bed. Am I wrong about that?"

Digging around in the top cupboard above the fridge, Jez pulled out a roll of paper towels and tossed it to me. I set it on the kitchen table and considered the question. "Nope. You're not wrong. He told me that he wants to be inner circle. Power wise, he brings a lot to the table."

"And what about the bedroom? Interested in hitting that? He's young so that probably makes him eager."

Since it was just the two of us enjoying some girl talk, I felt like I could be honest. "Can't say I'm not tempted. He's got this quiet, mysterious thing going on and a lot of power to play in. But I'm not sure he's earned a place in my bed just yet."

Jez laughed. "So you want to bang him but also need to justify it to yourself. You're a succubus. He's hot, young, and willing. What is there to justify?"

I picked up the paper towel roll and smacked her in the ass with it. "It's not that simple. I have to be careful with this stuff. I want to keep my circle small. I have to be picky."

"You've already claimed him, Lex," she pointed out. "You've picked. Holding out is some kind of twisted foreplay for you."

Pursing my lips, I half shrugged. "Maybe it is. Maybe I just want him to work for it."

"Now that I can get behind." Pausing, she peered into the next cupboard and laughed before pulling out a rolled-up Playboy that was older than either of us. Flipping through the pages, Jez raised a finely sculpted brow. "Damn, now that's a hairy cooch. Why did Kale keep this?"

Together we flipped through the pages and shared a few laughs. Getting to this moment hadn't been easy. We'd both gone through our own personal hell and emerged out the other side. These moments of girl talk and laughter, they were priceless. Now I knew just how priceless.

By the time we finished with Kale's place, it was ready for the cleaning crew Jez had hired to come by in the morning. A for-sale sign had already been stuck in the front yard.

The sleek black 1973 Camaro sat in the driveway. That car held just as many memories of Kale, if not more, than any other place.

Jez locked up the house and joined me. She plopped into the passenger seat and began to fiddle with the radio dials the moment I started the engine. "So where are we headed?" she asked, obeying when I pointed to her seatbelt. "The night is still young enough to have some fun. I think we've earned it."

"We have," I agreed. "I'm up for just about anything. Within reason, you wildcat."

Jez began to speak animatedly as she searched for an address on her phone. "There's this new burlesque club on the south side. Male and female dancers. Very sexy. Want to check it out?"

"Yeah, sure. Why not?" I maneuvered the Camaro through the streets, savoring the rumble of the engine.

If I had to name the last time Jez and I had gone out and done something normal that had nothing to do with vampires or demons, I probably couldn't do it. Trouble was coming down the wire. Soon. No time like the present to have some fun.

I could use the down time. Before I knew it I'd be up to my eyeballs in Sin City mayhem and immortal, twin flame chaos.

Truth be told, I could hardly wait. I had a little mayhem and chaos of my own to dish out.

~ ~ ~ ~

Don't miss Falon's bonus epilogue on the next page!

~ ~ ~ ~

BONUS EPILOGUE

FALON

How can you hate fuck someone who's crying? You can't. Unless you're a real piece of shit. I'm no nice guy. I own that. But I'm not that much of a piece of shit. So you hold them while they cry their fucking guts out because their whole world has just gone to hell in a handbasket. And you wonder, when the hell did hate fucking turn into this?

The night at the hotel, when Alexa fell apart in my arms, I'd wanted so badly to tell her what I knew. That she would come out the other side of the pain to find victory. Sitting on the floor of the shower with her, hot water beating down, I'd been in a near panic.

A woman's tears held a strange power over me. One that reduced me from an angel to a man. Speechless. Uncertain. Even hers.

I'd kept my mouth shut, knowing that to spill it at the wrong time would be folly. So I'd just held her and waited for the tears to stop. My God, that had been hell.

"Why are we here, Falon?" Alexa nagged me for the third time since we'd arrived. "I'm starting to think you're leading me on a wild goose chase."

We walked through the largest cemetery in the city, a small community in its own right. Prime pickings for those seeking a creepy graveyard vibe for whatever magical mischief they were cooking up.

I rolled my eyes and scoffed. "I have the same info you have. Smudge said a couple was walking through the cemetery and saw a group of dark robed figures. Probably your run-of-the-mill wannabe witches. Still, it could be the real deal. Someone has to check it out."

She turned deep brown eyes on me and frowned. Her lips twitched like she wanted to tell me to go fuck myself but held back. Most likely brewing up a better smartass remark to fling at me later.

"And why does it require both of us?" She nitpicked, unable to leave anything alone. "Pretty sure you could've poofed in and out of here in seconds and saved me the trip."

This woman severely tested my patience. She was everything I hated about those who walked between the worlds. Too ignorant to understand what they've been given. Too green to know how to properly use it. Undeserving. Not to mention annoying as fuck.

But son of a bitch did I want her. I've never known a succubus who embodied sex in all its possible forms quite the way she does. And I've known a few. She makes it an art.

From those piercing eyes—usually vampire blue when she's with me but I enjoy the brown wolf eyes too—to that luscious ass and sassy mouth, she drove me wild. I hated how much I loved the way she drove me. She just knew how to work me. How to touch, where to bite, and the woman rode me like it was her calling.

There was nothing about fucking her that I didn't love. Listening to her talk though? Now that I could do without.

And yet, even though I often found myself wishing I could be rid of her, rid of wanting her, I couldn't let him get to her. Bane. Underworld prince. Godless scum. The curse of my existence.

He'd taken the only woman I'd ever loved from me. Now he wanted the one woman I most loathed as well. What had cut the deepest was that Winter had let herself be taken. She'd chosen him in the end. Deceitful bitch.

Evidently that had not been enough for Bane. The underworld liked to talk. Bane had heard about Alexa and my tie to her. That had been enough to pique his curiosity. He didn't really want her any more than he'd wanted Winter. The thrill of the conquest enticed him, winning a rarity such as they were. Winter had been nothing but a prize to him. Being able to destroy me in the process had just been a nice bonus for him.

All in a day's work for those demon types.

Some might consider me among them. I don't bother to argue that. I am not one of the good guys. Although from time to time, I still fight the good fight. From the inside.

"Do you ever annoy yourself with that voice?" I asked with a smirk. "Maybe you don't hear it the way I do. It's kind of a nails on a chalkboard sound. You know?"

Alexa jerked to a stop in the middle of the walking path we followed. Hands on her hips, head tilted to one side, she oozed attitude. "You don't seem to have a problem with it when I'm begging for your cock."

The organ in question twitched at her mention of it. My gaze fell to her full, pouty lips. I wouldn't say no to having them wrapped around me right now.

"Well, no." I smiled dryly. "That's because you're begging for my cock. Would you like to beg for it now? I'm sure we can spare the time." I reached to pull her closer, knowing she'd fend me off with a defensive move.

Which she did, precisely as anticipated. Throwing an arm up, she deflected my touch, smacking my hand aside. "Better dial down the ego a bit, Falon." She strode on ahead, scanning our surroundings for any sign of a threat. "You've been on your knees begging me for more than an orgasm. You've fucked me until your soul bled. Isn't that what you said?"

The truth was… Alexa's voice was sexy as hell. A smooth, sultry sound with an occasional rasp of a wolfish growl that grabbed my balls and squeezed but went much further. Deeper. To a place I didn't like to share with anyone.

Not anymore.

Her lashing out at me, that seductive voice carrying on the light breeze, it did something to me. Something that made me hate myself and hate her. A little more every night.

"Look, I don't care who gets on their knees as long as one of us is doing some begging. Preferably you though. You've got more experience than I do, and it shows." I laughed when she flipped me a middle finger and stormed ahead.

I watched her walk in front of me, admiring the way she held herself. It had changed in the time I'd known her. She'd been somewhat of a yappy little dog when we first met. Lots of bark. A little bite. Her confidence had grown since then, as had her ability. Alexa had started to settle into her role as a leader among supernaturals. The regal wolf and the dynamic vampire, crammed inside the most annoying woman I'd ever known.

Now that her twin flame balance with Arys had been restored, she'd become the final version of herself. The true queen of light and dark.

She would need to embrace all that entailed in the battle ahead. With Lilah and Salem going full dark side, we were all going to find out what we were made of.

Terms of power and rank are a dime a dozen in the underworld. Princes like Bane are often born or recruited into their role. Others, like Lilah, rose to their ranks by taking out everyone who stood in their way. But for the most part, labels like that are self-appointed by bigshots trying to intimidate through name alone.

The night Alexa had turned Willow human, I'd watched her struggle. Doubt and failure had taken hold. It had been a good excuse to slap her, so I did. But the words had tumbled out, dredged up from somewhere beyond me.

I'd called her the queen of light and dark, effectively giving a name to what she'd become. A very rare few were permitted to command the powers of both light and dark. For the rest of us, it was a pretty cut and dried one or the other situation.

It was my job to know things. I went to great lengths to obtain information, and then I stored it away, using it only at the right time and never a moment too soon. The right information could make or break a person or situation. Getting close to Shya and others like him came at a price, but more often than not it was worth it.

I'd done a lot of terrible things to earn my place within The Circle of the Veil. Naturally, they expected me to keep it up. And I did. I was convinced that being paired with Alexa had been a punishment for screwing up with Shya. However, it gave me a reason to check up on her often, sometimes without her knowing. Although I didn't make a habit of that. It made me feel like a creep.

Alexa came to a sudden stop. She stared off into the dark, between the rows of headstones. "There's something here."

I followed her off the path, weaving between graves. One grave had an especially large headstone. Right in front of it was the remains of a salt circle. A quick perusal of the circle and it was obvious this had been legit magic. It left a residue behind, one that could be felt.

"Ritual magic," I observed. "Almost feels like someone was trying to summon a demon."

"Someone specific?" Alexa's eyes were wide as she jumped to conclusions.

Getting closer, I hovered a small fireball in my hand before releasing it over the circle. It allowed us to see the hastily kicked salt line, like someone had destroyed it in a hurry. Most likely when they'd been discovered.

Studying the inverted pentagram that had been scuffed into the earth, I walked around it from the outside. Demon summoning was pretty standard witchcraft. The majority of the time it didn't work, usually due to lack of experience and genuine power.

At first glance I almost missed it. Something small and shiny glinted in the light. I picked up the small, triangular talisman. Three snakes crisscrossed in the middle, their heads and tails creating six points within the triangle.

My skin crawled. "Yeah, someone specific."

I held the talisman up for her to see.

She took one look at it and swore, shoving a hand through her blonde and black locks. "It's hers, isn't it? Lilah."

"It's one of the talismans her followers used to wear to show they belonged to her," I explained, pocketing the thing for proper disposal later. "Word must be starting to spread that she's out of her cage. They're seeking her out."

"It's only a matter of time until she shows up." Alexa leaned heavily against a headstone and stared at the salt circle. "Maybe I shouldn't go to Vegas. Arys can go and I'll stay here."

I made a noise of disgust that had her glaring my way. "Don't be stupid. Right now is not the time for you and your twin to be apart. You may have restored the balance, but you're still strongest together. Do not divide yourselves."

With a sharp nod she grudgingly accepted my logic, which was how she always accepted my logic. On those rare times that she did.

"Go to Las Vegas," I continued. "I'll go between both cities. If anything happens here we'll know right away. I'll be here to deal with it until you catch a plane home. But I intend to be with you there as well."

Her mouth tightened into a fine line. She tossed her hair, revealing the mark on her neck. My mark. Why the hell had I done something so fucking stupid? I still didn't know.

Alexa was a Hound of God, more than capable of holding her own against the average demon. Bane was not the average demon. My mark was not enough to keep him from coming after her either, but it would lend her extra protection should she have to face him again. Though I planned to be there should that happen.

"How the hell are we going to deal with twin flame immortals who've gone dark side?" she muttered, staring absently across the cemetery, lost inside her thoughts.

"Oh, we're not," I assured her with a sadistic snicker. "You are. Don't worry. I'm sure you'll figure it out." I couldn't resist making things difficult for her.

The glare she shot me smoldered. She took the bait. "You're a real asshole, you know that? Why do I still put up with your crap? With allies like you, Falon, nobody needs enemies."

Chuckling to myself, I moved fast, appearing right in front of her. She gasped and punched my arm. Tipping her head up, I leaned in to kiss the silver feather decorating her skin.

"We're lovers, not allies. Don't mistake them for being remotely the same." Following the feather down her slender neck, I murmured, "And you know damn well why you put up with my crap. Same reason I put up with that god-awful voice."

Alexa surrendered to the night pulsing around us. To the fear that she needed to purge with me inside her. With her fingers in my hair, she hit me with that succubus aphrodisiac. My lips moved faster on her neck, a hand seeking out the warmth between her legs.

I'd come to know many things about her, both as an outside observer and from the inside, as her lover. I knew she was hot tempered but usually reasonable. New to so much power and authority but willing to learn how to handle it. I knew how to piss her off and how to make her plead my name.

But of all the fascinating, curious, and despicable things I knew about Alexa, of one thing I was especially certain.

The Queen of Light and Dark had yet to play her biggest role.

ABOUT THE AUTHOR

Trina writes urban fantasy that is dark and gritty with a twist of romance and horror but which is ultimately about people in dark places discovering who they are and what they're made of.

A lover of rock music, vampires and muscle cars, Trina is a dreamer who always secretly wanted to be a rockstar. She lives in Alberta, Canada with her bass player husband, ukulele playing daughter and small herd of cats.

Trina loves to hear from readers so don't hesitate to drop her a line on social media or via email. Find her info at trinamlee.net.

Printed in Great Britain
by Amazon